I0637119

A LOT TO UNPACK

PORTIA MACINTOSH

Boldwood

First published in Great Britain in 2025 by Boldwood Books Ltd.

Copyright © Portia MacIntosh, 2025

Cover Design by Alexandra Allden

Cover Images: Alexandra Allden and Shutterstock

The moral right of Portia MacIntosh to be identified as the author of this work has been asserted in accordance with the Copyright, Designs and Patents Act 1988.

Every effort has been made to obtain the necessary permissions with reference to copyright material, both illustrative and quoted. We apologise for any omissions in this respect and will be pleased to make the appropriate acknowledgements in any future edition.

A CIP catalogue record for this book is available from the British Library.

Paperback ISBN 978-1-80557-164-3

Large Print ISBN 978-1-80557-163-6

Hardback ISBN 978-1-80557-162-9

Trade Paperback ISBN 978-1-80656-012-7

Ebook ISBN 978-1-80557-165-0

Kindle ISBN 978-1-80557-166-7

Audio CD ISBN 978-1-80557-157-5

MP3 CD ISBN 978-1-80557-158-2

Digital audio download ISBN 978-1-80557-160-5

This book is printed on certified sustainable paper. Boldwood Books is dedicated to putting sustainability at the heart of our business. For more information please visit https://www.boldwoodbooks.com/about-us/sustainability/

Boldwood Books Ltd, 23 Bowerdean Street, London, SW6 3TN

www.boldwoodbooks.com

For my wonderful family

1

I sit up in bed, all of a sudden, and gasp.

Waking up is usually such a gentle process, sleepily stirring, slowly coming around as your eyes adjust to the light of day, but not today. Today it's like flicking a switch. Today I'm quite anxious though, to be fair.

I grab the glass of water from the bedside table, briefly disoriented by the fact I'm not on my usual side of the bed – well, Ben doesn't like to sleep next to the door, so he wanted to take the left while we're here at the hotel. I wouldn't read too much into it, except I remember the two of us watching a movie where the couple were arguing about who slept closest to the door, because that's who would apparently get murdered first, and he didn't say a word at the time, but I can't help but feel like his actions have always spoken louder.

I clutch my glass in both hands, about to down the contents, when something hits me in the mouth.

'Oh my God,' I call out.

I look down into the glass and there it is, bobbing around like an especially minging ice cube. A retainer – Ben's retainer.

'Ewww...'

Ben appears in the doorway to the bathroom, brushing his teeth.

'What's wrong?' he asks, toothpaste foam dribbling down his chin.

I hold up the glass.

'Your retainer is... in my water,' I tell him, not quite able to believe the words I'm saying.

'Oh, sorry,' he mumbles, totally unbothered, as he heads back into the bathroom to spit into the sink. 'I forgot the case. I didn't want to leave it on the hotel sink or sideboard. You never know what kind of germs are in hotels. If they shone a black-light in here the place would light up like a Christmas tree.'

Not from anything we did, I think to myself, setting my glass back down on the bedside table, pulling a disgusted face at it as I do.

'I didn't think you would be drinking it,' he says as he returns from the bathroom. 'It's almost time for the party. I'll buy you a fresh one.'

He'll buy me a glass of water. I'm one lucky, lucky lady.

We're in a hotel in Leeds – my hometown – and while Ben might be concerned that the germ count is off the charts, it's my stress levels that I'm worried about. We're up here from London, where we both live and work, for my cousin Hannah's engagement party, and while I'm sure her fiancé is lovely, and the party is going to be fabulous, I just know that I'm going to be plagued with questions about when it's going to be my turn, and Hannah can't hide her smugness that she not only managed to seal the deal first, but that she did it while she was still in her twenties. At thirty, sadly, I've missed the cutoff – I didn't even realise there was a cutoff because, news flash, there isn't.

Ben is staring at me, standing at the end of the bed with a

towel wrapped around him – but not around his waist, like you would expect. It's around his chest.

'I think you're nervous,' he says, sitting down on the edge of the bed, picking up one of his green trainers from the floor. 'You seem nervous.'

'I'm not nervous,' I reply. 'I'm just... mentally preparing myself. For what's to come. I already know it's going to be a whole thing because, for someone who usually likes to make everything about herself, I know that Hannah is going to somehow make this about me too.'

He raises an eyebrow.

'As long as we keep our heads down and just... smile and nod, we'll get through it unscathed,' I add.

He smirks and starts tightening his laces.

'You worry too much about what people think of you, Liberty,' he tells me.

'You're not wearing those, are you?' I ask, ignoring his comments, getting back to the task at hand.

'My trainers?' He wiggles the offending footwear at me. 'Yeah – it's a party in a garden.'

'It's a garden party with a dress code, at a luxury hotel,' I remind him.

'Exactly. Grass. Soft terrain. You need grip,' he points out. 'These are my smartest ones – I wear them in the golf clubhouse.'

'Golf?' I repeat back to him. 'We're toasting an engagement, not teeing off. I packed you some smart shoes – please wear them.'

'The dress code doesn't apply to shoes,' he replies.

'What are you talking about? Of course it does!'

He shrugs.

'Liberty, I'm telling you, you need to care less about what

people think. You'll never be happy if you're constantly worrying about appearances.'

This coming from the man currently tweezing his nose hairs in the mirror. With my tweezers.

'And you need to stop using my tweezers for that,' I tell him. 'They're for my eyebrows. Not digging around in your nose. Use the trimmer I got you.'

'I don't like it,' he says, inspecting the monster hair he just yanked out. 'It makes me feel old.'

'You need to care less about what people think,' I tell him, mocking his North London accent.

He finishes up and drops the tweezers back into my bag without giving them so much as a wipe. Then he steps into his suit trousers, still with his towel wrapped around his body, like I haven't seen him naked hundreds of times.

I finally swing my legs out of bed, avoiding eye contact with the retainer cocktail I sipped, and psych myself up for the day.

It's a lunch party, thank God, which means with a bit of luck it'll be over before we know it, and we can escape into the city for dinner and maybe a drink or twelve to decompress.

It's not that I hate my family – well, not all of them. I love my parents. But my cousin Hannah and her mum, Auntie Eleanor, are not easy to love. Not unless you like passive aggressiveness and feeling bad about yourself, at least.

I think the problem comes from Hannah and I both being only children, and the only two of our generation, so everyone has always compared us to one another, pitted us against each other even, and we've always been so different that that was never going to go well. Hannah was captain of the netball team, so bubbly and confident, whereas I was more shy and preferred to hide from the world by getting lost inside other worlds – books.

Everyone knew Hannah. No one knew me, and I liked it that way. But when you're unknowingly participating in a popularity contest, that doesn't work out all that well for you. At school I always got top marks – of course I did; I read every book I could get my hands on – so maybe that's why Hannah and Auntie Eleanor always leaned into other things being more important – things that would go with us into adulthood. Things like getting married first and/or before turning thirty.

Honestly? I try to let it go over my head. So what if I'm thirty? I have a job that I love, a good boyfriend, and we've talked about marriage (as a concept at least) and I'm sure it's on the cards, for the future, when we're ready. But why rush? I'd rather get married at fifty, when I'm sure, than thirty, only for it to end in divorce.

'Are you going to be a while, getting ready?' Ben asks, buttoning his shirt.

'I'll be as quick as I can,' I tell him.

He leans over to kiss me so I move my lips to meet his, only to realise he was actually leaning over me to grab his watch from the bedside table. His watch – a vintage Omega one that his grandad left him – really carries his outfit sometimes, to the point where, as uncomfortable as Ben might look in a suit, the watch adds a level of style and sophistication. Even I have to admire it. Apparently, the face used to be white, but they've all discoloured and changed over their lifetime, giving each watch a unique look. Ben's is a vibrant orange shade now, with a crackled pattern – sort of like tiger bread. I don't think he loves the look of it all that much, but he knows it's expensive, so I think that's why he wears it. And then, of course, he wears an Apple Watch on his other wrist, which undoes all the hard work of wearing a stylish watch. I love a smartwatch, but a man wearing a watch on each wrist looks mad.

'You'll be fine. Just smile and nod and drink all the prosecco,' he tells me.

That's not a terrible idea.

'Thanks,' I say, grabbing my dress, ready to become a blur of hair and makeup and clothes. If I only had time for one, I think it would be the makeup. Today definitely feels like a day for war paint. Today, I don't want to give anyone any excuse to say I wasn't present, or that I wasn't happy for my cousin – and I definitely need to make sure I don't give anyone any excuse to think I'm jealous. If anyone thought I was jealous of Hannah marrying Samuel, the kind of guy who lives up to the donkey in his name, I would be mortified. He's one of those guys who always manages to say the wrong thing, who puts his foot in it whenever he can, who always seems to find the words to offend.

Ben throws on his suit jacket like it's an old hoodie, tugging it over his shoulders with the sort of enthusiasm usually reserved for putting out the wheelie bin.

'Can I go watch the football in the bar while I wait for you?' he says, already halfway out the door.

'I won't be long,' I point out, unrolling my heatless curls. 'I only need to cake on my makeup and put on my dress...'

'I could catch the first half, please,' he says, giving me big sad eyes, like I'm keeping him from visiting a dying relative, not sitting in a hotel bar watching a bunch of men running around a field.

'Fine,' I say with a sigh. 'Go on then.'

'You're the best,' he replies, leaning in for a kiss that is mostly on my nose. 'I'll meet you at the party, I won't be late.'

And boom, he's gone – as fast as his trainers will carry him. Fantastic.

Ben and I have been together for a couple of years – living together for a few months now – but we work for the same company so we spend a lot of time together. Sure, there are things about him that drive me kind of crazy, but being in an adult relationship means overlooking those little things and focusing the stuff that matters. Nobody is perfect, right?

I head into the bathroom to get ready and immediately stop in the doorway because... wow. The place is a mess.

There are beard hairs pretty much everywhere. In the sink, on the sink, somehow under the sink. Oh, and I can't even count how many towels he's been through.

I tidy as I go – mostly so I can make my way through the room – moving the towels, flicking rogue beard hairs from my toiletries. Ugh, I hate the feeling of having someone else's hair sticking to my hands. I know it's only hair and that I'm not bothered about it when it's attached to him, but it's a bit grim when it's loose and everywhere... right?

Maybe I'm being overcritical. I think maybe I'm just irked about the trainers because would it really be so difficult to wear shoes for a few hours?

I apply my makeup and blast myself with hairspray, then check myself for Ben's hairs before I head back into the bedroom. I swear, I need a decontamination unit.

I take my green silk dress from the safety of the wardrobe, sighing as I admire the fabric. I suppose I should be grateful that his trainers are colour coordinated with my dress. At least we can style it out like we're doing a thing.

I finish off my outfit with gold jewellery and a pair of yellow heels and that's me ready. See, I told you it wouldn't take me long.

I grab my clutch from the dresser and spot Ben's shoes lying on the floor. His real shoes. I wonder about taking them to him, making out like he's made a mistake, so he has to put them on, but then we'll have to bring his trainers back, and I don't want to embarrass him, so I guess he's won this one.

Shaking my head, I grab my phone from the charger, to chuck it in my bag, when the screen lights up with a notification. It's a message that says 'Liberty, you should see this' and a picture from an unknown number. Curiosity getting the better of me, I click it right away, only to instantly close it again.

Oh my God, ew, I only saw it for a split second but it was unmistakably a dick pic. Who would send me a dick pic? No one I know, but they knew my name, so they know me, unless it's spam? Some kind of scam? We deal with these things at work all the time – maybe Ben knows what I need to do.

Why do I feel so shaken up? I guess I just wasn't expecting it to be there, for one thing, but worrying it might be something sinister has me freaking out.

And now I'm even more annoyed that Ben didn't wait for me because I need him. He's techy. He can look at this and tell me what I'm supposed to do. He'll sort it.

Well, he will when it's halftime, I imagine... Oh my God, if Hannah finds out I'm having a crisis at her party she will freak out, say I'm trying to steal her thunder or something, so I need to get to Ben before he gets to the party.

There has to be an explanation for this, right? I'm sure it's nothing.

...then why do I have a bad feeling about this?

2

I don't even think sliding down the shiny wooden bannister on my bum could get me down the hotel staircase faster than my feet are carrying me right now.

I know you might think it's only a dick pic, lord knows I've had a few (never solicited) sent my way by well-meaning (I'm sure) suitors while I've been playing the dating game, but something about this one seems so sinister. Not the dick in question (I didn't look at it for long enough), more like the dick who sent me it – although, while we're on the subject, they're never great photos, are they? I'm not saying I want to see them with more artistic merit (I don't want to see them at all) but a few seconds' thought to the lighting or the background – most notably what's in shot, because you're doing yourself a disservice by leaving the remote control for the TV in the frame. It really helps figure out a scale.

Anyway, I didn't look at this one for long enough to see if it was giving 'dead baby bird' or 'smart TV remote', because I was worried that if I left it open too long it might, like, I don't know, drain my bank account or something. Well, what little there is to drain.

I work as an assistant, for a firm of private investigators in London, and honestly the number of clients we get who are trying to track down the person or organisation who has scammed them is frankly alarming. This is why I need to find Ben. He works for the same company, in IT, so I'm sure he'll know what to do.

I scan the lobby, looking for directions to the bar, only to be stopped in my tracks.

'There she is...'

Shit.

'...our daughter who defected to the south,' Dad continues, joking for the most part, but he's one of those Yorkshire men of a certain age who are offended by the existence of London.

'Hello, darling,' Mum adds.

I head over to greet them with a smile, trying my best to mask my panic, because my mum has always been able to see right through me.

They're both dressed in their best – Mum in a beautiful, floaty peach dress, Dad in a navy chinos and blazer combo that makes him look like he just stepped off a yacht.

'You look gorgeous,' Mum tells me as she kisses me on the cheek.

'Thanks – so do you guys,' I reply.

I notice the look on Mum's face, almost like she's analysing me, as she steps back.

'Where's your Ben?' Dad asks me as he gives me a hug. 'Has he seen the score?'

He says this in a way that suggests something has happened – not that I care, or would understand even if he told me.

'I think he's watching it in the bar,' I reply. 'I was just going to get him, actually.'

'We'll walk with you,' Dad suggests. 'I want to see the look on his face – his team are taking a hammering.'

'Erm, okay, yeah,' I reply. 'I think it's this way...'

'Are you okay, darling?' Mum asks, linking her arm with mine. 'You seem a little flustered.'

'Oh, no, I'm fine, just... antsy about today, I guess.'

'Oh, I'm sure your Auntie Eleanor will be her usual cheerful self,' she says, the sarcasm impossible to ignore.

'That's what I'm afraid of,' I say with a snort.

Oh, how much simpler things were half an hour ago, when all I had to worry about was my wicked auntie and smug cousin.

'You've got that face on, like when you were a kid, and you were convinced you'd seen a "ghostie",' Dad teases me with a laugh. 'Have you seen one here at the hotel?'

More like a goolie.

'Really, I'm fine,' I insist – not sounding all that fine, to be honest. I really need to up my game.

'It's only an engagement party,' Mum reminds me gently. 'Not the Met Gala.'

'Let's wait and see how big Auntie Eleanor's hat is, eh?' I joke, trying to seem more like myself.

'That one she wore to our Tina's wedding was like a satellite dish,' she says jokily, though it actually was like a satellite dish. Big, white and round.

'Remember when I asked her if she got Sky Sports?' Dad says, laughing at his own joke.

It's been fifteen years since Mum's cousin Tina tied the knot for the second time, but Dad is unwilling to let anyone forget his brilliant joke.

'Liberty,' I hear my cousin Hannah's voice call out. 'Hey, have you got a minute?'

'Don't worry, we'll go get Ben,' Dad reassures me.

'Yes, we'll see you outside – don't worry,' Mum adds so only I can hear.

'Hey, Hannah,' I say, trying to seem enthusiastic, because I don't want her to misinterpret my stressing as disinterest in her day.

She's in white – because of course she is. A lacy, floaty dress with dainty heels and a necklace so delicate I can barely tell it's there. Very demure, very bridal. Oh, and Auntie Eleanor is here too, lurking just behind her, and yep, her hat is massive. A big yellow thing with feathers – like a bird has landed on her head and she hasn't noticed yet.

'Oh, hi,' I add as I spot her, trying not to sigh or let my face fall in any detectable way.

'Love the dress,' Hannah says in a voice that betrays her. 'Very... bold.'

'Ah, this old thing?' I joke awkwardly. 'Thanks.'

'Well, we appreciate you making the trip,' Auntie Eleanor says. 'Leeds must feel very... provincial now, compared to London.'

'I love coming home,' I insist. 'Just to breathe the cleaner air, have a cup of Yorkshire Tea made with Yorkshire water.'

I say this in a jokey way but it's true. You get the best cups of tea in Yorkshire, I reckon.

'Were you planning on wearing, like, a jacket or a shawl or something?' Hannah asks me.

I frown, confused.

'Erm... no,' I reply. 'It's going to be 28 degrees today. Don't worry, I've got SPF on.'

My attempts to lighten the mood are futile.

'It's not that,' Hannah says. 'It's just... you do have a tendency to, sort of, erm, pull the focus.'

My eyebrows shoot up. I quickly force them back down.

'I do?' I check.

'You upstaged Baby David at his christening,' Auntie Eleanor reminds me.

'I fainted,' I point out.

'How was he ever going to compete with that?' she replies, missing the point entirely.

'And then there's your interesting job – it's all anyone wants to talk about,' Hannah adds.

'Okay, well, I will avoid making small talk at all costs, and I can't imagine my bare shoulders will do much damage to proceedings but, if there's an issue, I'll go grab a jacket – how about that?' I suggest, holding my tongue.

'And make me look like the bad guy?' Hannah replies, unimpressed.

I don't know why Hannah thinks I live to upstage her (although my guess would be insecurities, because we all have those). Sometimes it's rational, I suppose, like when she thinks me talking about my job overshadows hers, but that's only because people understand her job, as a primary school teacher, because we all went to school, whereas the idea of a private investigator fascinates people – because everyone loves a nosy and gossip. Other times it's crackers beyond comprehension – like me 'outdoing her' in our GSCEs, even though I sat mine years before she sat hers. I promise you, I did it to get into uni, not so I could dunk on her in the near future.

'Anyway, isn't it party time?' I check. 'Let's go, hmm?'

'Right, yes, I don't want you making late for my own party,' Hannah replies – the implication being it's me who is making her late.

I hang a few paces behind them, not wanting to arrive with them, lest it be considered a hostile manoeuvre.

Outside, I skirt around the edges of the marquee, finally spotting Ben with an almost empty pint glass in his hand.

'It's afternoon somewhere,' he says, noticing the look on my face.

'Oh, I don't care about that,' I insist.

'Good, because your mum and dad are bringing me another,' he replies. 'I told them to get you a cocktail.'

'Thanks,' I reply, practically flinching at the first syllable of the last word.

'What's up?' he asks, sucking his cheek in on one side, rolling his eyes.

'I got a text,' I tell him.

'You have a friend,' he jokes. 'Well done you.'

'No, it wasn't from a friend – although they did seem to know my name,' I reply. 'It was... it was a photo.'

'Okay?' he replies. He doesn't sound all that interested, to be honest.

'A photo of... someone,' I continue.

'Who?' he replies. 'Come on, Liberty, I'm not in the mood for trying to decode your girl talk today.'

'Not a who – a what,' I continue, letting that remark go for now. 'A dick pic.'

I mouth the last three words.

'Oh, yeah, and who is sending you dick pics?' he asks, almost like he's teasing me, like we're a couple of mates.

I glance down at the ground, only to clock the trainers on his feet. God, they look dumb, but I've got bigger fish to fry.

I frown at him. He laughs it off.

'It sounds like a scam. Probably a virus,' he replies.

'Should I show someone at work?' I check. 'Maybe Tom – or I could ask Erica?'

'No,' he replies quickly. 'Just delete it. It can't do anything, it's only a photo, probably designed to get you to engage with the sender, so don't. Delete it, block the number – I'll do it for you. Give me your phone. Then we can get on with having a nice day, okay?'

I puff air from my cheeks, trying to make myself a little lighter, to trick my body into relaxing.

'You're right, you're right,' I reply. 'Not about us having a nice day, because, y'know, we're here, but about me deleting it and forgetting it. Sorry for overreacting. I think I've just heard so many horror stories at work, of people opening an email, then suddenly losing tens of thousands of pounds...'

'You don't have tens of thousands of pounds,' he jokes. 'So you're good.'

'Right, I'm deleting it now,' I announce, unlocking my phone.

'Let me do it for you,' Ben says.

'That's okay,' I reply. 'I'm a big girl.'

'Okay, but I don't want my girlfriend looking at another man's penis, so let me do it,' he insists.

I don't point out to him that he's always looking at other men's penises, if his search history is anything to go by. Not that I check up on him – if you have to check up on someone, you shouldn't be with them – but I had to use his laptop recently and that autofill can be a bitch.

'I've already seen it,' I remind him. 'And I'm going to delete it anyway. I won't even open it again, I'll just delete the message thread.'

'Right, okay, good idea,' he replies.

I appreciate him being – what? – gentlemanly and gallant, defending my honour or whatever – but it's a bit much, and so out of character. I'm a big girl, I can take care of my own dick pics. Well, now that I'm getting over the initial panic and violation, anyway.

'I'll delete it, we'll go to the party, and I'll never think of it again,' I say, clicking into the app like I'm simply checking the weather or something.

I swipe the message thread to the side, without opening it, first to block the sender and then finally to delete the messages, never to be seen again.

'There – done,' I announce.

'Good,' Ben replies. 'Because your mum and dad will be here with our drinks in a minute, so if we could stop talking about dicks...'

'A great idea,' I say, relaxing more and more by the second, but then I hit it, the stumbling block, the brick wall that's going to block me from actually relaxing.

'One more thing, actually,' I tell him, taking out my phone from my bag again, clicking into my photos because I've just remembered something. 'It autosaves images I receive to my camera roll, so I need to delete the offending photo from there as well.'

'I'll do it,' Ben says quickly, insistently, but it's too late.

Is that...? It is! It's not the penis in the small version of the photo that catches my eye, it's the watch, that distinct, one-of-a-kind orange watch face with the crackled pattern through it. I open the photo properly. It's on the wrist of the person holding the duvet up to proudly display their bang-average penis – yes, I've seen better and, yes, I've seen this one before. It's Ben's. That's his penis, his watch, and now that I'm looking closely, that's the duvet cover we have on our bed at home, so this has to have been taken very, very recently. And sent to someone else –

someone who felt the need to send it to me, to show me what Ben has been up to behind my back, I guess.

I look up at him. His face is ghostly pale.

He knows that I know.

'Liberty—'

'Right, here we go,' Dad's voice booms behind us. 'Drinks for everyone.'

I quickly lock my phone screen so no one can see what I'm looking at – not that I opted in to looking in the first place.

'Brilliant, thanks,' Ben replies. 'So, what do you think of the match so far?'

Ben pats my dad on the back, almost ushering him away from us, and my dad is always happy to talk footie so he follows Ben's lead.

Oh, that's so low, such a dirty trick, using my dad as a human shield. Then again, isn't that exactly the sort of behaviour you would expect from the kind of man who sends pictures of his knob to other people, behind his girlfriend's back?

I notice Hannah out of the corner of my eye, greeting guests, and I remember what she said about me allegedly stealing the attention, so I need to keep a lid on my rage, to get through this party, but the second it's over, and we're back in the relative privacy of our hotel room, we'll get into it.

But for now... I'm going to have to smile, make small talk, and pretend everything is fine.

Even though everything definitely is not.

3

I'm not sure what is the warmest – the sunny weather, my glass of prosecco that is heating up by the second or my blood, which is positively boiling.

My smile is in place, fixed so firmly it looks like it could be painted on. It doesn't move, not even a millimetre, not even when I drink. I need to keep it together, for Hannah, but I also need answers for myself. I want to confront Ben, and I won't make a scene, it will simply look like the two of us are having a nice little chat – except he knows I want to talk to him, so he's doing everything he can to prevent that from happening. Surely he knows all he's doing is buying himself time? It's a stupid strategy, because I'm only getting more annoyed by the second.

I have to hand it to him, he's doing a great job. Using my parents as human shields is – wow – chef's kiss.

'Ben?' I say, trying to intercept him outside the toilets. The outside area has its own toilet block so I've been hanging around outside it, like a weirdo, waiting for him to come back out. Impressive, really, that he's managed to hide in there for eighteen minutes.

'Ben, we need to talk,' I say, walking alongside him, synchronising my steps with his, trying to match his pace.

'Linda!' Ben calls out, grabbing one of my distant cousins from seemingly nowhere. 'Linda – Liberty was looking for you, she was just telling me how much she wanted to catch up with you.'

I mean, I absolutely wasn't, but now I have to make small talk with Linda for long enough that she doesn't feel bad, or like I don't really want to talk to her. My God, who knew this man was such a master of deception? I'm always in awe of some of the tactics they use at work to try to get the information or evidence they need for various cases. I always wish I could be all cool and secret agent-like, but I'm only an assistant, in the most admin-y way. Ben has clearly been taking notes though.

Small talk suitably chatted, I make my excuses and set about looking for him again, scanning the crowd, eventually spotting him with my Uncle Clive.

I sidle up next to Ben and gently place a hand on his arm.

'Can I borrow you, please?' I ask him.

'In a minute,' Ben replies. 'We're having an important conversation.'

'Give over, lad, we're talking about water butts,' Uncle Clive says with a snort. 'It'll keep.'

'Canapé?' a waiter asks, presenting us with a tray of incredibly fancy, super-tiny pieces of food. The kind where you can't work out what they're made of by simply looking at them.

Generously, I'd say Ben is only trying to get away from me but there's a strong chance he did what he just did on purpose – he's bumped into the waiter, sending the tray and its contents to the ground below. It doesn't make the loudest noise, it's landed on the grass, but a nearby female guest screams – that's the loudest noise, it turns out.

I notice Hannah staring at us, with a look on her face that says 'how did I know Liberty would be at the centre of the chaos?' but you can't blame me for this one. Well, I guess you can, technically, but no jury in their right mind would convict me today, given the evidence.

'I'll go get someone to help you,' Ben tells the waiter.

'Ben, wait,' I call after him, but he's off.

I keep on his tail, trying to stay as chill as possible, but the more he avoids me, the worse he makes things for himself. I'm going to be honest with you: as much as I would love to avoid the hassle of blowing my life up, I'm struggling to see a universe where I can forgive Ben for this. Well, why would I? He's a liar and a cheat – but I deserve an explanation. I don't know what he thinks he's going to achieve by running from me. Maybe he thinks I'll get tired or I'll calm down or I'll forget? Is he crazy?

As he passes my parents, back over towards the toilet block (his tactic can't surely be faking another wee, can it?), I notice my mum collar him. Yes, Mum, stop that man! Oh, and she's hooking her arm with his. He's not going anywhere for the moment.

'Liberty!' Mum says cheerily. 'I was just saying to Ben, Dad and I wanted a photo together, and his phone has the best camera. He always gets the best pictures.'

Ben and I have the exact same phone, and therefore the exact same camera, but he does seem to take better photos. I guess I know what he's been practising on.

'Yes, of course,' he tells them, taking a step back to get them in the frame.

They smile widely and obliviously as he snaps a few photos, and that's when it hits me – I know exactly what I need to do. Well, Ben isn't saying anything, and they do say a picture is worth a thousand words, don't they?

'I know, why don't I take a photo of all three of you!' I suggest with the most enthusiasm I think I've ever exhibited.

'Oh, that would be wonderful,' Mum replies.

I take Ben's unlocked phone from his hand before he can so much as blink and then my mum and dad stand on either side of him, wedging him in. He's trapped.

'I need to move back a little, a little more, just to get all three of you in,' I say as I edge away from them. I can see Ben's face on the screen and he looks terrified. It kind of gives me the ick, seeing him look so pathetic, clearly feeling so sorry for himself, because he's been caught out. Wah, wah, wah, etc.

'There we go,' I announce and then, without pausing for a second: 'Oh my, I need the loo real bad, back in a sec…'

I dart away with Ben's unlocked phone still in my hand, heading towards the toilet.

'Wait, Liberty, you have my phone,' he calls after me.

I pretend not to hear him and pick up the pace. There's a single baby changing room, much closer than the ladies', so I go in there and lock the door behind me.

'Liberty,' he calls out, banging on the door. 'Liberty, please, I need my phone.'

I don't reply. Instead I open up his camera roll and… oh my God. There are so, so many dick pics in here. I don't know what's funnier – that they all pretty much look the same, so why even bother taking a new photo, or the fact that he has more pictures of his knob than he does of me, his girlfriend.

So, who is the lucky lady, huh? The recipient of alllll these photos – presumably she's the one who forwarded the photo to me, I'd imagine to tip me off.

'Liberty, Liberty, please,' Ben continues.

'You can use my phone,' I hear my mum tell him.

'I need mine,' he insists as he carries on banging on the door – it sounds like he's hitting it even harder now.

I close his camera roll and I'm just about to check his messages when I notice something where the frequently used apps pop up. It's Matcher – a dating app.

Oh, that bastard. I know it wouldn't make a difference if he'd met someone and started swapping pics with them, but to download and use a dating app is so cold and calculated. It's cheating with intent. There's no other reason for having it.

I open it up and head straight to his inbox. Wow, he must have swiped right on every girl within a fifty-mile radius. So many chats, so many dick pics being pinged out into the network.

I fling open the door and press his phone into his chest.

'You're disgusting,' I tell him.

'What?' he replies defensively.

'What?' I reply, mocking his voice.

'Liberty, Ben, please, can we not do this at my engagement party?' Hannah says through gritted teeth – and with the scariest fake smile I've ever seen. She looks like a shark.

'Sorry, it's his fault,' I say.

'Liberty, nothing he has done can be more important than my day,' she says confidently.

Is she serious? Nothing at all?

'What about sending photos of his dick to everyone on Matcher?' I ask her, just loud enough for everyone around us to hear, because I want Ben to feel as mortified as I do.

'He's being doing what?' my mum squeaks.

I notice the tension building in my dad's jaw.

Okay, fair enough, I shouldn't have done this here.

I grab Ben by the arm and drag him away from our audience.

'Okay, let's talk.' He finally gives in. 'I can explain – I promise I can, but you have to hear me out. Let me finish, okay?'

I have to say, if I could pretend for a moment that the decisions I made now wouldn't shape the rest of my life, I would be fascinated to hear what sort of explanation he thinks he can give me that I will accept. But this is real, and it's happening to me, and only I know whether or not I can forgive him.

I remember, years ago, when my mum's friend's husband had cheated on her, and she was trying to decide what to do, my mum would talk to me about it. I was probably in my late teens, so my mum took the opportunity to share with me just how horrible men could be. I remember her saying that men did things that hurt, but that hurt could be recovered from, if you wanted to. She said the real worst thing a man could ever do to you was embarrass you, because that was something impossible to get over. Now, more than ever, I know that she was right. Well, they say time heals all wounds, but embarrassment is something else – I can still remember, clear as day, saying 'yes, mum' instead of 'yes, miss' during a Year 2 registration, along with every other time I've embarrassed myself ever since. No matter how many times Ben apologises, and even if he never does it again, I'll still remember every excruciating detail, every pitying look, every uncomfortable moment from today, and from all the days to come, because I can't make everyone here forget this, and I can't make myself forget it either.

'I don't want to hear it, Ben,' I tell him plainly. 'It's over. Can you just leave, please?'

'But we live together,' he reminds me. 'And we work together.'

'And I will figure all of that out,' I reply. 'Without you.'

'Liberty, you're making a huge mistake,' he says. 'You'll miss me – you can't live without me.'

'I'll miss you? I can't live without you?' I repeat back to him. 'Oh, yeah, how will I live without a dick-pic-sending, trainer-wearing, hair bomb of a man who thinks it's a perfectly normal thing to leave his retainer in my drink?'

'I explained that,' he replies. 'Come on. Who will do all the blue jobs, huh?'

Oh, look at him, trying to be cute. Pink and blue jobs were our fun little way of sharing out the household chores in our new flat. For example, taking the bins out, which I hate doing, we would joke was a blue job, whereas things like cooking and cleaning were pink jobs. Now that I think about it, basically every other chore was a pink job.

'Who will take the bins out?' he says, half joking, as he reaches out to take my hands in his.

I quickly pull back, so he can't get hold of me.

'Oh, no, not my bin man,' I say sarcastically. 'If the main thing you think I'll be missing is someone to take the bins out, then I guess I'll find a different one who knows how to keep his dick in his pants. Now just go, please.'

I can see from the sad look in his eyes and the droop of his shoulders that he knows he's fighting a losing battle, so he gives up and walks away, looking at his feet like a naughty little kid. Because of course he gave up without a fight. But did I want him to fight for me? Not really, because it wouldn't have worked, but seeing him give up only goes to show how little he cared about me.

He's right about something though – we do live together and we do work together. I guess I'll have to figure out what we do about that but, for now, I just need to exhale, try to calm down, and focus on the positive things. *What positive thing?* I hear you ask – the fact that I found out. Imagine if I hadn't, if I'd kept living with him, sleeping with him, all while he was up to God knows what behind my back.

The best time to see Ben's true colours would have been before I moved in with him. The second-best time is today.

And everything else, well, I suppose I'll figure that out tomorrow. But right now I need a drink.

4

If not getting a job was a desirable skill that you could put on your CV then I would, well, have a job.

If not having a job, a home or a boyfriend were desirable traits, I'd have more admirers than Dua Lipa.

If emotional baggage and trust issues are things you like a gal to have – give me a call, because I've got buckets of both. But, please, no Matcher flashers.

What I'm trying to say is that I have nothing. Well, after I broke up with Ben, and it was time to work out who got what, I knew that there was no way I would be able to keep working with him (and IT guy trumps assistant) so I had to leave. When it came to who got to keep the flat, well, that naturally went to the person who kept the job, because he was the only one who could afford it. So I was out on my arse – but my one blessing came in the form of my friend Jess's flat, which has been sitting empty while she is away travelling with her girlfriend, so she said I could crash here until she got back. It was a lifeline right when I needed one, and I figured I had plenty of time to bag myself a job before she got back... except it's November, and she's back just before Christmas, and I cannot land myself a job to save my life.

You would think there would be so many assistant jobs out there, because surely everyone needs an assistant, right? Except it turns out there are even more assistants out there looking for jobs and the competition is fierce.

I started strong, aiming high, applying for jobs that I liked the sound of. Working as an assistant to an editor at a lifestyle magazine, or at a luxury fashion boutique – I didn't even get interviews for those. Then I set my sights a little lower, applying for jobs in a cycle shop (I know nothing about bikes) and with a cultural heritage consultant (I don't even know that that is). Still not getting any bites, I applied for a job at a water treatment works (didn't get it) and even as an assistant to a touring psychic (she said she couldn't see us working together – I guess she'd know).

I've applied for so many jobs I've lost count but with each one, with each rejection, it's like a little bit of my confidence goes with it. That's why I'm bringing my A game today, because I actually have a job interview, with a tech firm – I don't know what they do exactly. The listing said the company would be revealed at the interview, so I'm hoping it's a cool tech company, like Apple, because imagine getting employee discount there.

I'm dressing for the job I want, in a black suit with a flash of red coming from my accessories, instead of the job I have – sitting on the sofa watching daytime TV in my PJs. I want to make a good first impression, because apparently that's every-thing, and you only get one chance to make it. I need to look good, sound good and be on time. It's rare I ever manage all three.

The fact that I'm walking into a skyscraper, in central London, bodes well for the calibre of job I'm here for – but not for my chances. Everything is glass or metal, screens or lights. I know I'm somewhere techy – and fancy, because even the security guards are wearing designer suits.

I'm trying to keep confident but I feel like a fish out of water here – which is ironic, because it does feel a lot like being in a fish tank.

Still, I head for the desk, tell them I'm here for an interview with Paige Pool, and listen carefully while she tells me which floor to head to. I'm usually one of those people who, when being given instructions, forgets the English language and how to use my ears, so I make a note in my phone. See, I'm a professional, give me a job.

I head to the lift – which is up a small escalator, for some reason – and step inside right as the doors are about to close. There's only one other person in there, a man, staring deep into his phone to the point where I almost feel like I'm intruding.

He's leaning back, effortlessly casually, against the mirrored wall, but not in a scruffy, lazy way – more like one of those sleek, sexy photos you see hot actors posing for that grace the cover of *Vanity Fair*. He is good-looking – it's impossible not to notice – with his strong jaw, his thick dark hair and his full eyebrows. He's in his late thirties, maybe, I don't know; he just seems to have that sort of genuine confidence that comes with having a handful more years under your belt, unlike lads in their twenties and early thirties who are still running on pure bravado.

I'm not sure if his eyes are smouldering or tired or both – if it's both, it's probably because he knows how to have a good time.

'Good morning,' I say brightly.

'Morning,' he replies, looking up for a split second before whatever is on his phone screen pulls him back.

No need for me to push any buttons; we're going to the same floor. As the lift starts moving, I try to relax.

I don't know why I'm admiring a random man in a lift. Well, I do, it's a distraction. I'm thinking about anything but my interview. Anything else would have been better, to be honest with you, because my hunt for a man is going about as well as my hunt for a job. It ain't.

The trouble I'm having is that, since Ben, I look at men in way more detail, and as soon as I put them under my microscope I realise I don't like what I see. Obviously there are the big things, the dealbreakers, the red flags that put you off a person. I'm not talking about that. I suppose what I'm doing is comparing every man I meet to Ben, not in a good way, in a bad way. In hindsight, Ben did so many things that gave me the ick – his poor hygiene, his laziness, the fact he cared about sport more than he did me. Now that I'm looking for icks, trying to make sure no one has any, they're all I can see. It's like I have this ick alarm in my head and it always goes off, usually sooner rather than later, and then that's that. Date over. I can't deal with it.

I mean, take the sexy man in the lift here. He looks good – he smells amazing – but I bet I'd find something wrong with him, either something he's doing wrong, or I'll just home in on something that can't be helped and let it ruin everything. Like, what if I hate his name? What if he's called Ronald McDonald, or Homer Simpson, or Michael Scott? Seriously, Ben has done a real number on me, because I start trying to work out what is wrong with a person right away, and, frankly, he doesn't have to have anything truly wrong with him, it might be because he has ice in his drink, or because he doesn't, or because he uses a paper straw that weakens in the middle and breaks in half and that is obviously a personal failing on his part, right? Right?

It just always feels like the moment is coming, like it's unavoidable. I'm starting to wonder if I should give up on dating for a while, because if I don't go on them then I'll never know what the thing was going to be that ruined it all. Sort of like a Schrödinger-type situation. I'll only wind up feeling frustrated with myself, if I peep inside the box, so why bother?

Then again, maybe that's how you live with regret. In the sort of words of Michael Scott, you miss all of the shots you don't take. For that I need to keep trying, to turn up knowing that it's going to be shit, but with the hope that this time it might not be.

That, my friend, is life until you die in a nutshell.

Hey, I already told you, Ben has done irreparable damage to me. I'm aware. But I don't ever want to find myself in that situation again, so I'm not taking any risks.

All of a sudden the lift grinds to an unexpected halt. Then the lights go out. Like, properly out. It would be pitch black in here, were the man in here with me not still staring at this phone. It lights up his face, like he's telling a horror story around a campfire. Two things – one, he's still gorgeous, even with the creepy lighting. Two, he seems completely unbothered by what's going on.

I, on the other hand, am very bothered.

'Fuck,' I blurt.

I think I hear him laugh, quickly and quietly. I turn to him.

'The lift has broken down,' I tell him, because I'm genuinely starting to think he might not have noticed.

'Yeah,' he confirms – still casual as you like. 'It happens all the time.'

'This lift breaks down all the time?' I check, because surely not?

'Yeah,' he says again.

'Then why would you get in it?' I ask in disbelief.

'Because it doesn't happen often enough to make me want to walk up thirty flights of stairs every day,' he says, amused.

It's hard to tell if he's an optimist or an idiot. Maybe he's both?

'Don't worry, it doesn't usually take them long,' he (kind of) reassures me. 'I think we almost made it all the way today.'

Sure enough the doors slowly open, letting light pool in from whatever floor we're on – except we haven't quite made it, we're between floors, so we're peering down at our rescuer.

'Morning,' she says.

'Morning,' the man replies.

'Ladies first, I guess,' she tells me, reaching up to take my hand.

So, what, I'm just supposed to jump out of the lift, into this random woman's arms? Beats being trapped in a lift, I guess.

I take a leap of faith and land on my feet – but I roll my ankle in the process.

'Ouch,' I blurt.

The woman sort of ushers me to one side.

'Come on, you know the drill,' she tells the man, all smiles.

'You should be less on the ball, it would give me a chance to sneak a nap,' he jokes as he hops out of the lift. He nails the landing because of course he does.

'Only two floors off today,' she tells him, like she's impressed. Then she turns to me and her smile drops. 'You'll have to use the emergency stairwell, over there. This takes time to reset.'

'Erm, thanks,' I reply, heading for the stairs, trying to walk off the pain in my ankle. I don't think I've done anything bad to it, but it's slowing me down a little.

By the time I reach my destination, I'm sweaty, hobbling still, and on my last nerve. I'm here though – and, oh boy, I'm not the only one. This place is like a holding pen for unemployed assistants; everyone here looks just like me. It's not like we all have the same physical features, but we're all tired, desperate, in the same boat. No one is chatting – I suppose because we all know we're in competition with everyone here. Only one person can get the job. A lot of people are going to be disappointed, to say the least. I'm sure I'll be one of them.

I find a free chair and take a seat. Looking around, I don't fancy my chances. Yorkshire is seeming closer and closer by the second.

I hear my name being called so I pull myself to my feet – I'm relieved to find they're both working.

I head into the large corner office where a woman greets me at the door with a firm handshake.

'Liberty?' she checks.

'Yes, hello,' I reply, trying to match her grip.

'Paige Pool, thanks for coming in today,' she tells me.

'Thanks for having me,' I reply – so stupid, like I'm here for afternoon tea or something.

'So, it's my company – well, half mine, anyway, so I'm the one you need to impress,' she jokes – I assume she's joking.

So she's funny, successful and beautiful. Her cheekbones are high, her skin glows – in a flawless way, not like mine, because I'm sweating from a combo of nerves, adrenaline and stairs. She's wearing a cream trouser suit and I could never. I spilt coffee on my leg, on the Tube, and if these trousers weren't black, you'd be able to see it. I'm certain I can still smell it.

'Please, take a seat,' she tells me, gesturing to the chair at her desk. She sits at the other. 'Impressive CV.'

Is it though? I guess she says that to everyone.

'Thank you,' I reply anyway.

'So your last job was at a private investigation agency?'

'It was,' I confirm. 'But I fancied a new challenge.'

And that challenge was not seeing my lying dick of an ex every day, but Paige doesn't need to know that.

'What was that like?' she asks. There's a sparkle in her eyes, like she's truly fascinated by the idea, and honestly this might be the most interesting thing about me, even if I was only an assistant.

'Very interesting,' I reply. 'Challenging, rewarding – no day was the same.'

But only in the sense that every day was the same. But, again, she doesn't need to know that.

'So, you were an assistant – assisting with cases?' she checks.

I don't want to lie but, really, it's so obvious that the specifics of the agency are what she's interested in, rather than me.

'Yes, I assisted with the cases,' I reply – technically true. 'Gathering things, liaising with clients...'

And by that I mean gathering coffees, and giving them to the clients.

'So you must know a lot about surveillance, covert operations, going undercover?'

'I do,' I reply.

I've seen every *Mission: Impossible* movie.

'Very interesting,' she replies.

'I'm also great at researching, compiling evidence...'

AKA googling and writing things down.

'You're good at reading people?' she checks.

'Very,' I reply. 'But I think you already knew that.'

Okay, I'm getting cocky. I need to turn it down a notch.

'Any experience with hacking?' she asks. 'What sort of clients did you have?'

I'm still using Ben's Netflix – I low-key feel like a hacker every time I log in to watch old episodes of *Gossip Girl*. Wow, she really is more interested in my old job than she is in me.

'I can't really discuss it,' I say, wondering if this is a test in confidentiality. 'But everyone from businesses to people in relationships used our services.'

'People in relationships – now that's interesting,' she says. 'Then let me ask you this, and be honest – what do you think of Matcher?'

I can't help but snort out a little laugh.

'Something funny?' she asks. 'Come on, say what you think.'

'I think we would have had fewer clients needing help with their relationships if Matcher never existed,' I reply.

'You sound like you hate dating apps,' she points out.

'I guess I do,' I reply. 'I've seen them hurt a lot of people.'

That might be the most honest thing I've said so far.

'Very interesting, then, that you would apply for a job at Matcher,' she muses. 'Fascinating, really.'

I purse my lips and try to stop my eyebrows from lifting of their own accord. Shit.

'You're an investigator, you're observant – you must have seen the sign on your way in,' she points out.

Yeah, I most likely would have, if I hadn't come up the emergency staircase... Probably. I'm not that observant, to be honest, not when I'm in a flap.

'And yet you still want to work here?' she continues. I'm not sure if it's a question or an observation.

'I'm a professional,' I say – I'm not sure either of us believes that.

'Well, thank you for your time, Liberty, we'll be in touch,' Paige says, clearly wrapping up our interview.

And I've blown it. My first interview in ages, and I've messed it up. I figured I might need some practice but damn, me and my big mouth. I was already exaggerating, fudging the truth, so why didn't I just lie about Matcher? Or say I had no experience with it? Why did I give an opinion – why, why, why?

As I head out, back towards the lift (which appears to be working again now – still, I think I'll take the main stairwell) I notice the large pink Matcher sign by the door. Fair enough, even I wouldn't have missed that.

So, I'm not going to get the job. I never get the job – but I'm reeeeally not getting this one, am I?

5

'Don't sound too devastated,' my mum says with a laugh.

'Sorry, Mum, it's not that I don't love the idea of living around you all again,' I reply. 'It's just that moving home feels like so, so many steps backwards.'

'People move all the time,' she reminds me. 'It's merely a coincidence that we're already here.'

'Except it isn't,' I remind her. 'I'm moving there because you won't charge me rent.'

'We bloody will,' Dad calls out from the background – what a fun way to find out I'm on speaker.

'We won't,' Mum practically whispers. 'Plus, it means you will definitely be here for your grandad's birthday, and maybe you can patch things up with Hannah?'

'Hannah doesn't want a patch-up, she wants a punch-up,' I joke – well, half joke. I'll bet she'd love to hit me.

'She'll come around,' Mum tries to reassure me.

'She'll – oh, Mum, I've got a call coming through, can I ring you back, please?' I say.

'Of course – go,' she replies.

I go straight from one call to another.

'Hello?' I say.

'Hello, Liberty? It's Paige Pool. We met earlier today,' she replies.

Do I act like I'm excited to hear from her? Do I play it cool? Do I pretend I'm trying to remember her? What do I do?

'Paige, hello,' I reply. 'I hope you've had a productive day.'

Oh, the cringe. What am I doing?

'Yes, thank you,' she replies. 'I've found someone for the assistant position.'

Crap.

'Great,' I reply. 'That's great...'

'It's you,' she replies. 'Although I'm sure you've already figured that out.'

I really hadn't, I'm not that optimistic.

'That's fantastic news,' I reply. 'I accept.'

'Well, wait until you hear the job description first,' she says – now that doesn't sound good. 'So, we are in the process of taking Matcher worldwide. It's been a slow process, but we're starting to feel like we have a good base in all of our key territories; however, our focus at the moment is on growth. The competition is tough.'

'I understand,' I tell her, because I do, in the vaguest sense.

'So, we send teams to different locations, for a number of reasons,' she continues. 'I need you to be on standby, in case I need you to go anywhere and... assist. Presumably, you're okay with travel? You have a passport?'

'Yes,' I say, as calmly as I can. I clear my throat. 'Yes, that all sounds fine.'

What I want to do is jump up and down screaming with glee because not only do I have a job, but it sounds amazing.

'I'm going to send you an email with all of the details, everything we need to set you up as an employee here, requesting all of the various things I'll need to set up potential trips for you. I'll also send you a link to our staff network. We're on WorkM8, I'm sure you've used it at your other jobs.'

I haven't.

'Sounds great,' I reply.

'But, for now, if you could just make yourself a silly user-name – most people have one – and only observe. Get a read on the dynamics. No posting in forums, just read. Only until you've met everyone in person. We have a strict rule about no dating amongst employees. It's a recipe for disaster.'

I hear that.

'Yeah, sure, okay, so when do you want me in the office?' I ask.

'I don't,' she says quickly. 'I need you to be on call, for when we do need you, for trips. We'll get you set up in the office soon enough but, for now, this is what we need you for.'

'But... will I still be paid? Or is it freelance?' I check.

I suppose I'll have to accept it either way but it's not ideal.

'You'll be paid,' she replies. 'It will all be in the welcome pack so have a read, send me what I need from you, join the group – and welcome to the Matcher family.'

'Thanks so much,' I reply. 'I really appreciate the opportunity.'

'Well, given your skills, and your honesty, you're exactly the sort of person we need,' she says. 'So, go celebrate.'

'I will, thank you.'

I need to ring my mum and tell her the good news – and the bad news, I guess, because now I don't have to move back home. Not yet, anyway. First, though, I'm straight into my emails, to see the details of the job. Okay, wow, it pays better than my last job, and I'm going to get to travel, and right now I don't have to do anything, just wait, and get paid. What a dream!

I download WorkM8, which looks like an app lots of businesses must use, and sign up. NewGirl feels like a good username, for now, given that I'm not supposed to be interacting with anyone.

I click around the different threads, reading what people are saying, and it does seem like a nice place to work. Everyone seems happy.

MRLOVEBYTE
Hello, NewGirl

A private message pops up from nowhere. Am I... allowed to reply to this? Was it only posting publicly that I wasn't supposed to do?

MRLOVEBYTE
Welcome to the team!

I feel bad, ignoring him. I'll keep it short and sweet, I'm sure that's fine.

NEWGIRL
Thanks!

I'll leave it at that. I already feel like I'm part of a team, though, and I'm excited. I have a job and not just any job, but what seems like it's going to be a great job. Perhaps my luck is about to change – and, ironically, because of Matcher again. Hopefully for good reasons this time though.

6

I can't believe this is my first time in Paris. Not that I know what I'm doing here.

It's not that I'm not excited about my new job, really, I am. I mean, I'd much rather work for a company that isn't peddling an app that is frankly where the scum of the earth go to try to touch each other, but beggars can't be choosers, and I've been begging for something.

I just need to focus on the positives – not only do I have a job but it's paying me to go somewhere I've always dreamed of visiting. Paris has always been at the top of the list; in fact, I've been talking about it a lot this past year, because I was trying to convince Ben we should go together. I didn't simply drop hints, I dropped full itineraries of all the places I wanted to go and the things I wanted to do there – it was practically a ready-made Valentine's Day or anniversary or birthday gift. All he needed to do was take the initiative and book it, no thought required (and being thoughtless was clearly his speciality). Why on earth was I settling for such a terrible boyfriend? Never again.

Anyway, I'm here now and my first impression is that it's big, beautiful but so busy. I suppose we always think of places as they look on postcards, or in carefully constructed movie scenes, but in real life there is no director, no one to keep tourists out of your Instagram shots or help you get tables in cute cafés.

It's hard to believe I'm here for work – mostly because I haven't been given any work to do yet. They've just shipped (well, technically flown) me to Paris, stuck me in a hotel and told me to wait. That's all Paige said to do, to wait, to hang out but not venture too far, to see if I was needed. She isn't even here, it's the other owner, apparently, so I guess I have to do as I'm told, to 'hang out' and see.

So that's what I'm going to do, that's my plan. I'm just going to amuse myself until I'm needed... if I'm needed. This job is so strange.

I like that my plan of action is to basically have no plan at all. That's my new plan of action for everything really, because in my recent experience, if you simply go with the flow and hope for the best then it's almost impossible to feel disappointed. Spontaneity, that's what we'll focus on. Well, what's more romantic than being (technically) whisked away to Paris and then having no idea how the night will turn out, the endless possibilities? It's a dream, and not only a dream come true, but a silly fantasy, because I was brought here by my job, not a man, and let's face it, if your man brings you here for V Day you'll, what? Walk around the overcrowded tourist hot spots, fork out a hefty wedge of brie for a meal and then probably feel so full you'll get about three pumps of missionary before he falls asleep and you attempt to watch French TV alone. Not that I'm still bitter since my break-up or anything...

Speaking of living in a dream world, I'm currently on my way out of my hotel, heading out to see the sights, doing my best impression of Carrie Bradshaw from *Sex and the City* – well, I'm taking inspiration from her Parisian outfits at least. I'm wearing a baby-blue tulle skirt – a big ruffly thing – and a cropped white jacket. I'd say I don't know who I think I am, but I do – the third-best *Sex and the City* girl (I'll leave it up to you to figure out my ranking for the others).

I am beauty, I am grace, I have poise, I have... Oh, mother-fucker, I've got my skirt caught in the revolving door.

The hotel is busy, of bloody course, so the door is moving pretty much constantly, and as much as I'm yanking away at my skirt, I can't break it free. At this stage I don't even care if I rip it, but it's a cheap thing from a fast-fashion website, not delicate couture, so it is unrippable. It's probably largely made of plastic – I'd have more luck melting it, versus ripping it, but with zero tools at my disposal, I can't do anything but keep walking around and around with the door. The occasional person steps in with me and generously I assume they don't speak English, realistically I think they're more likely ignoring the crazy English girl caught in the revolving door.

I need to keep calm – which would be much easier to do had I not just realised that each time the door goes around my skirt gets pulled in a little closer, so pretty soon I'm going to be up against the glass. Could I die from this? Because I think if anyone could find a way to die from this, it would be me. Shiiiit.

'Oh, for fuck's sake,' I blurt, yanking at my skirt again, to no avail.

Suddenly I know what I need to do – I mean, I kind of knew this was an option already, but I'd ruled it out for obvious reasons. I need to find a way to get my skirt off. Sure, I'll be here just, you know, in my knickers, but if my options are death by revolving door or flash and maybe get done for indecent exposure, well, I'd choose...

Hang on, I'm still thinking...

'*Excusez-moi*,' a man's voice interrupts me from my spiralling – no pun intended. Actually, scratch that, I'm the kind of girl who uses humour to deal with things when life gets hard; there's always a pun intended.

He's in the same – what would we call it? – door compartment as me, walking around in circles with me.

'You are English?' he asks in the most French French accent I've ever heard, if that makes sense. I know, I'm in France, but all I can think about is how much he sounds like Lumière from *Beauty and the Beast* – not to sound like the 'childless millennial Disney adult' I absolutely am.

'What gave me away?' I ask, smiling, because in Britain we keep calm and carry on, right? Carry on going round and round in a revolving door.

'It was when I hear – how you say? – "for fuck's sake",' he replies – and it sounds so, so much better when he says it.

'Ah, that'll do it,' I reply.

I just smile at him – far too calmly and politely really, given my situation.

'Can I 'elp you?' he asks, nodding towards my skirt.

'Oh, if you could, mate,' I reply, and I've never sounded more English. I don't even say 'mate' – what am I doing?

'I think we could stop the door,' he says, strolling beside me. We've done at least four rotations together now. 'But I fear the skirt may need to come off.'

I fear that too.

'Erm, yeah, I'm not sure how...'

'*Alors*,' he says, taking off his long coat before placing it over my shoulders. 'Wear this.'

I do as he says, fastening up his coat over my outfit.

'What now?' I ask.

The Frenchman reaches out and places his hands underneath my armpits. Then he lifts me into the air, somehow keeping up the steady pace of the still-moving revolving door, and I feel my skirt slowly being tugged from my body so I wiggle my legs to help it come loose.

Look, I know this is highly embarrassing, and I'm not coming across as my best self right now, but bloody hell, this is like something out of a movie.

Finally free, the Frenchman carries me outside, out to the street, where he carefully sets me down on the pavement.

'*Voila*,' he says with a grin, and I'm almost amazed my knickers didn't remove themselves too.

'You're my hero,' I tell him. 'My knight in shining trench coat. I can't thank you enough.'

'Your skirt...' he says, nodding towards the door.

Oh, boy, it's really mangled up now. Most definitely destroyed. Thank God it was only cheap.

'Ah, yeah, never mind,' I say with a bat of my hand – yeah, genuinely, now I'm trying to play it cool, like that whole mess didn't just happen. 'I'm sure someone in the hotel will take care of it.'

'A great attitude to have,' he says with a smile. 'I'm Henri.'

'Lovely to meet you, Henri. I'm Liberty,' I say, offering him a hand to shake, which is awfully formal given that he just lifted me out of my skirt.

'What are you doing here in Paris, Liberty?' he asks.

The way he says my name makes me melt – ironic, given how chilly my lower half is underneath the coat. October in Paris is not the time to be bottomless.

'Well, first things first, I'm going to buy a new skirt,' I half joke, although that might not be a terrible idea, because I only brought the one fancy outfit with me, and I can't exactly visit a fancy restaurant in my travelling or work clothes. 'And then, well, I'm seeing the sights. I'm here to write an article about why Paris is a great place to visit for a getaway, so I'm going to explore, find somewhere nice for dinner and... yeah.'

Yeah, I just came up with that. Well, I can't exactly tell him why I'm really here, can I? On call, for something that I might not even be called on for – for my assistant job at a dating app. It sounds made up. I want him to think I'm cool and chic like he is.

'Alone?' he blurts in disbelief.

'Yeah, well, I'm single, so...'

'*Non, non, non,*' he replies. 'We can't have that. Come, I know a beautiful boutique. We will get you a new skirt, and then I will show you the sights, and I will take you for dinner – let me show you the romance Paris has to offer. What do you say?'

'*Oui,*' I blurt, unable to hide the mild breathlessness I'm feeling, because wow. This man has game – and somehow he's fallen into my lap, semi-literally, and I'm swooning. 'Yes, I'd love that.'

Best to clarify, lest my French be as clumsy as myself.

'Come,' he insists.

Honestly? I think I might. It's the accent.

There are certain obligations when it comes to exploring Paris for the first time, and I feel like Henri has given me a tour money can't buy – or that money could buy, even, because it's like he's pulled our itinerary straight from a guidebook.

I would ask how I got so lucky, finding someone to show me the sights, but I could ask that question in more of a general way because Henri is a certified dreamboat. He's smart, he's funny, he's French – and he's drop-dead gorgeous. To look at, he isn't the typical Frenchman you would conjure up – not that I'm one for stereotypes; then again, I'm a single Englishwoman in her thirties who just got her skirt caught in a revolving door. He's tall and broad with blown-back sandy blond hair. He's dressed effortlessly smart in a blue suit, and he has his jacket back now because he helped me buy a skirt. Yes, he shopped with me – he even picked out a skirt for me. He even tried to pay for it. I didn't let him but he said he wanted to because it was his fault that when he saved me, he regretted that he couldn't save my skirt too. How bloody French is that?

We've been everywhere. The Champs-Élysées, the Arc de

Triomphe, then onto Montmartre to see Sacré-Cœur – and, of course, The Louvre is a non-negotiable destination. From there we went for dinner at the most charming bistro, where I consumed so, so much cheese – I had the best toasts de chèvre (that's fancy cheese on toast to you and me) and Crêpes Suzette au Grand Marnier (really hope I'm not butchering the pronunciation) for dessert – the boozy pancakes of my dreams.

Now we're strolling along the edge of the Jardin des Tuileries, because sadly it's closed now, but our hotel isn't far.

After Ben, and his wankery antics, I didn't think I would ever have a good time with a man ever again – and that I certainly wouldn't find one who wouldn't give me the dreaded ick. Since deciding that I was never going to settle for any icks ever again, it always feels like a matter of time before I spot one, but maybe, just maybe Henri could be different?

'Thank you for such an amazing evening,' I tell him sincerely. 'Not just for saving me, but for showing me the sights. I'll bet not many people get their own personal genuine French tour guide to show them around, buy them clothes, take them out for dinner – it's like a French fairytale.'

Henri laughs.

'You deserve – how do you say? – a hot date,' he tells me.

'Well, you are one seriously hot date,' I confirm. 'Ten out of ten. No notes.'

Finally, outside the hotel, we pause on the pavement. Even though we're obviously both going inside, this still feels like a natural place to say goodnight.

Unless...

I notice Henri lick his lips, like he's gearing up for something, his eyes darting between my lips and my eyes until he leans in and takes me in his arms, pulling me close, planting his lips on mine and... wow. Wow, wow, wow. He kisses French too, in case you were wondering, his tongue flicking mine lightly before going in for the kill, turning it into something more passionate.

Eventually, we separate, if only to breathe, and ooh la la.

Henri glances in the direction of the revolving doors.

'I see they've removed your skirt,' he points out.

'So they have,' I reply, giggling awkwardly.

'Perhaps, if you might like to come to my room, I could remove this one...'

Henri lightly grazes the back of his hand from my stomach down to my skirt, lingering between my legs for a split second. Not enough for anyone to realise what's going on, but spelling out exactly what he has in mind for me.

Pulling the trigger on moving on, in that way, is not something I have excelled at thus far – why am I being coy? To put it plainly, I haven't slept with anyone since Ben, and I'm not exactly sure why. It's not like I'm planning on living a life of celibacy, it's just that it's never felt right.

I guess I need to look at it this way: I'm in Paris, I'm on a dream date, with a really nice man. If not now, then when, right? Plus, I don't need to worry too much, because I'll be back in London soon enough, and Henri will stay here, so what does it matter if it goes disastrously...

'I'd love that,' I blurt in a breathy voice.

Theoretically, I would. So maybe a little fake confidence is what I need for the real deal to kick in.

'*Allez*. Let us go inside.'

Henri steps aside to allow me to walk through the door first, I'd imagine so that he can keep an eye on me, to make sure that no one or nothing gets to take off my skirt before he does. Inside the lobby, he takes me by the hand and leads me towards the lifts.

'Henry... Henry... Oi, Henry... Henry... Henry, oi, are you deaf, pal?'

Henri keeps walking but I turn my head and see that there's an Englishman hot on our heels.

'Erm, I think someone wants you,' I tell him.

'No, no, it can't be me,' Henri says, picking up the pace.

'Henry, pal,' the voice says, getting louder.

I notice a hand reach for Henri's shoulder. Henri stops and turns around.

'Deaf git,' the man says, laughing. 'I was going to say where were you, you missed half the conference, but suddenly it all makes sense. You pulled a French bird, eh?'

I can't help but cock my head as I stare at the man.

'Sorry, love, no offence, but they don't make 'em like you back in Milton Keynes, where we're from,' he tells me. He turns his attention back to Henri. 'Is this why you ducked out early? Did you plan this?'

I look to Henri. He's ghostly pale right now.

'Ehhh... no, I went for a cigarette,' he replies.

The man cracks up.

'Give over with the fake French accent, you'll offend your bird,' the man ticks him off.

I look to Henri but he can't return my gaze.

'Yeah, no, sorry, I bobbed out, but me and her just met,' Henri – well, Henry – explains.

Oh, my good God. Henry's voice is much higher pitched than he's been letting on – which hardly seems worth mentioning, given that he's clearly been pretending to be bloody French this entire time. His real accent is much different.

'I'll leave you to it, pal,' the man says, slapping Henry on the back. 'But have you still got your guidebook? I've lost mine. I want to go out, and it looks like you'll be staying in...'

He wiggles his eyebrows.

Henry says nothing. He takes the guidebook from his pocket and hands it to his friend, who soon makes himself scarce.

Okay, that's why the tour seemed like something out of a guidebook, because presumably that's exactly where it came from. Not from Henri, the sexy Frenchman, but from Henry, Milton fucking Keynes born and fucking bred, who obviously clocked me as a ditzy English bird and thought he'd try his luck.

'Liberty, I'm so sorry,' he says, his real accent still completely alarming to my ears.

Oh, God, this is why he sounded so French before. And why everything he said felt like, I don't know, like something you'd hear in a movie. I kept thinking to myself: wow, I can't believe the French actually talk like this, and now I know – they don't. They absolutely don't.

'I thought maybe, if you were English, you'd be looking for a Frenchman, and you wouldn't be arsed about some businessman from Milton Keynes, but we've had such a good time, haven't we?'

I mean, yeah, we have had a good time. It's been a lovely day, the food was good, the kiss was amazing, and Henri – I mean Henry – is a good-looking guy. But does any of that matter if he's a liar?

'What do we say we still go up ze stairs?' he says, playfully adopting his French accent at the end – which, now that I think about it, sounds so, so fake.

And just like that my ick alarm sounds, blaring in my ears, telling me to run. Why should I settle? His fake accent makes me cringe, no doubt about it, but more than that I hate that he lied to me, that he actively deceived me for hours. Oh my God, that explains why the waiter was so rude to him; he could tell he was faking it!

'You know, I think I'm just going to get an early night,' I reply, backing away.

'Liberty, come on, don't be daft,' he calls after me.

Daft! Oh, he's so ruddy, bloody English. I can't believe I didn't see it.

'No, *merci*,' I reply, subtly sarcastic, to let him know that he's blown it.

As the lift arrives, I step inside, alone, and press the button to close the doors. Just before they do, I notice Henry sigh heavily. He knows he's messed up and he's clearly feeling really sorry for himself.

I know, I could have still gone to his room, it's just one night in Paris and I'll probably never see him again regardless, but it is what it is, and when you get the dreaded ick, there's nothing you can do about it.

I told you, I refuse to settle, and I'd rather spend the night alone than be with Henry, who would probably have been groaning fencing terms to try and keep up the French act. Criiinge, no way, I'm not having it.

He's clearly taking the *piste*.

8

I'm on a nice, relaxing trip away in Yorkshire with my family.

Well, no, if I'm being totally honest with you, 'nice' and 'relaxing' are not words I would use to describe my current situation, but 'trip' and 'Yorkshire' are accurate, and I am here with my family.

Yesterday we celebrated my gran's eighty-ninth birthday and my grandad's twenty-third birthday with a joint party. I know what you're thinking – how does a thirty-year-old have a grandad who is only twenty-three? Reg, my lovely grandad, was born on 29 February back in 1936, and thinks it's cute (and it absolutely is) to only count the years when his actual birthday comes around, each leap year – meaning he's twenty-three. He is, however, eighty-nine years old too, which I think is far more impressive, but still, with no technical 29 February this year, he gets to be twenty-three for a little while longer, so he decided he would have a joint birthday party with my gran on her birthday – so long as we didn't mention him turning eighty-nine too. I would love to be so wilfully delusional when I'm that age. Just straight up refusing to age, that's my grandad. My gran, Elsie, doesn't mind people knowing her age – probably because she looks so good for it.

Gran and Grandad moved to the Yorkshire coast to enjoy their retirement in the sleepy coastal town of Marram Bay, but soon decided it wasn't sleepy enough, so they moved to Hope Island, a tidal island that cuts itself off from the rest of the country twice a day, only a mile from the shore. I was amazed when I first learned about it, the way it seemingly detaches itself from the rest of England, but trust me, you feel less into it once you realise you're trapped on a tiny island with your family.

So I'm here, with my grandparents, my mum and dad, my Auntie Eleanor, Uncle Clive (her husband), and then there's cousin Hannah and her hubby-to-be, Samuel, and as far as I can tell they still aren't speaking to me. I would say it had been awkward but, to be honest, with them and my auntie hardly speaking to me, it's been relatively peaceful.

I know what you're thinking: how's a working girl (so to speak) like me able to take a trip away with her family in the middle of the week? I'll tell you why. Because Paige still has me waiting in the wings, still not giving me anything to do, and it's so weird. It's like she hasn't found a use for me yet – but then why does she want me? It's not that I didn't have an interesting time in Paris, but in the end there was nothing for me to do there.

Paige didn't have to hire me. I'm assuming that I'll be replacing someone who hasn't left yet, and maybe there's just no work for me yet, because that's the only thing that makes sense. It's hard to complain, not when I'm getting paid regardless.

I grab my phone from my bag and fire up the WorkM8 app, the one they have us all socialise on. Oh, and I have a message!

MRLOVEBYTE

So, NewGirl, when am I going to see you
around the office?

I'm so intrigued by him. There's something so... I don't know,
exciting, about messaging anonymously with someone. I mean,
Paige did say I could only look, that I shouldn't talk to anyone
yet – and MrLoveByte, whoever he is, knows that.

My finger hovers over the keys. I know I shouldn't
reply, but...

My cheeks flush red as a call comes through from Paige. She
can't have known I was thinking about fraternising with
colleagues, can she?

'Hello?' I answer brightly, trying not to sound guilty.

'Hello, Liberty, how's it going?' she asks.

'Great, thanks, having a lovely time in Yorkshire with my
family,' I reply – well, if I'm lying anyway...

'You're in Yorkshire?' She sounds surprised.

'Erm, yeah, you said I could—'

'Right, yes, of course,' she replies. 'When are you back?'

'Tomorrow,' I tell her.

'That's good, because I need you to go to Canada,' she says
with the sort of casual tone you would send someone to the
corner shop for milk with.

'I'm going to Canada?' I reply, certain that's what she said,
but I can't quite believe it. Yeah, she's had me doing all sorts of
paperwork, for going to different places, but she's always made it
clear that it would be a last-minute thing, if I was needed or not.
I guess I'm finally needed.

'Is that a problem?' she asks.

'No, not at all, I'm glad to have something to do,' I tell her.

'I've been feeling a bit useless – is there anything else I can be doing? I want to help...'

'The best thing you can do is to be on call, should we need an assistant,' she replies. 'But, yes, okay, if we don't call on you to assist with things, what you could do for me is, wherever you are, I want you to use Matcher.'

'What, like... you want me to make a profile and swipe on people?' I reply – again, in disbelief.

'Yes, sign up, swipe, maybe meet a few people – you never know who you might spot on there – and then write me a report on each location you use it – how does that sound?' she replies.

It sort of sounds like she's inventing a task for me but, again, what else can I say?

'Right, okay, yes, I can do that,' I tell her.

'Great,' she says. 'I'll let you get back to your family. But straight back tomorrow to pack your things, yes?'

'Yes,' I reply. 'Looking forward to it!'

We say our goodbyes and I'm careful to dial back the enthusiasm to something a bit more realistic, but I'm so excited to be going somewhere, and doing something, even if it's still giving major red flags. Going to Canada sounds great – using Matcher sounds awful, but I guess I'll download it and give it a go. For my report. I suppose it could be fun though, to try it out, to go meet someone maybe... because as much as I love my family, I can't face another night of falling out over boardgames and dancing to Elvis songs until 2 a.m. – to paraphrase the man himself: no, thank you very much.

It's the first time we've all been together, since the engagement party, and I'd always thought the worst thing would be people talking about what happened with Ben and asking loads of questions, but what's happening instead is far worse. It's like people are talking about it, without actually talking about it.

They're asking about my love life, if I'm seeing anyone – if I've seen anyone, even, just for confirmation that I can still attract a man.

I suppose when you're bored, looking for an escape, and with everyone I love highlighting that I'm single, then a little boss-ordered time on Matcher might be exactly what I need to feel, I don't know, like I'm not as hopeless as everyone seems to think I am.

My brief look on Matcher was on Ben's phone and there were so, so many girls. Here though, on the island, I guess there aren't many takers, so all three (yep, just three) of my options are on the screen together. I suppose when there aren't that many people, if you get too swipe-happy, there's no one left.

Okay, so, three men. Wow, I feel like I'm on Blind Date. Let's see who we've got...

There is Arnold, from here on the tiny island. Tim, from here on the tiny island. And finally, there is Woody, from – you've guessed it – here on the tiny island.

Arnold, unfortunately, is in his late sixties, and the only daddy issues I have is that I thought mine was going to strangle me over a game of Scrabble yesterday, so he's an easy no.

Potentially an even easier no still is Tim. Not only do I get a bad vibe from the line 'no crazy chicks' but the fact that he's the local fishmonger puts me off because I'm imagining him being a bit smelly – but even if he likely isn't, his attitude stinks, so that's that.

Which means we have a winner: Woody, a thirty-two-year-old electrician with no immediate red flags on his profile.

I'll drop him a message, see what happens, and if there are as few women on this app, on this island, as there are men, I might just win by default too.

I'm alone in the kitchen, making cups of tea for everyone, when cousin Hannah walks in.

'Is that the Garfield mug?' she asks me.

'Yeah,' I reply.

'Remember how we used to fight over it, when we were kids?' she says with a laugh.

I remember that she used to kick off if she didn't get it.

'This mug is older than us – it will probably outlive us too,' I say instead.

'You're right,' she replies, her smile unnerving. 'Are you okay, after what happened at my... Are you okay?'

I feel like she stopped, right before she made it about herself, which I appreciate. I feel like she does really care.

'Ahh, I'm fine,' I reply. 'I'm sorry for the way it came out. It was just such a shock and I was really mad at him.'

'I get that,' she reassures me. 'I was just upset, because it was my day, but I've calmed down, and so I want to reinvite you to the wedding.'

I purse my lips – I didn't realise I'd been uninvited. Information my mum probably kept from me because she knew Hannah would calm down eventually.

'Thanks,' I reply.

'Let's just keep it a normal day – my day – yeah? I don't mind if you bring a plus one, but bring a good one,' she suggests.

'Sure,' I say. 'Thanks again.'

I did make a scene at her party and I am sorry. I have to do better at her wedding – I refuse to be messy, no matter what's going on in my life. Perhaps Matcher can help me find a decent plus one?

'Wait – can I have that cup?' she asks quickly, just in time before I put a sugar in the Garfield cup.

'Of course,' I tell her.

She takes her cup along with one for her mum.

Alone again, I notice my phone vibrating on the worktop and it's Woody, the only eligible man on the island, asking me if I want to meet up – wow – in twenty minutes. I mean, yeah, it's a small island, but that doesn't exactly give me long to get dolled up. Then again, beggars can't be choosers, on an island that is probably less than two square miles in size.

Am I nervous? No, of course I'm not, because this isn't a real date, is it? It's work.

Thankfully, being a local, he's suggested a place where we can grab a drink. A bar called DeepBlue, which sounds like a promising place to get a cocktail at least.

'How are those drinks coming along?' my gran asks, joining me in the kitchen.

'I think I've got one for everyone,' I reply semi-confidently. 'And that I've got everyone's order right.'

Gran casts an eye over them.

'Wait, who isn't having one?' she asks.

'Oh, me,' I reply. 'I'm going out – I have a date.'

'How did you know?' she asks, surprised.

'What do you mean, Gran?'

'How did you know about your date? Did your grandad tell you? I'll be honest, I thought you'd be dead against it...' she says, confusing me even more.

Erm...

'Grandad knows?' I check.

'He was there, when Marlena and I set it up. I was just coming in here to tell you – I'm so relieved you're okay with it,' she replies, rubbing my arm. 'I hate to think of you alone. I want you to be happy, and Marlena wants the same for Tom.'

Okay, one of us is confused, and while my gran may be pushing ninety, I'm pretty sure it's me.

'Tom?'

'Marlena's grandson,' she replies. 'She said you should meet him at seven, at the Anchor Inn pub, and that he'll be wearing a blue striped shirt. You're supposed to wear a red scarf, if you have one, so he knows it's you.'

Oh, God, no, I've just realised what's happening here. My gran has set me up on an actual blind date.

'You know what, Gran, I'm not sure I can make it,' I reply, not wanting to throw her kindness in her face. 'Do you think you could cancel for me?'

'Sorry, my love, I can't,' she replies. 'Marlena is on a cruise.'

'So, no way of contacting Tom?' I check.

'No, sorry,' she replies. 'But that's why we decided he should wear a striped shirt, so you can spot him.'

I wrap an arm around my gran and give her a squeeze. No, I don't want to go on a date with Marlena's grandson Tom, but I love Gran so much for thinking of me. I know how lucky I am, to still have both my grandparents around, given their age. Hey – here's hoping I get my genes from them.

'Okay, well, I'll get ready and I'll head out,' I tell her. 'Tell Hannah to help carry the drinks – I'll slink off, if that's okay? Save me having to tell everyone my business.'

'Got you,' Gran says, tapping her nose. 'Go, have fun. Marlena says he's a lovely young man.'

'Fab, thanks,' I reply.

Okay, so how do I manage this? I go to the bar, I meet Woody, and then what? What do I do about Tom? I don't exactly want to meet up with Marlena's random grandson, but I don't want to leave him standing there, waiting for me, if I'm not going to turn up. That's straight up mean.

I fire up the map on my phone and look at where the bar and the pub are. Okay, okay, I can work with this. Thank you, tiny island, because amazingly the map says it only takes less than two minutes to walk between them so, when it's time to meet Tom, I'll say I'm going to the loos, or to make a call, or something, and I'll duck out, leg it to the pub, tell Tom something has come up, make my apologies, then leg it back to the bar. I'm sure it will be fine, right?

I get ready as quickly as I can, throwing on a pair of jeans, a nice top and a leather jacket, pull on my favourite thigh-high boots, and slink out through the side door, lest I have to explain to anyone where I'm going.

I don't have to walk for long before I'm in the small area where all the bars, restaurants and shops are. There aren't many here really and I can't tell if I love it or I hate it. Being cut off from the rest of the country has its pros and cons, but if I had to choose right now, I would say I kind of like that everything is close together. Whether you want to pop to the shop, go out for dinner, or walk home – it's all so easy to do on foot. I like the convenience. Unlike in London, where sometimes you have to catch a train from A to B for the simplest thing.

And there he is, Woody, waiting outside the bar for me. It's a relief that he looks like his profile picture, because I've watched enough documentaries on Netflix to realise how often they don't. We all take a liberty here and there, with a flattering angle or a light filter, but it sounds like some people on this app would only be identifiable by their dental records, if they went missing, because the missing posters would be no use with the photos they had. I guess, for this reason, if I'm ever in a life-threatening situation, I need to make sure that I pout, so that when they find my body, and check it against my photos, they'll know it's me.

'Woody?' I check.

'Liberty?' he replies. 'Why, hello there.'

'Hi,' I say with a smile. It amuses me that he shakes my

hand. Oh-so formal considering we met on an app most people use for hook-ups.

Woody isn't much taller than me – which some shorter guys hate, but I didn't notice his face fall when he clapped eyes on me, so that's a good sign. He has wild curly brown hair that doesn't look like he does much to it beyond washing it, but he looks like he's dressed well, in dark trousers with a smart long black coat buttoned up to the top to keep the chill out.

He gestures towards the bar with his dark brown eyes.

'Shall we?' he suggests.

'Let's do it,' I reply with what I would call an encouraging level of enthusiasm, my way of letting him know that I'm happy to be here.

We've no sooner stepped inside DeepBlue when Woody leads me back outside, through a different door, onto some decking.

'I thought we could have our drinks out here,' he suggests. 'It's heated, peaceful and you can see the stars.'

Oh, boy, you really can. There's something about being out of the city, away from the lights, and looking up at the sky. You know there aren't more stars here, obviously, but the way they reveal themselves is something really special.

'Do you like space?' he asks me.

'The stars are beautiful,' I reply.

'Yeah, but do you like space?' he says again.

A waitress arrives to take our drinks order so I leave his question hanging in the air. When it's just the two of us again, he looks at me expectantly. Do I like space? I mean, yes? I suppose? I like looking at the stars but I'm not sure my passion stretches beyond that. Maybe I'm being a little overcritical of the man but, to me, asking a question like 'do you like space?' is a little bit like asking 'do you like dinosaurs?' We're not seven.

And yeah, okay, maybe I am being a bit harsh. I need to relax a little, to give Woody a chance, even if it is just for tonight.

'Space? Yes,' I reply. 'You?'

'Oh, big time,' he replies. 'I have all these apps on my phone, for tracking ISS – and Starlink, of course.'

'Oh, yeah, of course,' I reply, despite having no idea what he's talking about. I'll be honest with you, I think it's the strong Yorkshire accent, but initially, I thought he said 'ISIS', and I was so confused.

The small talk doesn't last long before Woody takes things up a gear.

'Shall we get our dealbreakers out of the way then?' he suggests, cutting to the chase. 'Worst thing about dating is all the time-wasting, when you were never really compatible, right?'

I'm sure 'time-wasting', as he puts it, isn't great, but I don't know, for me, when I think of the worst things about dating, ultimately sending intimate pictures to other girls, and men pretending to be French because they think you'll shag them, is up there too, although I suppose you could file both under time-wasting.

'Why not,' I reply with a smile. 'My dealbreakers are just, you know, the usual stuff.'

'Like what?' he asks.

I let the waitress place our drinks on the table before I carry on talking. I take a generous gulp of my Sex on the Beach, buying myself a little time to think about what I'm going to say.

'Just... no liars, no cheaters. I like people who are kind and polite,' I say, pausing again. 'I'm generally quite open to most people.'

Until that inevitable ick kicks in, of course. Perhaps tonight it won't happen?

'Kind of a cop-out answer, but okay,' he says before swigging his beer. 'I'm glad you like honesty, because I'm the kind of bloke who speaks his mind, who says what he thinks, whether people want to hear it or not.'

That's a red flag, right there. People tend to use 'speaking their mind' as a euphemism for being a bit of a dick.

'I can't cook, so I tend not to fancy lasses who can't cook,' he continues. 'No modern women.'

'No modern women?' I repeat back to him.

'No parrots either,' he jokes.

'Sorry, I've got to know what a modern woman is,' I say, laughing as I say the words.

'I mean that because I don't cook, I don't clean and so on, so I need a lass that will do those things for me really,' he explains in a tone of voice that suggests I must now fully understand and agree with him.

'I see,' is about all I can say.

'And no emotional women,' he adds. 'I can turn a blind eye one week of the month but, beyond that, I've no time for drama.'

And there it is, my 'ick alarm', sounding loud and clear.

Do you think I could get away with murdering him, out here, in the dark of night? Would anyone even miss him? Is there a jury in the world that would convict me? If I got a female judge, she'd probably give me a high-five.

'I'm really emotional,' I tell him plainly. I don't suppose I'm any more or less emotional than the next girl, no matter what week of the month it is, but I think we're done here. 'And really modern.'

'You don't seem all that modern,' he replies, his eyes narrowing.

My main takeaway from that is that he has no issues believing I'm emotional.

'Looks can be deceiving,' I tell him. 'I can't cook, I refuse to clean, I basically never shave my legs and even my vibrator has a vibrator.'

Woody sucks his bottom lip into his mouth as he thinks for a moment.

'You're taking the piss out of me, aren't you?' he replies.

'Well, now you're going to make me cry,' I say as I pull a silly face, like a baby about to scream.

'Okay, Liberty, let me say first of all that this behaviour isn't mature or ladylike,' he informs me as he stands up from his stool. He picks up his beer bottle and drains the last of the contents into his mouth. 'Like I said, I hate timewasters. We're clearly not meant to be, so I think I'm going to go.'

He does seem genuinely annoyed at me, which gets my back up a little.

'Oh, no, now I'm *really* going to cry,' I say sarcastically.

'I hope you find what you're looking for,' he says simply before leaving me.

I'd say I hoped he found the non-emotional non-modern woman of his dreams but I think she might be just that, a fantasy, nothing he's going to find with his eyes open.

I finish my drink and, as I do so, I realise that Woody has left me to pay the bill. Unbelievable.

What do I do now? I don't want to go back to my gran and grandad's, not yet – oh, shit. Tom. I'm supposed to be meeting him soon, at the pub. I was going to go and tell him that I couldn't stay but, I don't know, with Woody being a bust, maybe I could have one drink with him? It beats going home early, and it definitely beats hanging out with Woody.

Screw it, I'll do it, I'll go to the pub and meet Marlena's grandson. It's less than two minutes from here so I'll freshen up, maybe grab another quick drink, pay the bill and then head right over.

By the time I'm making the short journey from what seems like the only bar to the only pub, I'm ready to sit inside, so I'm delighted to see that they have an open fire lit. Oh, and that must be Tom, sitting at the table in front of it, because his stripy blue shirt stands out a mile in a room that is otherwise filled with plaid and tweed.

It's only as I approach him that I notice how familiar his curly brown hair seems, and as I peer around to get a look at his face, my worst fear comes true.

'Woody?' I blurt as our eyes meet.

'Liberty, what the fuck? Are you stalking me?' he asks.

'Oh, don't flatter yourself,' I clap back. 'I'm... you're... Your grandma isn't called Marlena, is she?'

'Yeah, she is,' he replies. 'Oh, God, tell me you're not Elsie's granddaughter...'

I can't help but laugh.

'Oh, no,' he says. 'No, no, no.'

You would think I'd be offended at how horrified he is, but it only makes me laugh harder.

I sit down at the table with him for a moment, just to satisfy my curiosity.

'Wait, I thought my gran said I was meeting someone called Tom though?' I point out.

'Yeah, I'm Tom,' he replies. 'Tom Wood – Woody to my friends. Nanna never mentioned your name, only that you were Elsie's granddaughter. You're supposed to be wearing a red scarf.'

'I don't have one. So, wait, you scheduled two dates for one night?' I check.

'So did you,' he replies.

'No, I scheduled one,' I correct him. 'My gran set me up with the other, and I didn't have any details to cancel.'

'My nanna is always trying to set me up too. She wants me to settle down, so she lines me up these blind dates with her mates' kids, or grandkids, and then tells me to turn up in a striped shirt so they can find me. Honestly, I think she's just worried about me being alone. She wants me to be happy, like her and my grandpop were when he was still with us.'

That's the first hint I've seen of something sincere and likeable from Woody. He isn't entirely detestable, when he shows his vulnerable side.

'I get that,' I tell him. 'My gran had the same sort of idea. She worries about me too.'

'Nanna told me that Elsie told her what happened to you,' he replies. 'With your ex. That's rough, that. No one deserves that. It makes sense to me now, why you're being so guarded with me. I'm sorry if I made a bad first impression.'

I am... disarmed. I wasn't expecting him to be nice, caring or understanding. Maybe he's not as bad as he seemed before? Is that possible?

'That's okay,' I tell him. 'I mean, we're here now, our grans wanted us to meet – we might as well have another drink?'

'Yeah, I'd like that,' he replies. 'Shall I get them?'

'Well, you did leave me to pay for the last ones,' I can't resist pointing out.

'You did tell me you were a modern woman,' he dares to joke. 'Take a seat, I think I know what you like now. I'll surprise you.'

Woody does seem like he's making more of an effort now so I make myself comfortable, taking off my coat to enjoy the heat from the fire, and when he comes back, we start chatting and it's actually nice. We don't go near anything controversial, or anything to do with relationships, we just chat shit and it's enjoyable. Perhaps Woody really isn't so bad after all.

After a while, I notice him look at his watch. Then he puts his coat on.

'Are you going?' I ask, surprised.

'No, no, I'm just cold,' he tells me. 'Carry on with your story.'

'Woody, it's boiling in here, are you okay?' I check.

'Yeah, I'm fine,' he says, slumping back in his seat a little. 'Carry on.'

I open my mouth, to carry on, but that's when I notice her, the woman at the bar, looking around like she's trying to find someone – and she's wearing a red scarf.

I look at Woody through narrowed eyes.

'Woody, do you have another date?' I ask him.

'What? No!' he insists.

'Then why have you covered up your shirt, and why is there a woman over there, in a red scarf, clearly looking for someone?'

'All right, okay, yes, fine, I did schedule in another,' he confesses quietly. 'I thought, if this one didn't go well, I may as well line up another.'

Oh, and there it is again, my ick alarm. I can't ignore it again.

'And if this one was going well?' I ask.

'Then I put on my coat, keep my head down, and wait for her to leave,' he replies. 'To be honest, I'd assumed with you being on the apps that we would have gone straight from the bar to my place. Anyway, it's a compliment, that I'm ditching her, to stay with you. I'm actually having a really nice night, and I think you are too.'

'It wasn't too bad, until I realised you'd lined up three dates for one evening, I watched you hide from one inside your coat, and I'm trying not to overthink what you just said about us going back to yours, but it's pretty safe to say that's not going to happen,' I tell him.

Woody frowns.

'Has she gone?' he asks me.

'What, your third date?' I check.

He nods his head.

'Yeah, she left, while you were hiding,' I tell him.

Honestly, this man. I can tell by his body language that he wants to go after her, now that he knows nothing is going to happen here.

'You want to go, don't you?' I ask, but I already know the answer.

He nods again.

'Go,' I tell him. 'I need to go to bed anyway.'

Woody doesn't need telling twice, he's off like a shot. At least he paid for our drinks at the bar this time.

Unbelievable. I get it, the man doesn't like to waste time, but three dates in one night? Wow. I know there aren't that many single people here but, even so, you could at least take a breath in between dates.

That's it for me, back to Gran and Grandad's, to get some sleep. I'll be up early to head back to London, to get ready for my trip, and then Canada it is. If there is one thing Woody has taught me about men tonight – by having me think about deal-breakers, things I do and don't want from a man – it's this: there is nothing more attractive than a man who lives far enough away that, when it's time to go home, you can leave him thousands of miles away. For me, knowing Woody is in Yorkshire, where my grandparents live, he'll always seem that little bit too close.

Canada here I come!

9

If I push any niggling questions to the back of my mind then it's official, I love my job.

I mean, so far, my job description has pretty much been to go to a place and be a tourist and piss around on a dating app. What's not to love about that?

I always thought dating apps would be really bleak – and maybe it would be, if I were actually using Matcher to find love – but I have to admit, it's kind of fun, swiping around, seeing who is out there. It sort of reminds me of when I was a kid, and I would flick through the Argos catalogue and circle everything I wanted. Was I ever going to buy all of it? Of course not. Groovy Chick bedsheets, a Furby and a clown pendant necklace – yes. But the pages and pages of Game Boys, Laser Challenge sets, swings, slides and roundabouts – in my dreams. It's like getting to try before you buy, but you're not actually buying anything, so you've nothing to lose.

I'm here, in Canada, as instructed, waiting on a call from Paige to say if she needs me. If! I know Matcher is a huge company, but I cannot for the life of me figure out why she would need an assistant on standby. They say if something seems too good to be true then it probably is – but why let that ruin a good trip, eh?

There is so much to love about Nova Scotia. I've been exploring for a couple of days now, seeing the sights, enjoying the local cuisine.

My favourite spot so far is probably Peggy's Cove. I was at the Yorkshire coast only a matter of days ago – a sight I've seen so many times – but this is something else. The iconic lighthouse sits atop rugged granite cliffs. There was something almost cinematic about the way the waves crashed against the rocks. It was so dramatic, violent even, in a way that reminded me just how brutal Mother Nature can be when she feels like it.

But then I also enjoyed exploring Halifax, visiting the Halifax Citadel National Historic Site. The views from the star-shaped fortress were so different to Peggy's Cove, but equally as beautiful. You got the most amazing panoramic views of the city and the harbour from the ramparts.

I'm sure I say this everywhere I go, but the only thing I find more exciting than exploring the area is exploring the menus, and Canada is not disappointing when it comes to cuisine. Personal favourites so far include the freshest lobster rolls I've ever eaten, blueberry grunt – which tastes a billion times better than it sounds – and of course poutine. Everywhere I go, I swear, it's always the cheese that gets me.

The only thing I don't love – and this is a me thing, for sure – is the cold late November weather. Oh my God, I've never felt cold like it. I don't think the mercury has risen above 5°C the whole time I've been here – and it's definitely dropping below zero. Luckily the locals are used to it, they're equipped for it, so indoors I feel fine. But then I step outside, into the icy winds, and it's like my breath is stolen from me.

Of course, the warmth from the locals goes some way to fighting the chill – quite literally, in some ways, as a very nice lady let me borrow her extra (yes, extra) scarf on one of my trips.

And now I'm back in my hotel. I've eaten, I'm relaxing, I've checked my phone a million times to make sure Paige hasn't asked me for anything. I do have a message from MrLoveByte though. We've been swapping a few messages, here and there. It's kind of nice, having some company, someone to talk to in an app other than Matcher – which I only use for work. I cannot stress that enough.

MRLOVEBYTE

Still loving the job?

NEWGIRL

Still not doing much...

I know we're in different time zones but I reply right away. He must be a night owl, because we always seem to time it right.

MRLOVEBYTE

Best kind of job, surely?

And he's up! Great, that gives me some company while I sit with my back to the radiator, trying to thaw myself out.

NEWGIRL

Maybe. Hey, I have a question for you. Have you ever actually used Matcher? Or does working on it put you off?

I wait patiently for him to reply, hoping I haven't over-stepped the mark.

MRLOVEBYTE

Are you not even going to ask me how my day is going? Haha! Straight to the hard questions. Yeah, I've used it. Off and on. Mostly off.

NEWGIRL

Interesting...

I wonder why that is.

MRLOVEBYTE

I go through phases where I use it. I download it, match with a few people, chat... maybe go on a date. Then I inevitably delete it and swear I'm done and I'm never bothering with it again... but a month later I'll find myself downloading it again. I tell myself it's for research. User perspective. UX insight. Field testing. Whatever it is I need to hear to feel better about it haha!

NEWGIRL

Haha! Have you figured out why that is?

MRLOVEBYTE

I guess... everyone wants to meet someone, right? Even the people who run the app that helps people meet people.

NEWGIRL

That's true. So, do you make work notes while you swipe, or can you keep the two sides of your life separate?

MRLOVEBYTE

Very much separate. If I start looking at it through a work lens... well... that's when I usually delete it. That or after I've had a crap date.

I admire his honesty.

MRLOVEBYTE

What about you? Are you on Matcher? Have you used it before?

NEWGIRL

Not until I got this job. Paige has me using it for 'research' – I'm not really sure what I'm doing but it's eye opening.

MRLOVEBYTE

So you're dating for work?

NEWGIRL

Basically. It's really weird. But it's my job, and I'm new, so I do as I'm told.

MRLOVEBYTE

You're talking to me though... when you told me Paige said you shouldn't talk to anyone...

NEWGIRL

You told me no one will ever know!

He did. When we were chatting, while I was on the plane, I told him Paige said I shouldn't chat to people yet, and he said it could be our little secret.

MRLOVEBYTE

They won't. We could always chat somewhere else... Maybe I should download it again. Who knows... maybe we'll swipe on each other.

NEWGIRL

Do you think we would match? And is that allowed?

MRLOVEBYTE

Well, Paige says no dating through work. But if we meet through the app... technically, that's a success story. She'd have to put us in the newsletter.

NEWGIRL

From HR to PR haha.

MRLOVEBYTE

Exactly. Although I do like a bit of low-level HR drama, it keeps the work day fun.

NEWGIRL

Sounds chaotic – maybe I wouldn't be your type. I think you'd swipe left on me.

MRLOVEBYTE

There's only one way to find out – I'm downloading Matcher again...

NEWGIRL

Why do I feel like I owe you an apology?

MRLOVEBYTE

Don't owe me an apology – owe me a drink.

I stare at my phone screen, wondering how to reply. I'm not supposed to be fraternising with my coworkers and yet here I am, low-key flirting up a storm with a man whose name I don't even know.

MRLOVEBYTE

Right... As fun as this has been, I do actually have to work at some point, so I'd better get on with that.

NEWGIRL

Same. Well, I think I'm supposed to be working. But since 'swiping' is the only task on my agenda, there's only one thing to do.

MRLOVEBYTE

Swipe wisely. And if you spot me... Well. Let's just say I hope I've picked a decent enough photo that you send me to the right and not the left.

NEWGIRL

So long as you're not in the gym or hugging a sedated tiger...

MRLOVEBYTE

Only a coward would sedate a tiger. I'd beat it fair and square in hand to paw combat.

I actually snort out loud.

MRLOVEBYTE

Speak soon, NewGirl.

NEWGIRL

Bye!

I do really appreciate his insights into Matcher – and his light flirting. It makes the days go quicker when there's nothing to do. Well, nothing but the only task I have left... To fire up Matcher, to see who is around, and to 'write a report', whatever that last part means.

I'm never sure if Paige wants to know about the functionality of the app, the general user experience or the calibre of men, so I give her a bit of everything.

Unlike when I was in Yorkshire, there are plenty of people to swipe through. I've got the swiping down to a fine art now, sometimes making split-second decisions on the look of a person, not even reading the details on their profile. I promise you, I would never be so quick to judge a book by its cover in real life, but on Matcher you have to learn how to streamline the process. I've learned how to read between the lines, when looking at someone's main photo. First of all, it's amazing how many men forget to take off or crop their wedding ring out of their photos, and being married is more than an ick, it's completely repulsive. I'm always quick to swipe away the gym bros – usually, if it's their main photo, it means that exercise, fitness and usually appearances mean far more to them than anything else, and I'm the girl who has eaten chips not once but twice today. Seeing people who like to travel always catches my eye... but if I see anyone posing for a photo with a sedated tiger or similar, ickkkk, no thanks – see the tourist sights, sure, observe nature in nature, but standing with your foot on a sleeping animal that could murder you if you gave it the chance just pisses me off.

I notice a message come from a match called Logan. He's got short dark hair and bright blue eyes. He's reading a book in his profile picture which, okay, is kind of a weird photo to exist when you think about it – it had to have been posed for – but there are worse set-ups. Reading his profile, I can see that his hobbies include sports – but sexy Canadian ones, none of the boring ones lads in the UK seem to be obsessed with – and cooking. Take me to watch hot hockey players and make me dinner after and you might be a winner – theoretically, of course. Just for work.

We swap messages, chatting about my trip, and Logan starts telling me about the things to do and the places to visit that I might not have thought of yet. When I mention that I've never been ice skating before, it floors him – I suppose such a thing is unthinkable here – so he invites me to the ice rink next to his apartment. He says, on an evening, they have these disco nights where they turn the lights down, crank the music and everyone has a nice time skating around casually, dancing – apparently it's super romantic. And then he asks me if I want to go.

It's something to do, right? Something to go in the report? Probably not, but I'm at a loose end, and kind of lonely. Solo travelling is all well and good, until you don't want to eat dinner alone, or sit quietly in your hotel room all night.

So we make a plan. I get dressed up – and then wrapped up – and head out to meet him. Ever the gent, Logan says he'll swing by in a taxi and collect me, so that I don't have to make my way there on my own, which is sweet.

Internet dating used to be this weird thing that only people with no social skills did, as a last resort, to try to finally meet someone. These days, especially if you're a millennial or younger, it seems like it's a given that pretty much everyone is on the apps. There's no shame in it... and yet it's still one of those things that, to people who seem like real adults, you don't tend to broadcast it. So Logan picks me up in a taxi and, in the presence of the driver, we talk like we've known each other for much longer than an hour or so.

'You do realise you're going to have to teach me to skate,' I point out. 'Like, before I can move a muscle, you're going to have to show me on dry land.'

'There's no real way to teach you other than to lace up your skates, get you out there on the ice, and just go with it,' he explains. 'You need to feel the ice beneath your skates, to flow, to find your balance and stay there.'

'Balance is not something I've had, historically,' I confess. I experience something similar to how I'd imagine it is when your life flashes before your eyes, except for me it's a speedy montage of all of the times I've fallen. From tripping over kerbs to stumbling over thin air, to actually stacking it on the ice – yep, I have previous – it seems unlikely that balance is something I'm going to be able to find tonight.

Inside the ice rink you can tell you're in a sporty place but, just as Logan said, the lights are low, there's a disco ball, Dua Lipa is pumping from the speakers. Here goes nothing.

Logan helps me on with my skates and then leads me out onto the ice. For the most part, everyone is going around in a circle, like they're on a track.

'We stick to the edges, to start with,' he explains. 'That way you can take it slow, no one will knock you.'

'I'll knock myself,' I joke. 'But okay.'

He takes me by the hand and sort of drags me onto the ice, moving me just slowly enough to keep me on my feet, but I feel like if he lets go of my hands, I'll drop to the ice in a second.

'Don't let go of me,' I say, my voice wobbling slightly.

'Don't worry, I got you,' he replies, laughing a little.

Logan looks like he skates even more confidently than he walks – which makes sense, as he explains to me how he's been playing ice hockey his whole life. He asks me about sports I played at school, and I don't know how to say that my most competitive sport was trying to get out of PE every week, so I just list the stupid girly sports they made us do. At our school, football was only for the boys, netball was the sport for the girls – and don't even get me started ranting about the fact that they made us play in skirts. Fucking skirts, for sport. When you're an insecure teen, with stretchmarks on your thighs, trust me when I say that you carry a lifelong vendetta against the angry woman with the whistle who made you repeatedly attempt the high jump in a pleated blue mini skirt.

'The more confident you are, the easier it is,' he tells me –

and he's right, I am finding it easier, and not only the ice skating. I suppose it's true of everything really, and we're told time and time again that men really rate confidence in a woman, so after an hour of flirting – and Logan making it perfectly clear that he's interested – I decide to be brave, to treat this more like an actual date, to take the bull by the horns. Well, the Canadian by the hips.

Look, I'm sure it was suave, sexy and sophisticated in another universe. In this universe, however, it takes Logan by surprise and as he backs up in a panic he starts to flap around – first backwards, then forwards, face down on the ice as he slides across the rink.

I don't have the skills to hurry over there, and as I watch other more capable people rush to his aid, I try to ignore the ick alarm going off in my head. Well, when someone does something embarrassing, but you already love them, it's fine. When it's someone new, yikes, the second-hand embarrassment is contagious.

Oh, boy. I can see from here that his nose is bleeding. The blood is flowing from his face, it's on the ice – it looks like something way worse has gone on. Not that falling and hurting yourself isn't bad, but a little blood goes a long way, so it looks more like someone has skated over his fingers and popped them clean off.

'I'm all right, I'm all right,' he reassures me as he approaches me, skating steady now he's back on his feet. 'You just startled me, is all.'

'Logan, I'm so, so sorry,' I say, placing my hand on his shoulder. 'Are you okay? Do you need to see a doctor?'

'I'm all right, really,' he insists. 'My pride hurts more than anything.'

'Everyone falls,' I reassure him. 'It's not a pride thing.'

'I wish I could tell them it was because you took me by surprise, when you grabbed my ass,' he replies as he examines the fingers that were pinching his nostrils closed. 'I think it's stopped – it's worse than it looks, I just have a sensitive nose.'

Ignore the alarm in your head, Liberty, you crazy person. There's nothing wrong with having a sensitive nose. You're clinging to this to find something wrong with this man, like you find something wrong with everyone.

'Can I help you home?' I ask. 'Help you get cleaned up?'

'Sure, thanks,' he replies. 'I don't live far from here.'

Logan is right, his apartment is walking distance from the ice rink – I guess that makes this his local. I hope he doesn't feel like he can't show his face here again. Jokes aside, there is no shame in falling. I'm glad he isn't truly hurt.

Logan's apartment is very much the bachelor pad you would expect of a single thirty-something man. I don't know what he does for a living – we didn't get that far – but whatever it is, it means he can buy a lot of tech.

'Nice place,' I say, turning to face him, only to see him peeling off his t-shirt to reveal his toned torso.

'Thanks,' he replies. 'Hey, I hope you don't think I fell down on purpose, to get you back here...'

He grins, showing me that he's joking. The thought hadn't crossed my mind, until he said it, and now all I can think about is the fact that I probably do deserve to be murdered for my naivety.

I can tell he's trying to lighten the mood though, and I appreciate it.

'Can I kiss you?' he asks.

Oh, boy. I've been so, so terrible at the dating game since my split. But I'm here, I do fancy him, and it could be a good way to test the waters. And it's only a kiss, right? If I mess this up, never mind, I'll be back in the UK before I know it. I owe it to myself, to try to move on... right? No, I'm not sure either, but it feels like what I'm supposed to do.

I nod my head.

Logan eases me back onto the sofa, and as my body sort of reclines into the mountain of cushions, he ends up sort of on top of me. He kisses my neck for a moment before kissing his way down my body, over my blouse, until he reaches my waist. He lifts my blouse, just a little, to kiss me on the stomach. It's kind of wetter and sloppier than I'm used to, and – no, Liberty, stop it. Stop being overly critical. Lie back and enjoy it.

It's only as Logan returns to eye level that I notice what's happened.

'Oh my God, you're bleeding,' I blurt.

I notice his eyes move to my body and then widen in horror.

'Fuck, shit, Liberty, I'm so sorry,' he babbles, climbing off me so quickly he inadvertently kicks his coffee table and then falls to the floor. Again.

The alarm bells in my head almost deafen me.

'I'll grab you a towel,' he says as he scrambles to his feet.

A towel? Is he serious? I look like fucking Carrie at the prom.

What I need is a shower but I guess I'll wipe the worst of it off here, and then head back to my hotel.

I was looking for a sign, to tell me whether or not I was ready to move on, and I'm clearly not ready. Better luck next time, eh?

I've never needed to literally wash a man out of my hair before, but here we are. There's a first time for everything.

10

I'm on my third trip for Matcher – this time travelling about as far as you can from the UK – and I'm still simply 'on call' waiting for something to do. To be honest with you, I'm sort of used to it now. I'd probably be disappointed if things changed. I'm being paid to go on holiday and use dating apps. Maybe that's it, perhaps that really is just the job, so I'm not complaining, I'm having a nice time... in Sydney!

Yep, I'm in Australia, and I'm loving it. It's a little bit strange today though, because it's actually my birthday, and here I am, spending it alone on the other side of the world to everyone I care about, but with my job position being... interesting, shall we say, I didn't dare turn down what is so far only my third assignment. I'm making the best of it though.

Breakfast at the hotel today was something else. I'm not usually one to rave about eggs – I've been known to get the egg ick – but these were poached to actual perfection, perched neatly on thick slices of sourdough that had been grilled, not toasted. That's an unnecessarily fancy step, surely, to grill your bread, but I'm here for it. The seasoned avocado that finished it off just sealed the deal. Easily a contender for my top five hotel breakfasts of all time – well, now that I'm staying in lots of hotels, I'm making a list (although this is only the third one so far, so it's not hard to get into the top five at present).

I'm having such a lovely time not working, seeing the sights, exploring everything the city and the surrounding area has to offer. I'm somehow doing my dream job, whatever it is, so in a roundabout way, Ben did me a favour, because I never would have left my old job were I not leaving him too. Sure, there were easier, less embarrassing ways to get here, but I'm at my destination now – so why stress over the turbulence?

It's been such a busy few days and I'm positively knackered – mainly because everything I have done has involved so, so much walking.

I have hiked around the Blue Mountains National Park, which was so beautiful, but to me felt more like a climb than a hike. I've strolled around Sydney Harbour, taking in the sights of the Opera House, and the bridge – which I also walked up, which again also felt more like a climb than a walk, but that might be because they strap you into a harness and you walk up high, across the metalwork. I was nervous, at first, especially doing it alone, but being alone is something I'm starting to get used to. I shouldn't miss out on things just because I'm single, right?

That said...

Today, in an attempt to feel like I'm at least doing some work, I have been swiping and chatting on Matcher, and there's one guy I've been talking to for a few days – Liam – who seems nice and normal so we agreed to meet up for a stroll on Bondi Beach. Yep, more walking, but we're having a lovely time so far. We're taking it slow (in every sense) and chatting as we go.

It's December, so it's summer here, which was lovely but

surreal to touch down to, after leaving the chilly weather back home. It's positively hot – and so is Liam.

I know what you're thinking: did I swipe right on him because he looks exactly as you'd expect a Bondi Aussie to look? Absolutely. Is his accent driving me wild? It certainly is.

Liam is a lifeguard, and while he may be wearing a vest on his top half now, most of his pictures were of him in his work uniform – shorts. Nothing but shorts. So I know there's a toned swimmer's body lurking underneath that top.

'I'm much happier walking along the beach than I am going in the sea,' I tell him.

'If everyone thought that, I'd be out of a job,' he jokes. 'Fancy grabbing some food?'

'I'd love to,' I reply. 'What do you recommend?'

'Fish and chips,' he suggests.

I laugh to myself. I've come all this way – travelling about as far as I can from the UK – and I'm going to have fish and chips for my lunch.

'Sounds great,' I reply.

To be fair, the fish and chips here are not at all like they are back home. They have so many different types of fish on offer – they even do lobster – and it's in breadcrumbs, not batter, which is a nice change – so long as the UK authorities don't take my passport off me for saying so.

'It's my birthday today,' I tell him, realising I haven't yet mentioned it. 'I'm pretty sure, anyway. I forget what the time difference is, so maybe it's not technically my birthday back home, but it's my Aussie birthday.'

'What?' Liam blurts. 'Happy birthday!'

'Thanks,' I reply.

'So, you're alone in Sydney for your birthday?' he checks. 'Wait, isn't it your thirtieth birthday then?'

'No, I'm turning thirty-one today,' I reply.

'I was gonna say, my mum would've been mad as a cut snake if I'd spent my big 3-0 on the other side of the world,' he tells me, popping a frankly massive chip in his mouth.

I have been messaging with my mum, and I told her I would call her later tonight, for a proper chat. The plan is that, when I'm home, we'll have a big party – probably while I'm there for Christmas, but after Hannah's wedding, so she doesn't think I'm only doing it to steal her thunder. It's not like it's my 'big' birthday, is it?

I've noticed Liam talks about his mum a lot. I don't know how recently she passed away, but you can tell she's on his mind. It's sweet.

'I don't know, it's kind of cool, being here,' I tell him. 'And, to be honest with you, I didn't do anything special for my thirtieth anyway, so I don't think it would have been any different.'

I remember, at the time, Ben saying thirty wasn't really a milestone. That after twenty-one there was nothing to be proud of by simply ageing. He said that at that point it stops feeling like counting up, and it starts feeling like counting down. I remember my blood running cold when he said it, because I don't feel old, but he made me feel like we were on borrowed time, that our days were numbered. I suppose, when you think about it, when you view life as that short, it makes sense to live life like there are no consequences for your actions.

I disagreed with pretty much everything he had to say on the matter (which should have made me realise we were completely incompatible) because I think ageing is a privilege. Looking back, I can't remember what we did agree on. We certainly didn't agree on whether or not we should show our genitals to other people, I know that much.

I wonder if he'll do that to his next girlfriend, if he'll sneak around behind her back, or if that was just something special he did to ruin my life. Actually, you know what, I'm going to give myself my birthday off from thinking about any of that. Ben isn't welcome in my thoughts today, even if I am slagging him off.

'My mum threw me a surprise party, at a restaurant in town, it was great,' he tells me, snapping me out of my thoughts. 'She didn't get on with my ex-girlfriend, so it meant a lot to me, that they planned the party together. But, hey, she was right about her. She always told me, when she thought she saw something that didn't seem right with my ex – her intuition was spot on, but that wasn't anything new. I remember, even when I was a kid, she would tell me that you could tell a lot about a person from their hands.'

Liam takes my hands in his, turning them, looking them over.

'I think you'd pass the test,' he says with a smile.

'That's really nice,' I tell him, smiling back at him. 'When did you lose her?'

Liam raises an eyebrow.

'How do you mean?' he asks.

'When did she pass away?' I say more clearly.

'Liberty, she's not dead,' he says, sounding almost offended. 'What made you think she was dead?'

Erm, the fact that you talk about her all the time, in a way that would be sweet if she had passed, and you were missing her, but now that I know she's still alive it seems kind of creepy.

'Oh, sorry, I must have misunderstood you,' I reply.

I give my head a little wiggle, the alarm bells going off in my ears like tinnitus that won't quit. I just need to ignore it, because I'm doing it again, I'm being overly critical. Oh, what's Liam's big crime, loving his mum too much? Come on. I'm being ridiculous. He's a great guy, he's fun, he's gorgeous, we're having a lovely time together, it's only a holiday romance at best, and it's my birthday. Even my 'ick' alarm should take my birthday off. Plus, in a few days, I'll be safely back home, on the other side of the world, and I'll never see him again. That's what I'm focusing on, while I'm here, because it takes the pressure off. It's not a big deal if I mess up. I get to go home after. All I need to do is enjoy myself and not worry about the details. How hard can that be?

'Ah, that's okay,' he replies, batting his hand. 'So, it's your birthday, how are we celebrating?'

I glance down at my food, then back up at him.

'Nah, this is lunch, we should go out for dinner,' he suggests.

'Oh, okay, I'd love that,' I reply.

'We could go out in Sydney, just give me a couple of hours, I can organise something special,' he tells me.

I smile, relaxing again.

'Don't go to any trouble,' I insist. 'I thought I'd be spending it alone, so doing anything is a step up from that.'

'You deserve to do something special,' he says, taking my hand again, squeezing it.

It is very sweet, when he holds my hand, but it is making it harder for me to eat, and this food is delicious.

'Aw, thanks,' I reply, picking up my can of Coke with my left hand so that I can have a drink.

'It's just my luck, that I meet a girl so perfect, but she's from the other side of the world, and she's going home soon,' he says. 'You know what though, tell me if you feel it too, but I reckon we could make it work.'

I cough and splutter, choking on my drink.

'Sorry, it went down the wrong way,' I say as I catch my breath. 'You were saying what, sorry? Making what work?'

'Me and you, doing the long-distance thing,' he replies.

For a second I stare at him. He has to be kidding.

'I know, it will be hard, but I think it's worth it. Let's see where this goes,' he suggests with a level of enthusiasm that is frankly alarming.

I thought Australia, the actual other side of the world, would be somewhere I could meet someone, have a nice time with them, see how it goes, and then head home as free and single as I arrived. Sort of like a test. I thought this because the only way I could meet a man who lived further away would be if I got a booty call from someone aboard the International fucking Space Station (yes, I did google ISS right after my date with Woody, and now what he said makes a lot of sense).

I feel so cheated. Seriously, I've come all this way, thinking I could relax, have a commitment-free time, enjoy myself – and yet here we go again. The alarm is sounding, and every reflex I have is telling me to run from this man who is clearly crazy – or to use his own words: mad as a cut snake.

I didn't want to spend my birthday dwelling on why I can't seem to pull the trigger on moving on. I – ironically – come on these trips so that I don't have to unpack anything. Ugh, and now here we are.

Obviously, I shouldn't go to dinner with this man. His intense relationship with his mum seems ever more crackers, now that I've seen how quickly he's trying to get serious with me. Honestly, if you can't rely on a beach lifeguard to be the kind of guy to shag his way through every tourist he meets, then what has the world come to?

'I'll just check, make sure my boss doesn't want me to do anything this evening,' I tell him, grabbing my phone, doubtful that there will be anything there, but certain I'm going to lie that there is.

'Only a monster would make you work on your birthday,' he points out.

Then a monster is what I'll make out like she is, because there is no way I'm spending the evening with this guy.

Oh my God, I don't believe it, there's an email from Paige, saying I'm needed at a dinner this evening, with an attachment including the details. I have work – actual work to do – and I'm not disappointed at all, because this gets me off the hook.

'Oh, no, I do have to work tonight,' I tell him – rather conveniently, but it's true – but I don't sound as disappointed as I had intended.

He narrows his eyes in disbelief.

'Really?' he replies.

'Yeah, honestly, look, here's the email,' I tell him, showing him my phone, sounding like I can't quite believe my luck.

Poor Liam. I feel bad now, but it never would have worked. If he's going to entertain a future with anyone then he should pick someone who is a) geographically accessible, because the UK and Australia are about as far apart as you can get and b) someone emotionally available, because I so clearly am not.

Whether I'm doing it on purpose or not, things just never seem to go right. My dates are like Groundhog Day. Sooner or later I'm icked-out and I'm running for the hills (or my flight home) – there are always red flags or, worse, beige ones, and I can't see beyond them.

Is it always going to be like this? Me going on dates, wondering what's going to be wrong with whoever I'm seeing? What big fat flaw or itty-bitty ick is going to be the thing that sees me retreating? I feel like I'll always find something, even if things are going well, some little thing to obsess over, to call the whole thing off.

Maybe I'm broken, but I can't worry about that now.

I have a job to do.

11

MRLOVEBYTE

Where are you hiding, NewGirl?

I'm not sure if he's giving Joey Tribbiani from *Friends* or Joe Goldberg from *You*. Is he flirty, or frightening? There's a fine line – well, there is when you have an ick alarm as sensitive as mine. I'm pretty sure it's charming, I'm just resisting, as always, but I don't feel like I've having a very good run with men at the moment, so you'll forgive me for swearing off them.

NEWGIRL

I'm hoping I'll get to meet everyone soon. Paige is keeping me busy.

Maybe I shouldn't have done that but I'm bored, sitting alone in a restaurant, waiting for my job which, it turns out, is not really a job. I suppose the fact that it seems so silly is the reason why I'm happy to bend the rules, just a little.

MRLOVEBYTE

Ahh, you must be beautiful then.

NEWGIRL

What makes you say that?

MRLOVEBYTE

Because she hides the beautiful women away –
she's got a real bee in her bonnet about no one
in the office having relationships (except her). I
thought Matcher was supposed to be about
finding love?

Oh, well, that's interesting. And an insight into Paige that I wasn't expecting. Ludicrous, though, to suggest Matcher is a place for finding love. Give me a break.

NEWGIRL

I thought Matcher was for finding hook-ups?

MRLOVEBYTE

I'm not opposed to that either.

NEWGIRL

It's my birthday today!

MRLOVEBYTE

Oh, and I haven't even got you a present.

NEWGIRL

You don't know my name – how could you have
known my birthday?

MRLOVEBYTE

That's a good point. I'm sure I can think of
something to give you when I see you…

I can't help but smile at my phone. He's cheeky.

I wonder if he's right, about Paige, or if he's just slagging off the boss – something I could see myself doing, if I had someone here to talk to, because as much as I'm enjoying being here in Sydney, the task she has finally set me (beyond just, y'know, swiping on her dating app) is not really a task at all.

She wants me to sit in on a meeting. Sort of. Actually, no, not at all – she wants me to sit next to a meeting. Yep, there's a meeting here, tonight, in the hotel restaurant, and Paige has booked me a seat at a table where I can observe the meeting from a distance (she's told me what table they'll be at) but that I have only to watch and make notes. Under no circumstances am I to interact with anyone, because apparently I'll 'disrupt the flow' of the meeting. I shouldn't even let them know I'm there, she said. So I just have to sit here, waiting for them to arrive, and then... what? Watch them eat dinner? Again, I can't complain, because it's an easy job and they're paying me for it but, I don't know, as far as job satisfaction does, I don't really feel like I have any – I don't really feel like I have a job.

I'm making a real meal of it (no pun intended), mostly because I'm bored. I've got my notebook and a pen, ready to jot down important notes like 'everyone ordered the steak' or 'one person sneezed'. Still, it's a nice restaurant, with a cosy vibe, decorative wooden beams, low-key romantic lighting. If I were to make one note, it would be that this isn't an ideal setting for a meeting. Next time they should choose somewhere with more light – and no pianist.

It's nice though, and the views out over Sydney Harbour are stunning. I'm making the most of looking out of the window while I can, before my role switches to staring across the room at a table, watching people like a creep.

I'm also making the most of the fact that this is a restaurant, and I don't have to pay for anything, and really, ordering food is the only cover I have, so I guess I'll just have to keep it coming – well, I wouldn't want to look out of place. I'm sampling the local seafood, and drinking cocktails, and I haven't even looked at the dessert menu yet, but I reckon I could order those back to back all night, if I needed to. Let it never be said I'm not dedicated to my job. Plus, you know, it is my birthday, and I am spending it alone. I may as well keep myself company with food – and it means the waitstaff come over more. I'm just trying to forge some company.

Oh, could this be them? Two people are being shown to the table – the one I'm supposed to be watching. I can see a woman – a beautiful Bondi blonde. Like, I'm blonde, but my colour comes out of a series of bottles in a North London hairdressers. This woman is a real blonde, the kind of colour that only comes from winning a genetic lottery and living her life in the sun, swimming in the sea, running on the beach, and probably drinking smoothies – ones with green stuff in.

She's wearing an evening dress, not really the kind you would wear to a meeting, but I suppose it is evening, and we are in a restaurant. I don't know if she's the client or the person from Matcher or what, until I see who is pulling out her chair for her – a man, *the* man, the one I got stuck in the lift with. So I would imagine he's the reason I'm here, the one I'm on hand to assist, if he needs me, which so far he hasn't.

He's wearing a suit – an expensive-looking one – and a watch that looks like it's worth more than my life. I can't believe he's the one I'm here to watch.

He takes his seat, smiling at the blonde, and they start talking. Then laughing, and she's got her hand on his arm, like he just said the fuuuuunniest thing. Nothing is that funny, is it? I don't think a man has ever made me laugh like that – not unless you count Jimmy Carr, and even then, he was talking to a theatre full of people, not just me.

I squint, as though that's going to make it easier to hear, but I can't tell what they're talking about. I can only try to read their vibe, but I'll tell you this: neither of them has so much as an iPad, a sheet of paper, a notebook – nothing.

It doesn't look businessy. It looks flirty. They're talking, laughing, looking relaxed and yet somehow like they're still on their best behaviour (so if it is a date, it's an early one). Then again, no one seems to find the need to be their best self on first dates with me, so why would this guy be any different?

Why on earth has Paige sent me here? Why does she have me watching him from afar like this? And what the hell am I supposed to report back to her with? The two of them seem happy together. Totally comfortable in each other's company. They're getting on like a house on fire if I'm being honest with you. There's... a familiarity, maybe? Does Paige want to know about that? They are definitely holding date levels of eye contact, that's for sure – but then again maybe that's a business move? How would I know? The girl who lied her way through an interview to bag a job that is seemingly not a job at all.

I grab my cocktail and drink as much and as quickly as the straw will allow me to. Maybe I am going to have to order a dessert or two, because they've only just got here, and they don't look like they'll be moving any time soon.

I pick two: something mango, and something chocolatey. I'm doing vital work here.

By the time my dessert arrives I could swear they're leaning in toward each other. She's twirling her hair. He's smiling like she's just told him something filthy.

I'm not sure what exactly Paige is expecting to hear from me, what kind of details she wants to hear, but whatever is going on at that table, I dunno, it's not like any business meeting I've ever sat in on.

Perhaps, when I report back to Paige, I'll have a better idea about what exactly it is she wants to know, and then I'll work out exactly how much to tell her.

My phone buzzes on the table, making me jump for no reason other than the fact I'm trying to be incognito here.

I pick it up, unlock it and see that I have another happy birthday message – all of the other ones have made me smile, but not this one. This one is from Ben.

BEN

Happy Birthday

That's all it says. Nothing else. No apology. No kiss at the end. No punctuation full stop. I'm not saying a full stop – or even an exclamation mark – would have compelled me to send a polite reply but, come on, guy, that's a poor effort. I suppose I should just count myself lucky that he didn't send me a photo of his knob with a lit candle sticking out of it – now that would have been effort.

Ugh. I already said I'm not doing this today. The man is still living rent free in my head and not only should he not be there on my birthday, he shouldn't be there at all. In fact – there – I've blocked him. We should be blocking more people from our lives, and not just their messages, but their entire person. I know I'd be a lot happier if I blocked people.

I need to focus, get back to the task at hand, and think about what I'm going to tell Paige.

And while I do it, seeing as though I need to sit here a bit longer, more food for me, I guess...

12

I'm at Matcher HQ today – and relieved to tell you that the lift is working. It's funny, when the man I got stuck with said he would rather chance it breaking down than take the stairs every day, I thought he was crazy, but when I arrived here this morning, walked into reception, my entire body feeling stiff from the freezing December weather outside, it made sense. The thought of walking up all those stairs, well, it made me roll the dice on the lift without batting an eye.

Should I be nervous, that Paige has called me in? I guess because so far my job has been, well, not very jobby, it feels like a red flag to be invited here to talk, especially when I've just got back from Sydney.

'Hello,' I say brightly, stepping into Paige's corner office.

'You've caught the sun,' she points out. 'Look at your tan.'

'Yeah, I could definitely get on board with living six months here, six months in Australia,' I joke – although I could.

'Sit,' she tells me, pointing to the chair on the other side of her desk. 'I got us coffees and pastries.'

Okay, so this is either really good news, or really bad, because she's either trying to soften me – or – the blow from whatever she's about to say.

'Lovely,' I reply, holding my nerve.

I don't know if I feel penned in or exposed, here in her office, which is basically a glass box in the sky. I'm a little unnerved by the fact that all of the walls are glass, meaning everyone else in the office can see right in here, so if I have an emotional outburst, everyone will see. Cool.

'So,' she begins, her face giving nothing away. 'Tell me about the dinner in Sydney.'

I sit up a little straighter.

'The meeting,' I say, suddenly feeling uneasy about what I'm supposed to be reporting on. 'Well... it was two people. A man and a woman. They arrived together, chatted, ate dinner...'

'Were they... close?' she asks, her word getting shorter and sharper.

'They sat next to each other,' I say. 'They were chatting, laughing...'

My voice trails off.

'Did it look like a meeting?' she asks.

'It looked like a dinner,' I reply.

This doesn't feel professional, it feels personal. What the hell have I got myself into?

'Did they leave together?' she eventually asks.

I don't know what else to say, apart from...

'Yes.'

'Bastard,' she blurts softly.

She stares at me for a moment, then exhales.

'Liberty, I have a job for you,' she says.

'Okay...'

'I need you to go to New York,' she replies. 'This week.'

I try not to smile. I've always wanted to go to New York. It's one of those iconic places you see in movies and TV shows, and somehow you feel like you've been, like you know your way around. I can't believe I'm getting to go there.

'I can do that,' I reply. 'Usual drill? Being on call? Observing?'

'No,' Paige says. 'This time it's different, I need you to work. Really work. Long hours. Whatever it takes.'

'Assisting someone?' I say, cautiously.

She shakes her head.

'Not exactly,' she tells me. 'I need your specific skillset. Your experience working for a private investigator.'

Ah. The experience I mostly exaggerated in my interview. I was an admin assistant, not a trainee investigator, which I think might be what Paige believes I was doing there.

'Right,' I say, nodding like I believe I'm the person for the job, when in reality the only thing I cracked at my last job was a mug. 'Of course. I'm happy to help.'

'I've made a big mistake,' she says, lowering her voice. 'But I think you can fix it – you're my only hope.'

'Okay...'

'The man you were observing, in Sydney,' she begins, 'was Jordan Bill. He's my business partner. And until very recently, my husband.'

'Oh... right,' I reply plainly.

That has surprised me. I don't know why – we all have exes. Yikes, it was bad enough for me, having to work with Ben, but imagine owning a business with someone, and trying to separate.

'Our divorce is done and dusted – but only just,' she tells me, which explains why she wasn't happy about him having dinner with another woman. 'The only thing left is to divide the business. It's all civil on paper, but really we're at war. I won't bore you with the finer details of it. We've divided certain things up – basically he's taking the US division and I'm keeping the rest – but Matcher is my baby, and I'll be running most it alone moving forward. The UK is what I care about the most, where it all began. If he wants to gad about in the US then fine, let him have it, so long as the main business remains mine.'

'Well, that's good,' I reply. 'That you're getting to keep the UK, working here, running things as usual.'

I say that but she's not making it sound like it's good.

'Except...' She sucks in air and puffs her cheeks. 'I've made a mistake. Only a small one, a silly one really, but it is going to ruin everything. I'm not in the best place, thanks to our split, and I may, in temper, have done a "find and replace" on all of our Ts and Cs, to get his name out of the day-to-day business, but I didn't stop to think about the harm that would cause. Again, I won't bore you with the details, but it turns out removing every instance of his surname – Bill – also removed all instances of the word "bill" – let's just say the "employment bill" is a mess, and it affects everyone, their rights, their benefits. It affects you, Liberty.'

'I see,' I reply. 'That's not great, then.'

That... that sounds like a lot. I know divorces can be messy, but damn, she's found a way to make it worse.

'Not great? It's a disaster,' she snaps. 'Without it, most of our contracts are void. No maternity leave, no sick pay. And if Jordan finds out, he'll use it to drag me back to the negotiating table. Or worse, he'll take the business outright, and the first thing he'll do is clean house and sack everyone who was loyal to me – and that means you.'

Bloody hell, I will never rage-delete anything ever again.

'That man has taken everything from me, but this business...' Her voice begins to crackle with emotion. 'This business is the only thing I have left. He cheated on me, you know. Moved on instantly. And now he's clearly screwing every female client and associate put in front of him. Well, I'm not going to let him screw me again.'

As someone who was betrayed by the man I lived with, worked with – the man I thought I was in love with – I get it. I know the heartbreak, the rage, and the unbearable feeling of failure that things didn't work out, even if it wasn't my fault.

Jordan sounds like Ben, but worse. A real piece of work. I don't want him to take Paige's company from her, out of sheer girl code, but I also don't want to lose my job. I've only just started to feel like I'm getting my life back on track. I suppose Paige feels a similar way.

'Okay then,' I say confidently, whipped up on her behalf. 'What exactly do you need me to do?'

'Jordan is flying to New York for his last few meetings on behalf of Matcher and he'll have the contract with him,' she explains. 'He promised me he would return with it signed – we're so close – but it has the new terms in and that's where the words are missing. I'm doing this for all of you, for all of you, I swear. So I'm assigning you as his assistant. He'll say he doesn't need one, but you'll be there anyway, so just ignore him. I've booked the rooms, you'll be in the one next to him, and I've made sure you're in first class on the plane too. You'll be by his side the whole time which should give you the perfect opportunity to swap out the contract he has with the correct version, without the missing words. Simple, really.'

Simple – maybe if I did actually have skills one might boast if they were a private investigator but, beyond Facebook stalking exes, I'm not much of a spy. What Paige is asking me to do is tantamount to espionage – corporate espionage, just, y'know, for the greater good.

'How am I going to get close enough to him to swap it?' I ask. 'He's not going to leave it lying around, surely?'

'In his room, he will,' she replies. 'It isn't hard to get close to him. He loves getting attention from women – he's addicted to it. Flirting with him will get you far – pretend you're interested in him, seduce him but, and it is a big but, do not sleep with him.'

'It would never come to that,' I reply.

Believe me when I say that the reason I'm not going to sleep with this random man for a work task isn't because Paige told me not to, it's because I'm not going to sleep with a random man for work. I do not need this job that badly.

'He's charming,' she warns me. 'Dangerously so. Do you think you can pull it off?'

I would've thought that would be off the table too.

'There will be a big bonus waiting for you when you get back,' she tells me. 'And a full-time job, of course.'

'Don't I already have that?' I ask.

'I hired someone else, for the assistant position in the office,' she explains. 'I hired you specifically for this. I sent you to all of those locations to be on call if I needed you – if I needed you to spy on Jordan for me. That's done now. But if you come through for me on this...'

Great. So the reason the job seemed too good to be true is because it was. She's had me on standby, stalking her ex, and now she needs me to do her dirty work, because she's made a mistake. I don't want to lose my job (but only in the way that anyone who needs money to live on needs to keep their job) and I do want to help her, but most of all I just really, really want to go to New York. Apart from stalking (and low-key seducing) her ex, everything else sounded amazing.

My mind is telling me no, of course it is, but do you know what is telling me yes? My overdraft. My need for independence. My annoying little habit of needing to eat food to survive.

'Okay,' I tell her. 'I'm in.'

13

Does it feel a little bit like I'm selling my soul to go to New York? Yeah, a little bit, but it is a damn sight cheaper than paying the hefty price with money.

And, you know, there's money and then there's moneeeey. Flying to New York, staying in whatever their equivalent of a Travelodge is, ain't exactly cheap, but it's more doable than flying first class, staying in a fancy hotel next to Central Park. I'm going to get a taste of the high life – perks of stalking a CEO, or whatever he is. The big boss, with the big money, and the big old expensive taste.

I'm here, at Heathrow airport, and it doesn't matter how many steps I take, I'm constantly finding myself feeling baffled when no one stops me. I mean, come on, there's no way anyone is looking at me and believing I can afford to be here. Everyone around me looks like they're wearing clothes by a who, not a where, and unless we're suddenly counting George (of Asda) as a designer, I don't think I have anything that qualifies.

Still, with big money comes big respect, so even though I look I've wandered into the VIP area by mistake, the fact I have a ticket means that everyone is treating me like royalty. And here's me thinking everyone is going to *Pretty Woman* me on sight... but that could be because I'm wearing over-the-knee boots which, in hindsight, probably weren't the best shoes for flying, but I was thinking of how cold it is here, and how cold it will be there.

I'm not saying I've got impostor syndrome, but even going through security is making me nervous, and I know that's my passport.

Checking in and passing through security takes minutes – I'm through in a flash, which is something I could get used to – and now I'm in the first-class lounge, and it really is first class.

You know when something as simple as the lighting makes a place seem expensive? Or the kooky décor? I've never seen life-sized horses with lampshades on their heads but here they are, standing proud. They work though; they seem at home (although I suppose they do technically live here). I just feel like I'm in another world, a world where the drinks are free and diffusers are pumping delicious fragrances into the air. The last time I flew, a crappy porn star martini cost £27 and the room smelled like the puke of the stag do at the next table.

There's something, I don't know, strange – but not in a bad way. I don't know, it feels a little bit like stepping back in time. I can see men in suits reading newspapers – the big broadsheets, not a cheeky *Daily Star*, and women (who, frankly, look like supermodels) serving them drinks.

'Is it your first time flying?' the employee at the gate asks me when it is time to board.

'Erm, no,' I reply, but I'm definitely giving off nervous energy. I should probably say something, lest he thinks I'm up to something. I could've lied, just said yes, but my passport would contradict that – is this a test, to see who is potentially dodgy, or am I overthinking it? It is definitely the latter.

'It's my first time in first class,' I explain.

'Lucky you! You're going to love it,' he insists. 'We only have eight first-class seats and you've got one of them.'

Wow, only eight? The last time I flew, there were eight people within touching distance.

I'm greeted by a flight attendant who says she will lead me to my seat. I follow her through what I assume is business class and, honestly, it looks great, I would have been more than happy with this. Then again, I would've been happy in the cargo hold, if it meant a free trip to New York.

'Here we are,' she announces and... oh my God.

'Wow,' I blurt.

She smiles.

'This is your suite. Get settled in, have a glass of champagne, and I'll be back to see if you need anything,' she tells me.

What else could I need? I've got my own little pod. My own private little space with not one, but two windows. There's a generously sized TV and some kind of console that controls it. There are so many buttons – some for adjusting the seat too – I'm terrified to press any, because who knows what they do? It could be anything from ejecting me with a diamond-encrusted parachute or summoning Tom Hardy to read me a bedtime story (in case you ever wondered what my idea of luxury was).

On my table there is a little bowl of nuts and a glass of champagne. I suppose I should raise a toast to Ben, really, because when you think about it his tragic little dick pics are the reason I'm sitting here today.

'What's so funny?' a voice asks me – I must have been laughing to myself, like an evil genius – as though this was my plan all along, rather than me being incredibly lucky to land on my feet.

I look up and see Jordan – Paige's ex-husband – standing next to me.

'Oh, nothing,' I reply. 'Hello.'

He narrows his eyes at me.

'Hello,' he replies. 'We've met before...'

'In the lift,' I remind him. 'At Matcher HQ. It got stuck.'

'It always gets stuck,' he replies as he settles into the pod next to mine. 'Oh, yeah, I remember you. You were freaking out.'

He says this like it's surprising.

'Yeah – the lift was stuck,' I remind him.

'Yeah – it happens all the time,' he says in a similar tone. 'So, you're Paige's minion, huh? Has she sent you to check up on me?'

'What? No,' I insist.

Now it's his turn to laugh.

'Relax, I'm only kidding,' he tells me. 'I told her I didn't need an assistant. She thinks I'm useless. Still, at least you get a trip out of it, eh? A nice break from the office.'

I probably shouldn't mention that I haven't worked in the office yet – or that I've been stalking him around the globe.

He pulls off his jumper to reveal a soft-looking grey t-shirt that matches his grey comfy tracksuit bottoms – the kind that can make a girl feel powerless.

'Are those to stop you getting a DVT?' he jokes, nodding towards my over-the-knee boots, as he takes off his own shoes.

'What? Oh,' I reply. He's making fun of me.

'There are slippers, in there,' he tells me. 'PJs too, if you want to make yourself at home.'

'Thanks,' I reply.

How will I ever take a regular flight again? Without slippers or PJs. Sounds awful.

'Is there anything I can do for you?' I ask him. 'Anything you need me to look over, check...'

'I don't need an assistant, really,' he insists. 'But thank you.'

It was never going to be that easy, was it?

'Well, I'm here if you change your mind,' I remind him.

It's only a few seconds before two flight attendants appear out of nowhere and they're on him like a rash.

'Can I get you anything, Mr Bill?' one asks him.

'Would you like another glass of champagne?' says the other.

'I have everything I need right now, thank you,' he replies, flashing them a winning smile.

Oof. There's that dangerous charm Paige warned me about. He's that devastating combination of gorgeous, charming, confident, living his best life – but aren't they always the ones who are total dogs? Paige made it sound like he would sleep with anyone who batted their eyelashes at him. I need to make sure I keep my eyes still and open – like a shark.

I glance over at him, unable to stop one of my eyebrows from rising. So much for being shark-like.

'What?' he asks with a grin.

'Nothing. You just seem... popular,' I reply.

'I am,' he says, deadly serious. 'Flight crew love me – I'm a good passenger.'

'Ohhh, is that it?' I say.

'If you need anything, and you want me to ask them for you, give me a shout,' he jokes. 'That way you know they'll say yes.'

'So, you're my assistant now, eh?' I dare to joke.

'Certainly looks that way,' he replies. 'What's your name, boss?'

'Liberty,' I tell him.

'Like the statue,' he jokes. 'I guess you're going to the right place. I'm Jordan.'

He reaches across the aisle to shake my hand.

'I know,' I reply. 'Just because, you know, you're my boss.'

Not because your ex-wife made you my mark or anything.

'Right,' he says with a laugh. 'How long have you been at Matcher?'

'Since that day, actually,' I reply. 'So still the new girl.'

He smiles.

'Well, it is a great place to work,' he replies. 'Our employees are always happy, our benefits are great.'

Not if I don't swap these contracts, they're not.

'The lift really is the only downside,' he adds. 'But sometimes it's a nice break.'

I laugh.

'I'm enjoying it so far,' I tell him. Well, I am; so far it's pretty much only involved going on holidays and crap dates.

'Good,' he replies, pulling out a laptop. 'I'm going to try get some work done once we're in the air. I always try to beat the jetlag but I always get it wrong.'

'Okay, well, I'll leave you to it,' I reply. 'I think I'll watch a movie.'

I say that, but I can't seem to stop myself watching him. Everything he does is cool. Unbothered. Stylish, even. Like he's a model for the airline. The poster boy of first-class travel.

I do feel sort of bad for him, and for not being honest with him, but it's not actually going to cause him any harm. I'm fixing a mistake. Righting a wrong. I'm doing this for my job, for Paige, for women everywhere... maybe.

I need to stick to the plan and it will be done and dusted before I know it, and Jordan will be none the wiser.

Just as soon as I realise how I'm going to do it, that is.

14

I have to keep pinching myself because I'm here, in the Big Apple, the city that never sleeps – sort of like me, on an eight-hour flight. I didn't get a wink. I think I was too excited.

I'm in the back of a car with Jordan, the one that is taking us from the airport to the hotel. I'm not saying it's swanky, but the driver is wearing a hat.

We're currently crawling through the thick Manhattan traffic but I'm happy to take it slow, to take in the sights. Outside the window, it's all yellow cabs, steam coming up from grates, towering skyscrapers – exactly as I imagined it.

It's December so it is cold, like it is back home, but somehow the novelty of being here makes it seem not so miserable. Christmas is coming, so everywhere looks so festive. I feel like I could be in a Hallmark Christmas movie right now – let me out of the car, so I can go outside and have my meet-cute with a hot local.

'Is this your first time?' Jordan asks.

'What?' I reply.

'In New York,' he clarifies with a smile.

'Oh.' I laugh, feeling my cheeks warm. I wonder if I'm being a dork. 'Yes. But I've watched a lot of *Sex and the City*, so I feel like I pretty much know my way around.'

He raises a brow, clearly amused.

'I haven't seen it,' he replies. 'But I'm sure it is a very accurate representation of the geography.'

'I already feel like I'm in it,' I say, dreamily. 'Don't be surprised if I go full Carrie while we're here.'

'That wouldn't surprise me at all, because I don't know who that is,' he replies. 'Though the only Carrie I know is from that horror film.'

'I've probably got form for both,' I joke.

He laughs again, properly this time, and I can't help but smile. He's hard not to like – until I remember the things Paige told me about him. I need to not like him, ideally, because it will make it easier to sneak around behind his back without feeling so guilty.

The car turns off Central Park West and slows in front of a beautiful old hotel – The Van Doren, with its timeless stonework and luxury vibes. It overlooks the park – it doesn't get more Hallmark than that, does it?

A doorman in a burgundy coat and hat opens the car door for me, and the moment I step out, the cold nips at my nose like it's mad at me. I wrap my coat a little tighter and glance up at the building. Boy, it is big. Obviously we have tall buildings in London but, here, it's different. Everything just feels so... big.

The second we step inside the lobby, it's like being wrapped in a blanket, the revolving door doing the most to keep the chill outside. Now that I think about it, that's the first time I've used a revolving door since Paris. I'm glad I didn't realise beforehand, or I would have overthought it.

The marble floor is polished, the gold fixings are gleaming, and the Christmas tree might be the biggest one I've ever seen in my life. It stands tall, allowing the spiral staircase to wrap around it, and it seems to go up and up and up.

Jordan handles the check-in, chatting easily with the concierge while I hover by the tree, unable to resist snapping photos already.

Jordan joins me, followed by a hotel employee pushing a golden trolley. He loads our bags onto it before escorting us to the lift.

'So, romantic getaway?' he asks, pressing the lift button, in an attempt to make small talk with us while he shows us to our rooms.

I open my mouth, then close it again. I don't know what to say.

'Probably not,' Jordan replies, beating me to it. 'She's my colleague. We're here on business.'

'Oh, my bad, sorry,' the man replies.

'Not a problem,' Jordan reassures him.

Colleague, that's interesting. Not assistant. Not employee. I don't know what it means, it's just... yeah... interesting. Like we're equals.

The lift doors open and we step out into the corridor. I still can't believe I'm here, with Jordan, doing what I'm doing. I mean, who do I think I am? I know who Paige thinks I am, some kind of super sleuth. A sneaky tactical operator – probably a master of disguise. I mean, she must, to have so much faith in me. Perhaps I'm not as crap at job interviews as I thought. I clearly impressed her. Then again, it wasn't doing the interviews I was struggling with, it was getting them in the first place.

I still have no idea how I'm going to do this. I haven't been more than a matter of feet away from Jordan since he boarded the plane, but the contract must be tucked away in his bag somewhere, just like the one Paige gave me is tucked away in mine. Really what I need him to do is fall asleep, in an armchair, with his hand ever so lightly gripping it, so I can sneak in and swap it, without waking him, like I'm in an old TV show. Like it's the perfect crime. He's not going to carry it around with him, though, is he? I suppose I should be grateful that they're dealing in physical copies or contracts and not digital ones, because I am without a doubt a worse hacker than I am a private investigator, and I'm clearly a terrible, terrible private investigator.

'Here we are,' the hotel employee announces, unlocking a door. He steps aside to let Jordan by. 'You too, ma'am,' he prompts me.

'Oh, right, okay,' I reply.

Christ, tell me we're not sharing a room. Sure, it would make finding and swapping the contract much easier, but I cannot share a room with this man. Oh, God. And there's only one bed – a big one, but only one nonetheless. This can't be happening.

'We're supposed to have two rooms,' Jordan points out – clearly he doesn't want to share a room with me either.

'Yes, of course,' the man replies. 'Two rooms with an adjoining door. Right here.'

The hotel employee reaches out towards a door I hadn't noticed and unlocks it.

'Ma'am, your room is through here,' he tells me.

'Why do we have adjoining rooms?' Jordan asks him.

'That's what was booked, sir,' the employee tells him.

'Interesting,' Jordan says. 'She can't have meant to do that.'

We both look to him.

'Sorry, just thinking out loud,' Jordan replies. 'So, it locks, right?'

'Yes, sir, it locks,' the man tells him. 'It's basically two separate rooms, with separate bathrooms, phones and so on. The door locks on both sides.'

'Well, that's okay then,' Jordan tells him. 'Thanks. Here, I have your tip.'

As Jordan pays the man for his help I saunter into my own room. An adjoining door, that's handy. Getting back through it though, that might be a problem.

I don't know why I was expecting my own room to be less spectacular than Jordan's. They are next door to each other. Maybe it was the adjoining door that threw me, like this might be a small connected room for the help or the kids. But no, it is exactly the same as Jordan's. Just as big, as luxurious – and it's all mine.

This place is nice – really nice. Easily the nicest place I've ever stayed in. I dread to think how much it costs, and how much the first-class plane ticket cost, and I'm well aware I'm only getting such special treatment because this is how Jordan does things, and Paige wants me on Jordan, as much as I possibly can be. I shouldn't get used to it... I could though. I really could.

It's a big, bright and spacious room. So light and airy, but super cosy too. I can't believe I'm going to have this big bed to myself – you could easily fit four of me in there (but three more of myself wouldn't be my first choice of bedmates. Having my own voice in my head, once, is more than enough).

I walk over to the window, slowly, allowing the view to reveal itself a bit at a time. I pull the heavy curtains all the way back, exposing the whole window, revealing that view – Central Park.

We're on the Upper West Side and, from way up here, you can see everything. It's so strange, the way the park stretches out, so flat and so massive, in the middle of the city. The trees are bare, having dropped their leaves for the winter, but it makes the scene no less beautiful. I can see so many people, all buzzing around, seeming so busy, probably working, Christmas shopping, sightseeing.

I let out a long, slow breath. It's bizarrely relaxing, watching the world go by through the glass – sort of like the chilled-out feeling you get when you visit an aquarium. So much to see, so much beauty, but nothing really happening. Just the slow and varied passage of time. Something different to see wherever you look, but nothing notable to pay too much attention to.

This really is the holiday of my dreams – except it's not a holiday, is it? There's so much I want to do, so many places I want to go, and so much I want to eat. But I can't, I have to stay hot on Jordan's heels, hanging around him like a bad smell, to be ready to make the swap whenever the opportunity arises.

I hear a knock. Not on the door, though. On the wall.

'Hello,' Jordan says, poking his head through our shared door.

'Hello,' I reply, making my way over to him, casually, like I own the place.

'I'm sorry about... this.' He nods towards the doorway between us. 'It must've been booked by mistake. Paige wouldn't put you in such an awkward position on purpose.'

Except she absolutely would. In fact, she's counting on it.

Still, I smile, like I don't know any better.

'Don't worry about it,' I insist.

'It locks on both sides,' he says, fiddling with the latch to demonstrate. 'So there's no way either of us can open it without the other person unlocking their door too. It's basically two separate rooms, in practice. If we keep it shut.'

'Great,' I reply. 'Unless of course you need me for anything...'

He raises an eyebrow.

'For working in the middle of the night?' He laughs. 'I think

I'll manage – but thank you. If we had an employee of the month, you would be well on your way.'

He's definitely mocking me.

'I'll leave you to settle in then,' he says, backing away.

'Okay,' I reply. 'See you later.'

He closes the door between us. Then I hear the distinct, purposeful sound of it locking on his side. He really doesn't want this door opening.

I'm coming across as too keen. Too eager to please. I'm probably giving him the ick, by seeming so try-hard.

If Paige thought an adjoining door was going to make this easier – help me to get closer to him, to worm my way into his trust and then his room – she is seriously mistaken.

I lean against the door. Oh, yeah, that is solid. That's not opening for anyone, unless they open it for me. It's sort of like… vampires, I guess? They can't come in on their own, you have to invite them in. Only then can they cross the threshold and bite your neck. Not that I'm planning on biting Jordan's neck, although I'm not exactly opposed to the idea, in concept. I need to confess something, but we have to keep this between us, because I'm ever so slightly embarrassed by it. I haven't had sex with anyone since Ben – I haven't had a date go well enough – and it's building itself up to be a big deal in my head.

You can't forget how to have sex, can you? Or, like, your body can't shut up shop, because it thinks you went sexually bankrupt? I'd say I was asking for a friend but at this point we both know I'm talking about myself. I'm starting to worry I might be allergic to doing the deed, because I seem to find any reason to be put off from going to bed with anyone, and because sometimes I'm so uncomfortable about it I use phrases like 'doing the deed'. If my ick alarm could go off for myself, I'd probably be deaf by now.

Anyway, I think it's affecting my brain, firing off signals when I'm around attractive men like Jordan for too long, like my body is asking: why aren't we pouncing on him? Oh, the audacity of my body, to think it can simply demand whoever it wants.

I'm only here to screw Jordan in one way: sneaking into his room, swapping out the contract, restoring balance, making sure he has no leverage over Paige.

This is going to be so, so much harder than I thought.

15

I'm not sure room service counts as experiencing the local cuisine, I don't know, maybe it does, but either way, my first taste of New York was exceptional.

The plan was to take it easy after we landed. Get cleaned up, get some rest, try to adjust our body clocks to the new time. I say 'we' like we were doing it together. No, that's what Jordan said he was doing, so that's what I did too.

So I had some food delivered to my room. I am not exaggerating when I say this: best cheeseburger and fries I've ever had in my life, and the hot fudge sundae I had to top it off was perfection too.

And then I laid there, drumming my hands on my bloated stomach, racking my brains for ideas, until I fell asleep. I didn't have much luck, to be honest with you.

Here's my thinking... The adjoining door is pretty much a nonstarter. Jordan locked it from his side, loudly and deliberately, after once again reminding me that he didn't want or need my help. Even if I could get him to open it temporarily, he isn't going to invite me in, and he definitely isn't going to say he'll nip out to give me a bit of alone time to rifle through his baggage, is he?

Then I started wondering: What would Tom Cruise do? I think it might have been the jetlag, but still, I gave it some thought.

I mean, obviously, he would climb out the window, shimmy across the building, *Mission: Impossible* style, and sneak in through Jordan's window. Two problems there. One is that I completely lack the physical strength and skill to pull that off without dying. The other is that even if I could make it to his window alive, it's not going to be open; it's December, so there's no way I'd get inside. Tom always had tech. The closest thing I have to a gadget is a watch that sometimes tells me when I've ovulated.

As I said, I probably should have tried to sleep more on the place.

But I'm up and at 'em now, well rested, and at Matcher US HQ.

Jordan is currently in their meeting room – which only has glass walls, of course – and I am sitting outside, watching, and feeling a bit left out. Well, as he keeps reminding me, he doesn't need me for anything. We're not the only two here from London, there are other members of the UK team in there, it's just me he's leaving out in the cold. So to speak. I'm grateful I'm allowed in the building. It's nippy out there today.

The office is a lot like the London one – contemporary, stylish furniture and minimalist décor – except it's bigger, taller, and flashier. And best of all: the lifts work. Which is fortunate, because we're so much higher up here, and (similarly to scaling a building) I lack the physical skills required to climb so many flights of stairs.

I glance through the glass wall again. Jordan is standing at the head of the table, sleeves rolled up, his hands moving as he talks. Everyone is laughing. Honestly, you would think he was doing stand-up, not holding a meeting. I wonder what he's saying, what they're all finding so funny. Perhaps they're all giddy about how popular the app is, how many people are using it, with no regard for how many people are winding up collateral damage in the process.

I can't get a read on his body language, not really. Obviously he's magnetic. His charm is impossible to ignore. He's so laid back, he isn't trying too hard, but because he knows he doesn't need to. Understandably, it's the women who are drawn to him the most but the men hang off his every word too. He's got the entire room eating out of the palm of his hand.

What I find the most interesting of all is that, despite him being so handsome, charming and successful, he doesn't make anyone nervous. It's like he has this way of making everyone woman feel like she has a shot with him (by all accounts from Paige, they do) but I suppose it's kind of nice. It clearly makes people feel good about themselves, and it makes them want to be around him more.

I keep reminding myself what Paige told me. How he uses that charm. How he uses people. And Matcher, for all its romance-y pink branding and 'happy ever after' slogans, is used for hook-ups, for pervs to get their kicks – like Ben, sending photos of 'Little Ben' to everyone in a twenty-mile radius.

I wonder how many people are using this app to cheat on their partners? To deceive? To manipulate? How many Bens are out there, sliding into DMs with their unsolicited dick pics and secret girlfriends? And how many people are using it to try to find love? Imagine you're some poor, innocent individual swiping, thinking you're going to meet the person of your dreams – how are you supposed to know if people are really who they say they are? If they're married? If they're a good person? If they're a serial killer, even, because you never know.

Trying to pull a switcheroo on Jordan's contract might feel unethical but, when you think about it, he's creating and promoting a platform that gives bad people an easy way to hurt those they supposedly love. He isn't a poor, innocent bystander.

I wouldn't usually call myself a doe-eyed romantic, and to each their own, everyone is entitled to live their lives the way they want to, but after what Ben did to me, dating apps scare the shit out of me. Would he have been sending those pictures to women if he hadn't met them via an app? He was never the type to get chatting to girls in bars, it took me long enough to get him to open up and be more confident with me, so it had to be the app that emboldened him, that gave him the anonymity, that made him feel like he could do whatever he wanted, and fuck the consequences.

Perhaps I'm being grumpy, because I'm annoyed that I'm the only one not in the room. Why has Jordan left me out here, when the other UK team members are in there with him? He's bathing everyone in his charm and attention and they're basking in it. Am I actually jealous, or simply frustrated that I'm getting nowhere with him?

The problem is that Jordan doesn't trust me, but I really need him to, which is further proof that he shouldn't trust me... God, what a mess.

I watch him for a little longer before aimlessly scrolling and swiping around on my phone, looking for something to busy myself with. I've doomscrolled every app and social I have, Duolingo is done for the day, and I've run out of lives on all the dumb games I play when I can't sleep.

Then I check WorkM8. Oh, I have a message.

MRLOVEBYTE

How's it going, NewGirl?

I can't help but smile. I still don't know who this guy is – assuming he is a guy, from the name – but I like getting his messages. It weirdly makes me feel less alone at Matcher.

His username is interesting. Obviously it's a pun, byte with a y, as in gigabyte, and love because Matcher is supposedly where you find it. In any other context it might come across as a bit sleazy. Then again, maybe that is just my ick alarm, prematurely firing off a warning shot, in case I was even thinking of going there.

NEWGIRL

So far so good... I have a question though.

I pause. Should I actually ask him this? The question that is on my mind. I mean, I can't ask Paige. I definitely can't ask Jordan. But I'm curious. Ah, well, I've already started asking now.

NEWGIRL

Is Matcher ethical? Do you think everyone has good intentions?

I hit send and I have no time to wait for a reply, or to second-guess myself, because the meeting is over. Everyone is standing up, still laughing, slowly filtering out of the glass room.

Jordan spots me and heads over, still so easy-breezy.

'You're still here?' he points out.

'Of course,' I reply, trying not to sound too enthusiastic.

'I'm sure I've already told you this...' He pauses to grin. 'I don't need an assistant. You're good. I release you.'

He does a funny little gesture with his hands, as though he's trying to push the air, to blow me away.

'Why don't you go sightseeing?' he suggests. 'You can't have seen it all in *Sex and the City*. There must be new stuff to discover.'

It's on the tip of my tongue to mention the spin-off show – until I realise he means the city itself. Almost embarrassed myself there.

'It's okay,' I reassure him with a smile. 'I'll hang around. Do my job. Just in case you need me – you never know.'

'Oh, but I do,' he replies.

He laughs, shakes his head, and walks away. I don't think he quite knows what to make of me – to be honest, I don't know what to make of him.

He knows something. He must. It's like he's keeping me at arm's length on purpose, as if he can sense that I have an ulterior motive.

One thing is for sure: I can't get close to him through work. He's never going to let that happen. I'm going to have to get creative. I have no idea how. It's like an escape room (except, you know, I'm trying to get into a room, not out of one) and puzzle that I just can't crack. There must be a way though. There must be.

My phone buzzes with a notification.

MRLOVEBYTE

That is a big question, NewGirl… Do you want the short answer or the honest one?

NEWGIRL

Honest – always!

Okay, well, that's officially got my attention. I wonder what he's going to say...

16

There's something about the streets of New York that makes you feel like you're walking through a live theatre performance at all times.

Everywhere you look there's something to be gripped by. If it isn't the scenery, it's the people – like the couple I just saw arguing in the street.

'You said the Hamptons were off-limits this weekend,' she hissed – I could tell she looked angry, even from behind her designer sunglasses (and, yes, it is December).

'Now suddenly we need to go?' she continued.

'I didn't say that,' he shot back. 'I said we should reconsider depending on the weather, and the weather is clearly in favour of Montauk.'

'You're seeing her again, aren't you?' she snapped suddenly – I wish I'd had popcorn with me.

'Oh, for God's sake, Tori, let it go, it was five years ago,' he replied.

'The first time,' she clapped back.

I kept walking, obviously, but it took everything in me not to slow to a crawl and fully tune in. Rich people fight differently. There's no mention of doing the dishes or taking out the bins.

I suppose I should be counting my lucky stars that having no man in my life means not getting cheated on in the Hamptons, and having zero arguments generally. Come on – I'm not actually jealous of two people, with a clearly messy relationship, arguing, am I? I don't want that. It would be nice to have someone to hang out with though. Doing all of this alone isn't as much fun as it would be doing it with someone else.

What am I doing? I'm hiding behind a plant.

I'm trying to think if I've ever had to hide behind a plant and, nope, I think this might be the first time. I might feel sort of tragic, were I not hiding behind a plant in New York. If you're going to be a weirdo, at least be a transatlantic one.

From where I'm lurking, I have a perfect view of Jordan. Well, perfect in the sense that I can see him from here, and he can't see me. Not perfect in the sense that, you know, I'm hiding behind a fucking plant, in a hotel bar, where if someone were to notice me, they would almost certainly ask me to leave – if not kick me out. If not deport me.

In hindsight, maybe I didn't need to hide. Jordan knows I'm here now; we're both staying in this hotel – it wouldn't be weird for me to be in the bar too. But perhaps he would behave differently, if he knew I were here? Maybe he suspects Paige of sending me to spy on him? And even if he wouldn't act all that differently, knowing that I was watching him, he would have even more reason not to trust me, and I really need him to trust me.

I was sort of hoping he would have the contract with him – maybe in a bag or a briefcase – or lying on top of the bar where I could simply snatch it up. Ha. Chance would be a fine thing. No sign of anything though. I'm sure he mentioned something earlier about not needing me because he was having a meeting tonight. I suppose it's true, he has met someone, but I'm not so sure how businessy it looks.

It doesn't help that his meeting is with an absolutely beautiful woman. She's tall, elegantly dressed, with glossy black hair. Her eyes are sparkly and her teeth are perfect, and the way she throws her head back when she laughs could be kind of dorky, except she's making it work for her.

But it doesn't mean it's a date, and not a business meeting, just because she's beautiful, right? Just because they're drinking cocktails, in the evening, laughing at each other's jokes – I'm not jealous, I'm curious.

Okay... maybe I'm a little bit jealous. Everyone wishes they had someone, right? Someone good though, obviously.

I'm not spying on him for Paige, I'm looking for my in, to switch the contracts. The chink in his armour. When he takes his eye off the ball. An opportunity – like him dropping his keycard or leaving his jacket just far enough away from him that I can grab it, see if his keycard might be there.

And yet...

I find myself squinting, trying to read their body language, guessing at what they're saying.

Oh... my... God, Jordan, you're so strong and so funny...

And rich too, baby, wanna get out of here?

I mean, I'm only guessing (or maybe projecting, if we're being honest) and Jordan doesn't even sound or talk like that, but that's how it looks from where I'm sitting. Well – hiding, anyway.

She leans in. Flashes a smile. Her hand brushes Jordan's wrist as she laughs.

Okay. She's definitely flirting. That's what I'd do – if trapping myself in a revolving door or assaulting him at an ice rink failed, anyway.

Is Jordan... is he leaning back? Is that him pulling away or just reclining in a way that says: hop on my lap, baby.

Again, that isn't how he sounds or talks.

If I'm jealous of anything it's because, going off what Paige said, Jordan is a bit of a dog. Any woman, any time, sounds like his type. And, again, not jealous (I'll keep saying it until you believe me), but he can hardly look at me. My very presence in New York annoys him. He wants nothing to do with me. How am I repulsing, by all accounts, the UK's number one top shagger? Am I unattractive? Forgettable? Am I too annoying? What is it about me that has made him look at me and instantly dismiss me?

Maybe I seem needy? Clingy, even, I am trying to get close to him – and I suppose I am spying on him right now, which is a bit intense. Perhaps if I back off, play hard to get? Not to get him to shag me, just to get him to trust me, enough for me to swap the contracts.

It's hard not to wonder what Ben thought of me, in the end. There must have been something missing, for him to do what he did, but even when I rumbled him, it wasn't like he wanted things to be over; he wanted us to stay together. I wonder if he would have promised never to do it again, or tried to talk me into opening up our relationship or something. One thing I do know for sure is that, if we had stayed together, I would probably be stalking him right now, because there's no way I ever would have trusted him again.

Jordan laughs again and I flinch, snapping out of the pity party I was about to throw for myself. The woman is smiling, sipping her drink slowly, eyes locked on his face. He smiles back, and it's hard to tell but...

Shit!

As I lean forward to get a better look I push the plant too far. A branch reaches out and swipes a glass off a table, causing it to smash.

I quickly dart out of the way, behind a wall. I think I might have got away with that one.

I wait for a few seconds – maybe even a minute – before I slowly emerge from my hiding place. Luckily they're back to their conversation, which gives me time to get out of here. I think it's probably best to call time on... whatever this is. It's not helping.

I'll leave him to his business meeting, or his date, or his whatever – what do I care what it is? Because unless it's the kinda thing where everyone puts their contracts in a fruit bowl and picks a different one out, it's not going to help me.

17

Suddenly it makes sense, why they call it the city that never sleeps, because while it may be dark outside now, it seems no less alive out there.

I'm standing at my hotel window, looking down at the street below, watching cars and people, everyone going about their business. I suppose it's busy everywhere, in the run-up to Christmas – but isn't it funny how some places just seem more festive? London and New York always feel so alive with festive cheer, but a big part of that is the dark evenings that allow the festive lights to shine brighter, and the freezing cold weather that makes the hot chocolate hit different.

My phone buzzes on the table in front of me. I grab it quickly, worried it might be Paige checking up on me again. I don't know how many messages I've had from her already, asking if it's done. I must have really, really oversold myself in my interview, if she thinks I could have made the switch already.

Ooh, it's a WorkM8 notification, from MrLoveByte…

MRLOVEBYTE

The truth? Okay. Matcher's not unethical. Not in theory. But people are. They lie, they cheat, they ghost. They use the app for all sorts of things it wasn't built for. Same as anything in life, don't you think?

I do think. That's exactly what I think. People are always going to people, and if you give them the tools to make it easier then they will take them, for better or worse. Look at me, for example, because I'm here to do something for Paige, for a good reason, but I'm not in love with the way I'm having to do it. In fact, I kind of hate it. Because whether it's for a noble cause or not, how I'm doing it feels wrong, because really, what it boils down to is me conning Jordan. Sneaking around. Waiting for the perfect moment to rummage through his belongings. That's not noble. That's desperate. Then again, I guess that's what Paige is, desperate to save the company from a mistake she made when she was feeling hurt. I do get that.

So here I am, because I said I'd do it. Because someone needs to. Because if I back out now, then who is going to be able to take care of it? The clock is ticking.

I just want to get on with it and move on with my life. I want to stop lying, stop sneaking around, because I'm clearly crap at it, even without the moral dilemma.

I glance toward the adjoining door and chew my bottom lip.

There has to be a way to get him to open that door, there just has to. But not only open it, oh no, I need him to open it, leave it open, and then go somewhere else, leaving me with enough time to make the switch.

I glance back at the balcony door. Yes, I know, I've already ruled out going Tom Cruise, I'm not about to try to climb into his room, or fling myself over the edge so he has to come and save me, but it could be useful. In fact…

Okay, I've got it. As I open the door, the cold winter weather hits me like a wave of razor blades. My God, it's even colder up here than it is down on the street. Then again, I wear my coat on the street, and it's less jarring walking out from reception than it is opening up this floodgate in the sky.

I stumble back as it briefly takes my breath away – I think it's just the shock – and then I get into character and go to bang on the adjoining door.

'Jordan,' I call out. 'Jordan? Jordan, I need your help.'

My initial idea was to tell him that I'd somehow managed to get my door stuck open, and that I need a big, strong man to close it, except it moves so easily and so freely, it would definitely seem suspicious, and even if it didn't, he would have it closed in an instant.

Even as I'm banging on the door I'm not entirely sure what I'll say, but my plan is to tell him that something ran in through the open door, like a spider or a mouse or something, and that I need him to get it out. Surely if I act all girly and squeaky, he'll feel obliged to help me, it's the gentlemanly thing to do. I know, I'm going to seem pathetic, but some men like that, right? To feel like the big man, the hero. Truthfully, if a spider did come in here, and it was big enough to bother me, I'd take a size seven heel to it myself, and as for a mouse, well, I wouldn't want some random rodent in here, but it wouldn't scare me. Not that I'd be offering it a bite of my food, but it wouldn't turn me into a damsel in distress.

'Jordan,' I call out again, adding a little more urgency to my tone. Not enough to scare him, but enough to know I need him.

'What's wrong?' he calls from the other side of the door.

'I… I need your help,' I say, breathless. 'I'm scared.'

I hear the door unlock, then it swings open and... oh, God.

There he is, Jordan, standing there, in nothing but a pair of boxers.

He gives me a bit of a grin, the kind that says: my eyes are up here. I already knew he had eyes though, what I didn't know was that he wore tiny, tight-fitting boxers, and that his body looked like it had been carved out of marble by a sculptor who had a real thing for bulging muscles – bulging everything, really. And then there are his tattoos. So many of them, all over his body, that you would never get to see unless you saw him without his clothes on.

'What's the problem?' he asks.

I can think of a few now...

'Liberty?' he prompts me. 'What's wrong?'

'I, er...'

I, er, have forgotten how to speak, because you look like an underwear model – but I won't say that out loud. I need to pull myself together.

'I have a situation,' I say.

He looks at me with a face that suggests he'd already gathered that.

'I opened the balcony door for some air and... something ran in. I think it was a spider. Or a mouse maybe.'

'Well, which one? You couldn't tell?' he replies.

'I panicked,' I tell him. 'It just... it ran in, scurried across the floor, and now I can't find it, but it's in here somewhere. You have to help me.'

He narrows his eyes, arms folded now, which only highlights his biceps and his pecs.

'Liberty. How exactly would a mouse get to your balcony? We're on the fourteenth floor.' His brow furrows. 'Don't mice hibernate?'

'Okay, then it must have been a spider,' I blurt. 'A really big one! A mouse-sized one. And it's loose in my room. You have to help me!'

He sighs, rubbing a hand over his face.

'Okay. Fine. Where did you see it last?' he asks, clearly not into the idea of helping, but not feeling like he has much choice.

'Somewhere,' I say vaguely, already stepping past him, into his room. 'Honestly, I can't look at it again. I'm so frightened. I'll just wait in here, while you look for it.'

'No, Liberty, wait,' he replies. 'You'll have to help me. Spot me – in case it sneaks up on me.'

'Sneaks up on you?' I repeat back to him.

'Yeah,' he replies. 'While my back is turned...'

'You'll be fine, just squash it, or chuck it back outside if you're that way inclined,' I tell him.

'Liberty, I, er... I'm scared of spiders,' he confesses.

'You're what?' I reply.

'I'm scared of spiders,' he says again. Then he laughs. 'Why are you looking at me with that judgemental face? You're scared of spiders too.'

'Well, because I'm just a girl,' I joke.

'What an old-fashioned way of thinking – you should talk to someone about that casual sexism,' he replies, and it gets my back up. Imagine being called a sexist by a man. He's probably joking too but it still annoys me.

He's smirking as he stands there, all smug and shirtless. He's getting under my skin in a way that makes me want to slap him and kiss him at the same time.

'I'll help you,' he tells me. 'But you have to keep an eye out too, okay?'

'Yeah, okay,' I reply, trying to think of my next play.

We both tiptoe around the room for a few minutes, trying to

track down the non-existent spider. Eventually, I get bored of pretending. This is never going to work.

'There!' I say, pointing vaguely at the balcony. 'It ran outside. I saw it.'

'Really?' he asks, looking deeply sceptical. I suppose it's hard to believe the problem could be solved so easily – especially when it's hard to believe the problem was real in the first place.

'Yes! It's gone. You did it. You must have scared it off or something. Quick, close the door,' I say.

He walks over, scanning the carpet – just in case – as he goes, and closes the door.

'Well, there you go,' he says.

'Thank you,' I say, trying not to sound breathless. 'You're very brave.'

He laughs.

'Goodnight, Liberty,' he says as he heads back to his room. 'I'd keep the door closed if I were you. It's freezing out there.'

'Thanks – goodnight,' I call after him as he closes the door behind him.

I hear it lock – of course I do. He probably thinks I'm crazy.

Brilliant. So not only did that not work, but I've made myself look insane, I've embarrassed myself and I've seemingly outed myself as a female sexist. Oh, and as a fun little bonus, my room is now positively Baltic, thanks to the door being open for so long.

I climb into bed, wrapping my blankets around myself, trying to warm up. I don't suppose this could get me into Jordan's room, could it? Saying mine is too cold? No, definitely not, that sounds like a come-on. Like an uninspired porno story-line. I'm sure that would only make things worse.

I guess I'll have to think of something else – something other than how good he looked in just his pants.

18

I got up early today – probably the earliest I've been up, well, ever. It wasn't even light outside, that's how early it was.

So I'm up, I'm dressed, and I'm ready to get my stalk on. That's my plan for today. With Jordan insisting I shouldn't even turn up at the office today, and instructing me to do my own thing, because he's busy, well, I started to wonder – busy with what?

This is what they don't show you in fancy secret agent movies: the waiting. So much waiting. You never see James Bond sitting on the end of his bed, waiting, or Ethan Hunt loitering next to an adjoining door awkwardly, listening for signs of life.

Well, that's how I do it, baby.

I've had no less than three coffees from the machine in my hotel room, to the point where my stomach is starting to complain, and I'm buzzing. Now all I need is for Jordan to get up, go out, and do whatever it is he's going to do – and hope, at some point, he says or does something that gives me an idea how to sneak into his room. Unless he's carrying the contract around with him – although I don't know if that would be easier or more difficult to pull off a swap.

I am spectacularly unqualified for basically everything, but I'm here and I'm doing my best.

Eventually, I hear it, the soft clunk of a door opening. It's him, he's heading out... It's go time!

I slink out of my room slowly and quietly and follow him – keeping my distance, of course – to the lifts. He gets in one so I wait for the next one, hoping I don't lose him in the few seconds I'm not going to be able to keep eyes on him.

Thankfully I arrive in the lobby only seconds after he does. He doesn't glance back as he heads out which is lucky for me, because I'm not sure where I'd hide in the wide-open space.

Outside, he walks like a man on a mission. It's not easy, trying to keep up with him, and keep enough distance so that he doesn't see me.

As he turns into a coffee shop, I make a very dramatic dive behind a newspaper stand not too far away. I can see him inside, queuing up, waiting to place his order. It looks like he's getting a takeaway coffee and a muffin, and while I've definitely had enough coffee, I'm so hungry. What I'd give for a muffin right now.

My stomach rumbles right on cue. The big, loud, dramatic kind of noise when your body is not only complaining, but pining for something.

He sips his drink, oh-so casually as he strolls out the door, and carries on down the street.

I might have had enough coffee, but what I'd give for something warm to hold on to. My hands feel like ice.

As he walks, he peers into shop windows. First a bookstore. Then a vintage record store. He doesn't look like he's looking for anything specific, more like he's browsing.

I stay back, blending in with the tourists, the people Christmas shopping, and those on their way to work. I'm just another random person in a crowd of hundreds of random people. I'm completely incognito.

All of a sudden he crosses the street. He doesn't think about it; he darts for the crossing, to the point where I have to pick up the pace just to keep up with him. He doesn't walk for long before he reaches another crossing and heads back over the road again. Is he lost or something? Still, I follow him, keeping my distance, but trying to keep up.

Soon enough he crosses again – okay, what is he doing?

I pause, ducking behind a tree. What the hell is he doing? Is he actually lost? Is this some weird cardio thing? Is this how he pumps up his muscles, by playing Chicken in New York? Or does he not know what to do with himself? Or is he meeting someone, but he can't find them...?

He stops. Looks around. Tilts his head, almost like he's deep in thought. Then he carries on.

I'm hesitant to keep following him, because the vibe is just plain weird, but in a weird way it only makes me more determined to follow him because, I swear, the man is up to something. I have to know what it is.

Why, yes, I am questioning my life choices. My toes are numb, I'm starving, and I'm literally stalking a man. But I can't resist the urge to see it through, to figure Jordan Bill out.

I wrap my scarf a little tighter around my face, to keep my nose warm, and carry on.

Jordan veers off into the park and heads along the winding paths. He seems like he knows where he's going now, and what he's doing.

I keep back, clinging to the trees, but doing my best impression of someone casually enjoying a wintry park stroll... alone... while so very blatantly stalking a man.

He stops briefly by the fountain, glances around, his eyes scanning the space, so I duck behind a wall, crouching down, pretending to tie the lace of my boot which, in fact, has no laces.

When I dare peek again, he's on the move. This time toward a huge, ancient-looking tree with a hollow in its trunk.

I slow down, trying not to crunch too many dead leaves beneath my feet as I get closer. Jordan looks around again, like he's checking no one is watching, and then he sticks his hand into the hollow of the tree. What? I pause mid-step, one foot frozen in the air like I'm playing musical statues at a kids' party and 'Agadoo' just stopped. He's rooting around in there (no pun intended), and I can't tell if he's taking something or leaving something, but whatever he's doing looks undeniably dodgy.

I give him a moment to leave before sneaking over to the tree, my heart thumping in my chest. I genuinely have no idea what I'm going to find in there – like, what could it even be? Is he into something bad? Am I going to get myself in trouble, if I touch it?

I know, I should leave well alone, I'm out of my depth, but I have to know.

I reach the tree, feeling around, my numb fingers bashing into the sides as I clumsily try to find whatever might be in there... but there's nothing. Just bits of tree, some melted ice (at least that's what I'm optimistically telling myself it is), but nothing of note.

'What are you doing?' a voice asks, causing my soul to jump out of my body for a second.

I squeal, partly because he's startled me, partly because he's rumbled me.

It's Jordan, because of course it is. He's staring at me, grinning, but the look in his eyes is one of genuine confusion.

'I'm just... Nothing,' I insist, rather pathetically.

'Nothing?' he replies. 'Because from where I was standing, it looked like you were elbow deep in a tree.'

'I thought I saw a red squirrel,' I tell him, like it's the most normal thing in the world.

'So you thought you'd – what? – high-five it?' he replies, clearly not buying what I'm trying to sell.

'Okay, fine, I saw you do it first,' I confess. 'And I thought it was weird, so I just, you know, had a bit of a look and a feel.'

He laughs at me.

'Oi, it's not funny,' I tell him. 'You're being really weird today. You can't blame me for checking up on you...'

He laughs harder and it boils my blood ever so slightly – simmers it, I guess – even in this chilly weather.

'You're following me,' he says.

'No, I'm not,' I reply.

'Liberty. You've been tailing me since the hotel.'

Shiiiit.

'You're making it sound like I'm being creepy,' I snap – although I've no right to be so defensive because it is creepy to stalk a person.

'Because you are,' he teases. At least he's finding it funny. 'Why are you following me?'

'I wasn't. I was just... walking. Coincidentally. In your exact direction,' I offer up.

'And into a tree...'

'Okay, maybe I was a little curious, and following you... a bit,' I reply.

'Obviously,' he replies.

'But you are acting weird,' I insist.

'Because you were following me,' he says, snorting with laughter. 'When I noticed you I thought it might be funny to mess with you, to do weird stuff, to see if you followed me. When I saw you with your arm up that poor tree I knew it was time to put you out of your misery.'

'That is so sneaky,' I say, annoyed.

'So is following me!' he claps back. 'Look, it's cold out, and you're going to follow me anyway so... do you want to grab brunch?'

'What?' I blurt.

'Brunch,' he says slowly and loudly, like I might be hard of hearing. 'That's my plan anyway, so you might as well sit with me, if you're going to stalk me – maybe you'll find what you're looking for?'

'Are you sure?' I check.

'No, but I'm hungry,' he jokes. 'So, do you fancy it?'

'Yeah, definitely, I'm starving,' I tell him. 'And I promise I'm not a weirdo, or a stalker – I'm not like Joe from *You*.'

'From me?' he replies, puzzled.

'Joe Goldberg, from *You*, the TV show,' I explain.

'Do you ever think you watch too much TV?' he jokes – well, he's laughing, so I assume he's joking.

I've seen an almost embarrassing number of TV shows and films set in New York over the years. *Sex and the City*, *Friends*, *Gossip Girl*, *When Harry Met Sally*, *The Devil Wears Prada* – even watching *Home Alone 2* as a child made me sick to visit. It's like the city's been quietly living in my head for years, drip-fed to me through glossy screens and quippy dialogue.

'Months of unemployment will do that to a girl,' I reply.

I don't tell him that binge-watching anti-love shows and

chain-eating chocolate buttons was what got me through my break-up.

'Do you think it's too early for pizza?' he asks. 'It is basically lunch time...'

'It's never too early for pizza,' I reply.

'Great, I know a place that does the best pizza in Manhattan, and it's not far from here,' he says.

As we stroll for our pizza, we make small talk about the weather – like I wasn't just literally stalking him like a maniac. I notice that he hasn't really pressed me on why I was following him, which is interesting.

The pizza place is kind of low-key. No gimmicks, no unnecessary fanciness – but it smells terrific, like melted cheese and Italian herbs.

'Take a seat, I'll order,' he replies.

'I'm not sure what I want,' I say.

'I'll surprise you,' he replies.

'Okay,' I say and, yes, I'm into the idea. Excited by it, even. Normally I would think the idea of having a man order my food for me would piss me off, but I want to see what Jordan chooses.

I slide into a booth, watching him as he heads to the counter. He points at something on the board as he chats with the woman serving him. A minute later, he comes back with two bottles of soda and two enormous slices of pizza. They're piled high with toppings, mostly vegetables, and they look so good.

'So,' he says, twisting off his bottle cap and taking a sip, 'what were you really doing following me this morning?'

I take a sip of my own drink, trying to play it cool.

'I was just... watching to see where you were going,' I tell him. 'It's pretty obvious that you don't want me here, and I'm supposed to be assisting you, so... I was just making sure you weren't leaving me out of anything to do with work.'

'It's nothing personal,' he insists. 'I know, you have a job to do, but I really don't need an assistant, and to be honest with you, I sometimes wonder if Paige is asking people to spy on me...'

'Oh, that's not what that was,' I say, although I'm sure he can tell I'm lying about something.

'So you're not going to report back and tell her you saw me in a tree?' he jokes.

'Would she believe me if I did?' I reply. 'The only thing worth reporting to anyone is how incredible this pizza is – my God.'

'I thought you'd like it,' he says with a smile.

I don't know, something about that – him thinking of me – makes my stomach do a little flip. Whatever it is, it's not part of the plan. None of this is part of the plan.

We sit in easy, comfortable silence for a few minutes while we eat. There's something sexy about the way he eats – the way he devours his food, like he's in love with it.

'Do you take all your stalkers out for lunch?' I ask, breaking the silence.

'Only my favourites,' he jokes.

Oh, I like his little jokes, they're so charming – which is a dangerous thing to think.

I can't afford to like him. I can't afford to feel charmed by him. I'm not here to be his friend, I'm here to get into his room, swap the contracts, and then head back to my life with my job still intact.

And yet...

As he tells a story about the weirdest things he's seen in Central Park over the years – all weirder than my sticking my arm in a tree – I catch myself laughing too hard. Watching the way his eyes crinkle at the edges when he's knows he's being funny.

I feel like I'm in trouble here, because he really is charming, and if the roles were reversed, he would've had me already. In the gotcha sense, that is, not *had me* had me.

Although... No! I can't think like that. I can't fall for his charm like everyone else. I'm here to do a job.

Or try to, anyway.

19

There's a certain kind of bar that only really exists in New York City – well, if TV shows and movies are anything to go by. Super sexy. Candlelit within an inch of its life. Moody even. Like you could be here for an illicit affair with a married man or a cop in need of a post-work whisky – or maybe even both. It's a real one-size-fits-all sort of place.

Why am I here? Well, neither of the above reasons, that's for sure. I'm here because I need to be somewhere, because Jordan clearly has no work for me to do, and because I'm going a little crazy on my own.

'Another?' the barman asks me, nodding towards my empty glass.

My plan was to try a few different cocktails, but with so many to choose from – and given that I'm in New York – I defaulted to a Cosmopolitan and, to be honest with you, it's just easy to get another.

'Yes, please,' I reply.

I know, I'm very much at risk of being asked: why the long face? But nothing feels like it's going to plan.

I take my phone from my bag to pay and notice I have a message from Paige.

PAIGE

Is it done yet?

LIBERTY

Not yet.

PAIGE

Liberty, come on. This is important. I need you to pick up the pace.

She must realise I'm trying? Does she think I'm just sitting around sipping cocktails? Okay, yeah, fair enough, I am right now, but I really have been trying my best.

LIBERTY

I know, but I can't risk getting caught, and he's not making it easy for me to get close to him.

PAIGE

Please try harder. If you can confirm he has the right version, I'll step in and press him to sign. But I'm not reaching out until I know he's seen it, otherwise he might sign the wrong one and we're screwed.

What can I say?

LIBERTY

I'll try.

PAIGE

Try harder.

Oof. I am so very clearly displeasing the boss – so that makes both of them – but wow. She must realise what an impossible job she's tasked me with. I would love to see anyone do a better job, because: how? How is a person supposed to do this? Short of stealing a housekeeping uniform, and a keycard, and then waiting until he's out to slip in and make the swap – obviously I'm not going to do anything illegal for a job. Is Paige really expecting me to?

'Here we are, ma'am,' the barman says as he sets my drink down in front of me.

'Thanks so much,' I reply.

'I can tell you're not a New Yorker,' a man says as he takes the seat next to me.

I glance sideways. A man with way-too-white teeth, a blazer that's just slightly too tight on the biceps, and hair that says 'I woke up like this' but definitely involved a diffuser and three separate products.

'I'm from the UK,' I say politely.

'I knew it. I knew you were British,' he replies. 'I've got a good ear for accents. I love an English accent. Where are you from? Are you Scottish?'

'The north of England,' I tell him.

'That's Scotland, right?'

It's really not.

'No, below Scotland, in Yorkshire – in England,' I correct him.

Perhaps I should have just said yes.

'You sound kinda funny,' he says – rather rudely, in my opinion.

'Oh, yeah?' I reply, not at all interested, but what's a girl supposed to say in response to that?

'Yeah... sorta... I don't know.' He thinks for a moment. 'I love England. I love *The Crown, Downton Abbey*, Kate Middleton, Posh Spice. Your accent doesn't sound the same...'

Hilariously he sounds almost suspicious.

'Ahh, well, I'm not from where Posh Spice is from,' I tell him. 'I'm actually from where Scary Spice is from.'

'I see,' is all he says. 'I like the posh accent. Like, Emma Watson posh. Have you seen the *Harry Potter* movies?'

'Erm, no,' I say, not giving him anything to work with. Turns out he doesn't need it.

'I just love all things British,' he continues. 'I've just always had a thing for Brits, you know? It's the accent. Not yours, the proper one.'

'Right.'

'Don't get me wrong, you still sound British,' he reassures me as he waves over the barman. 'Can I get a beer?'

'Sure,' the barman replies.

'Would I be drinking lager, if I was in the UK?' he asks me.

'Do you like lager?' I reply.

'I like British things,' he says. 'I have tried Carlsberg.'

I don't have the heart to tell him that's from Denmark. Actually, I do, but I really want this conversation to end.

'So.' He leans forward. 'Do you live in London?'

'Yes,' I reply.

'Near the Queen?'

I wonder if he knows we have a king now too. Honestly, I'm not even going to go there...

'No.'

'I love London. Black cabs, red buses, Big Ben...'

'Yep.'

'Man, your culture is so classy,' he continues. 'And I love the way you guys say, like, al-yoo-min-ee-um. And choo-na, when you have it on baked potatoes with beans from a tin. It looks so gross, but you eat like wartime stuff, right?'

Does this man really think I'm sitting in my manor house,

next door to the Queen, where she's eating tuna and beans in a jacket potato, with Posh Spice, while Big Ben bongs in the background? I'm starting to think he really does.

'Do you live in a cottage?' he asks.

'A flat.'

'A flat,' he replies, trying to copy my voice. 'Do you watch *The Great British Baking Show*? You guys call it *Bake Off* though, don't you?'

What is this? What's going on here? He's turned up, low-key offended me, he's interrogating me about Britain generally, like it's all one big London. Is he serious?

'I dated this girl, Sarah, from Clapham,' he tells me, although he pronounces it clap-ham. 'And Donna, I don't remember where she was from, but she worked for a company that made crumpets.'

Every now and then his accent slips into what I would imagine is supposed to be an 'English' one, but he sounds more Bean than he does Bond.

'We had an intern who was English, but she wasn't interested...'

'Do you only date English girls?' I joke.

'Basically,' he replies.

Wait, what? I know this isn't a date, I don't even know this man's name, but I'm going to call it. Here is it. Here comes the ick.

'Yeah!' he says proudly. 'It's just my type. The accent. The attitude. So posh but feisty, you know? Like classy but could also tell you to sod off if you burn the bangers and mash.'

I have no words.

'Say something British,' he prompts me.

I don't.

'What are you, one of those Beefeaters?' he teases. 'Come on, say something, anything. Tell me about how you make cups of tea or how you guys all love Boris Johnson? He is so funny...'

'Right, I'm off,' I tell him, knocking back the last of my drink.

'I'm off,' he says to himself. 'I haven't heard that one before.'

'No, I'm actually off – I'm going,' I tell him.

'Was it something I said?' he replies.

'It was literally everything you said,' I point out.

I grab my bag to leave. As I'm walking away, I swear I hear him say 'bloody hell' in the most exaggerated accent.

Well, that's a first. I've never been interesting just for being English before. Not that I liked it – being treated like a souvenir or something.

Perhaps going out drinking alone isn't for me. Plus, I've got a job to do, and if I don't get it done soon, Paige will be furious. I'll be 'brown bread'. And I really don't want that.

20

I have a plan... well, sort of.

I have an idea, is what I probably should say. I don't know if it's a good one, but it's the best I've got, and I need to try something.

My big idea? Cake.

Wait, no, hear me out. I know, I've had a few Cosmopolitans tonight, but I promise you this is me thinking straight. It's not as silly as it sounds. I'm basically going to use Jordan's strengths against him. His cool guy persona, his easy-going nature, his popularity.

I've ordered a cake to be delivered to reception – I went on a food delivery app, chose a cake, and then wrote a message saying for it to be delivered to reception, but that Jordan would have to come down and collect it. What that will do is – step one – get Jordan to leave his room.

Then – step two – I'm going to listen for him leaving, to go down and get it, and that's when I'm going to sneak into his room.

So, if there's one thing I've noticed about Jordan, it's that he doesn't check his door is locked; he walks through it and leaves it to close itself – he's that cool. I'm not cool at all. I'm the kind of person who locks the door, then checks it again, then double-checks. And even then, I'll still spend the whole day wondering if I left it wide open, but no worries if I have, at least it will be easy for the fire brigade to get inside, to put out the fire from the straighteners I'm usually pretty sure I've left on...

I might be an anxious girlie but that's what's going to make me good at this. I have all bases covered. So I'll hover in the recess where the door to my room is, listen for him leaving – thankfully the lift is in the other direction – and then try to stop his door before it closes, so I can nip inside, make the swap and boom. Job done.

So I wait, not for long – just enough time to question whether or not my plan is too dumb to work – but then I hear him leaving and, sure enough, he leaves his door to close itself, and he's far too cool to look back. I manage to stop it just in time, right as it's about to close, and that's it. I'm in.

The contract – the one I need to swap in – is safely stuffed down the back of my trousers. Well, I thought just in case Jordan caught me in the act, I didn't want to have any damning evidence on me. The plan is to make the switch, then stuff the contract with the errors down my pants, and then try to get out of here without getting caught.

What will I say if Jordan does catch me in here? Honestly, I have no idea. I need to make sure it doesn't come to that. I have unlocked my side of the adjoining door though, just in case.

Another fatal error I could make would be to try to swap the contracts, but get them mixed up, and leave the room with the one I came with, so I've made the slightest fold on one of the back corners.

I haven't read it. Not properly. I skimmed the first page after

Paige gave it to me, but it was all legal jargon and boring corporate stuff. It just looks like a contract. But hopefully my little fold helps make sure I leave here with the right one.

He has a desk, and it looks like he's been using it, because his things are laid out on it – so neatly though. I'll bet he's the kind of guy who puts his clothes away in the wardrobe, when he stays in hotels, whereas I'll live out of my suitcase the whole time I'm here.

I start carefully opening drawers, lifting papers without shifting anything too much. It seems like everything has its place, so I don't want him noticing if something has been touched.

There's a folder so I lift it open with one finger, like I'm trying to be careful not to leave fingerprints, as though he's going to have any way to dust for them, even if he is suspicious.

I hear it. Shit. A sound on the other side of the door. Footsteps. Then a voice – Jordan's voice. He's back already.

I go from nought to panic in about two seconds – I'm surprised it takes me that long to be honest with you. I think I'm mistaken but, no, that's his voice, and that's the noise the door makes when you pop your keycard in to unlock it.

So what do I do? What can I do? I hit the deck and crawl, like a worm, on my stomach, until I'm tucked away under the bed. And I do it just in the nick of time. He's here. He's in the room. And I'm trapped.

'Yeah, I was on my way down for it, but they sent someone up with it,' he says to whoever he's on the phone with, chill as ever.

I try to press myself flatter to the floor, holding my breath, as though those things might help me to be invisible. This is bad. This is really fucking bad.

Then he pauses.

'So you didn't send it?' He laughs, a little confused. 'Not that many people even know I'm here. Who would send me a cake?'

He laughs again, softer this time.

'Okay, bud, see you then. Bye. Bye.'

It's just me and him but he's quiet now, now that he's off the phone.

The bed above me creaks as it dips a little, under Jordan's weight. He must be sitting on it. It makes me jump, but I do my best to keep quiet. I grit my teeth, trying to keep as still as I can, to be as silent as humanly possible, but my heart is pounding and I'm convinced he's going to hear it.

I've really fucked this one up, huh? I'm not sure it could have gone worse. Even failing epically from the get-go would have been better, because at least I wouldn't have been caught, it just would have been a case of back to the drawing board.

What am I going to do? I can't stay here all night, can I? How will I ever leave? What if he knocks on my door for some reason? And, truly, I've never needed a wee so much in my life, but I'm certain I only feel this way because I know I can't go right now.

And of course I left my phone in my room, like an idiot, or I could've messaged him, asked him to meet me somewhere, lured him out again. I thought I was doing the right thing, leaving it. It seemed like something I might accidentally leave behind – I thought I was being so smart. It's probably worth remembering that I seriously exaggerated in my interview. I'm not actually good at this stuff, but I'm doing my best.

My only hope is the adjoining door. I unlocked my side earlier, just in case. But reaching it from here? I'd have to cross the room, and he would definitely spot me, crawling out from under his bed, like something from a horror movie.

The bed creaks again as he stands up.

I watch his feet as he walks to the desk. I hold my breath. Did I leave anything out of place? Anything that he might spot? Shit, I definitely moved that folder a bit. Maybe he won't notice? There's no way he can tell I touched it, right?

He turns and walks across the room again, eventually going into the bathroom, but he doesn't close the door. Well, why would he? He thinks he's in here alone, obviously.

If his bathroom has the same layout as mine – which, why wouldn't it? – then everything in there is around a corner. Which means if I'm quick – and I'm talking lightning fast – I might be able to make it to the adjoining door, but I have to decide if I'm going for it right now.

Well, what else am I going to do?

I launch myself from under the bed, half-crawling, half-sprinting across the carpet, probably looking like some kind of demon. I practically dive at the adjoining door, fingers fumbling over the little lock. It won't turn, it won't bloody turn – but then then it clicks. I fling the door open, slip through, slam it shut behind me, but maybe a bit too much force because it makes a bang.

Shit. Please tell me he didn't hear that.

I lock it on my side and back away like I'm in *The Shining* and my crazy husband is on the other side of it.

I pull the contract out of my trousers and push it under my bed, then I stare at the door, wondering if he noticed, waiting to see if I got away with it.

I swear, I actually start relaxing, but then I notice the handle moving, like he's trying to open it.

'Liberty?' Jordan's voice, muffled but clear enough to hear, travels through the door. 'Liberty, are you there?'

Oh crap.

'Yes?' I call back, trying to sound cool and casual, but I practically squeak the word out.

'Did you just open this door?' he asks.

'What? No,' I reply.

'I could've sworn I heard a door,' he says. 'And it's unlocked on my side now. I definitely locked it.'

'Weird,' I say, cringing. 'No, it wasn't me. I was... washing my hair. I was in the shower.'

There's a pause.

'Oh, okay. Can you open the door for a minute?' he replies.

Oh, for God's sake, no, I bloody can't, because if I do then he'll see that I'm bone dry. Unless...

'One sec,' I call out.

I bolt into my bathroom, fling off my clothes, and dunk my head under the cold tap. It's freezing and it's getting in my eyes, my nose, my mouth – I need to look wet though.

Then I throw on a robe and get back to the adjoining door. I unlock it, open it, and hope that nothing seems off.

'Are you okay?' he asks, his brow furrowed.

'Yeah, fine,' I say, breathless. 'Why?'

'You look...' His voice trails off, like he's not quite sure what he's looking at.

I glance at the mirror next to the door. The water has made my eye makeup run all over my face. I look like a raccoon that's joined a metal band.

'Oh,' I say simply. 'I forgot to take my makeup off before I showered.'

He's still staring but he's smiling a little now too.

'What can I do for you?' I ask. 'Do you need something for work?'

He laughs.

'Do you ever take a minute off? No, it's not work. Someone sent me a cake. No idea who, but it's too much to eat on my own.' He lifts a white box in one hand, and then pulls the other out from behind his back to reveal a bottle of champagne. 'Want to share it with me?'

'I'd love to,' I reply, because I really would. I'm not sure how this plays into my clearly not very good strategy, though.

He steps into my room, walks past me, and sits down on the edge of my bed. I swear, his foot is practically on the contract, where it's still sticking out a little.

'Do you have glasses?' Jordan asks as he opens the bottle.

I glance towards the sideboard to see two unused water glasses still sitting there. I grab them and bring them over, too scared to leave him alone, next to the contract, for too long. Even if he doesn't know it's there.

'So... you said someone sent you a cake?' I say, holding out the glasses, ready for him to pour the champagne.

'I guess so,' he replies, twisting the cork until it pops with a satisfying sound. He doesn't flinch – I probably would've screamed, but my nerves are definitely getting the better of me tonight. I hold the glasses out while he pours, trying to keep my hands steady.

'So I take it you know Paige and I are recently divorced?' he says, leaning back against the headboard like we're old friends catching up.

'Erm, yeah, I've heard... bits and bobs around the office,' I say, as neutrally as possible.

'Part of me wondered if she sent the cake,' he replies. 'She knows I'm here. And it's red velvet. My favourite.'

I chose red velvet because it's my favourite too.

'But then I remembered she hates me,' he jokes, and gives this little half-laugh that's not entirely convincing.

'Do you really think she hates you?' I can't help but ask.

He pulls a face.

'Well, I haven't had many divorces – this is actually my first,' he says, sort of jokey. 'But it's been messy and... I suppose it makes you feel like you hate each other, when you're scrapping over books, records – company stock...' He laughs. 'But we don't hate each other. We just don't like what we have when we're together.'

'That makes sense,' I reply, and it really does. More than I expected. I know, I didn't get divorced, but break-ups are break-ups.

'What about you?' he asks, taking a slice of the (thankfully) pre-cut cake. 'Have you ever been divorced? Or are you married – I forget sometimes people stay together.'

I laugh.

'No, not married, and I never have been, but I split up with my boyfriend this year,' I confess, taking a slice of cake – so glad I get to eat some, seeing as though I paid for it. 'We were living together but... yeah, it didn't work out.'

'Was it mutual?' he asks, sucking icing from his fingertips – and it's oddly sexy.

'Erm, not really,' I say, stabbing at the cake with my fork. 'I guess, technically, he decided to send photos of his penis to other people, and I decided to break up with him, so... mutual in the sense that we both stuck a knife in. Made sure the relationship was truly dead.'

He lets out a low laugh.

'Wow, yeah, okay, that'll do it,' he replies. 'Sorry to hear that. He sounds like a wanker.'

'Quite literally,' I joke. 'Yeah, he was, and it wasn't very nice, when I found out, but it opened my eyes. It showed me I could do better. That I should aim higher next time.'

'The bar sounds like it was low,' he replies. 'So... go way higher.'

'Believe me, I will,' I tell him. 'I didn't realise it at the time, but he did so many little things that... wore me down. Things that made every day harder.'

'It sounds like you're happier without him, then?'

I go quiet for a second too long.

'Or not?' Jordan adds gently.

'No, I am better off, definitely,' I say, forcing a smile. 'It's just... hard to move on.'

'I understand,' he replies.

I wonder if he really does though. He doesn't seem like someone who's struggling to move on. Then again, maybe that's just the face he puts on for the world. Maybe he's just better at hiding it than I am.

I polish off the last bite of my slice of cake. Honestly, considering I ordered from the first place I could see – it's not like I checked reviews or anything – it was incredible.

'I'd better let you go,' Jordan says, finishing his champagne.

'You don't have to,' I say quickly, surprising myself. I'm actually... kind of enjoying this. Hanging out with him.

He gives me a smile.

'I'm sure you need to dry your hair,' he reminds me.

Ah, yes, my hair – I guess I need to actually wash it too, or it will dry like straw.

'Oh, right, yeah,' I say. 'And finally take my makeup off.'

'Yeah.' He chuckles. 'You look like you've been water-boarded.'

I laugh too – mostly because I kind of have, just by my own hand.

He walks to the adjoining door.

'Goodnight, Liberty.'

'Goodnight,' I reply. 'Thanks for the cake.'

'Anytime,' he replies.

He closes the door behind him. Then, after a second or two, I hear him lock it.

Okay, so I didn't manage to swap the contract. The mission continues to be impossible. But I did get a slice of cake, a glass of champagne, and a surprisingly decent conversation out of it.

It might not be what I set out to get, but I'm happy it's what I ended the evening with.

And there's always tomorrow...

21

Today Jordan is doing a talk at some business event, where people have travelled from far and wide to hear him talk about the place dating apps have in modern society.

Thinking about it, dating apps aren't really that new any more, are they? Online dating has been around forever, but the apps were something new, something fresh – something everyone who was anyone was doing. But, shit, that was like ten years ago. I feel a million years old now.

It's a big room, with rows and rows of people, all here to hang off Jordan's every word. The lights are low, and the spotlight is on him. He's wearing one of those cool headsets that sits on his ear and hovers in front of his lips.

He looks good up there. He's wearing a white shirt and a smart pair dark blue trousers – if you didn't know why you were here, you could think he was a sexy pop star or a motivational speaker. I've never known someone so confident and charming. It fascinates me.

'So, I know what you're thinking, here's one of the people

who started Matcher – the hook-up app,' he begins, grabbing everyone's attention.

The room chuckles in recognition.

'And, yes, okay, some people use it that way,' he continues. 'But, really, we didn't invent the hook-up. People have been hooking up since the beginning of time. It's not a new concept but, like with anything, technology has only made it easier.'

'Thank you,' a male voice calls out from the audience.

'And you're welcome,' Jordan jokes, not letting it throw him off. If anything, it just makes him seem even more relaxed.

He starts walking slowly across the stage, quietly owning it.

'But, contrary to popular belief, that's not exactly what we had in mind. What I care about – the reason I'm standing here today – isn't just the hook-ups. It's the connections. Because for some people, Matcher isn't about one night. It's about that first step towards a lifetime of happiness. A first step for people who lack confidence, who don't do well in loud bars or at social events. People who need the shield of a screen to feel comfortable opening up, until they feel like they've found someone they want to meet in person.'

It's an interesting thought to consider, that Matcher is filled with men with the most confidence or the least.

'And then there are people who have just moved to a new town or city, who don't know how to go out and meet people – how the hell does anyone do that? Because let's be honest, it's impossible to meet people as an adult. For love, for friendship, for anything really.'

He stops centre stage now, his eyes scanning the crowd. I could swear he was looking right at me – or maybe it just feels that way. He's doing such a good job of appearing to talk to everyone. It feels intimate. Like he's speaking only to you.

'My focus is, and always has been, on creating safe spaces.

Safe spaces where people can connect without fear, without pressure, and – most importantly – without feeling like they have to change themselves just to be chosen.'

The room quiets. Everyone – including me – wants to know where he's going with this.

'So how do we do that? How do we make dating feel human again?' he continues. 'It's a scary time to date – scarier than ever, and tech, anonymity, AI... it's not making things any easier. There will always be people who use these tools for bad, people who aren't who they say they are, people who will love you and leave you – and block you. That's a relatively new part of the process. People who, no matter how hard you try, won't believe you're good enough. But what if I told you that, beyond everything we've got going on behind the scenes to keep you safe, there is one tip I can give you that will change how people view you – because it will change how you view yourself?'

You could hear a pin drop. Jordan smiles, like he's about to let us in on a secret.

'It's going to sound corny, so hear me out,' he starts with a chuckle. 'The most valuable thing you can do, first and foremost, before you even download the app, is to know your worth. First of all, remember that not everyone is going to be everyone's cup of tea. Not to sound like a very British cliché.'

Even when he's being serious, when he has the entire room holding their breath, I love the way he still gets a laugh.

'So I want you to think about it this way,' he continues. 'You can buy a bottle of water in a UK supermarket for, what, less than a pound? I'm going to guess it's the same here. But... go to a train station and it's £2.50. Go to a festival or a concert, and that same bottle might cost you four or five quid. But here's the thing – it's still the same water. The only thing that's changed is the demand, and to the right person, at the right time, it's worth it. Whatever the cost.'

Another pause. I glance around. People are nodding in agreement.

'Some people will drink from the tap, for free, and that's fine. But what I care about is helping people find the ones who see them, who value them, who think, yeah, okay, that's worth the price. And I'm going to make it my mission to give people the tools to weed out the timewasters. To cut through the bullshit, the ghosting, the games – so that someone doesn't only see you, they see your worth too.'

People clap, cheer – a few people even stand up. It's the kind of reaction you only get when someone says something everyone has been waiting to hear. Even I'm clapping, and I hate Matcher. I suppose, with the right effort, it could be an app used for good, not just for a good time.

I guess I'm also applauding Jordan for surprising me, for saying the last thing I expected him to say. I knew he was charming, sure, but I thought he'd be swiping Matcher with the best (or the worst) of them. I didn't get the impression – especially after talking to Paige – that he was someone who believed in love. Really believed in it.

Maybe he does – or maybe it's good for business to say he does – but, either way, he's won over the room.

It's the first time in a long time that I've heard someone talk about the dating game and thought, I don't know, maybe it's not so hopeless after all.

22

I didn't choose the corporate espionage life, the corporate espionage life chose me, and I really, really don't think I'm cut out for it.

I'm sitting on the plump, luxurious grey carpet of my hotel room, legs crossed, demolishing one hell of a club sandwich that I just ordered from room service. Even the crisps (or should that be chips, given I'm in the US) are incredible.

Why am I down here? I always like to sit (or lie) on the floor, when I'm having a pity party, wallowing, thinking about my life choices.

I have come to the conclusion that I'm struggling with not one but two issues. First and foremost, I don't know, the lying, the sneaking, the trickery – it's just not me. I know, I know, I'm doing this for Paige, righting a wrong, no one is going to get hurt, everyone's job will be saved, blah, blah, blah. I'm trying to focus on the positives, on doing what my boss is telling me to do – because that's what having a job is, right? Doing shit you don't want to do, for money, so you can pay your bills and eat.

Being so underhanded, though, it's just not who I am, and

the biggest spanner in the works is that, the more I get to know Jordan, the more it feels like some sort of betrayal, to be trying to trick him. I'm sure Paige knows him much better than I do, she was married to the man after all, but he doesn't seem like an unreasonable person to me, he seems like someone who cares. Can he really not be negotiated with? Surely he would be decent about it?

And then of course, aside from feeling morally conflicted by the task at hand, the second problem I'm having is that I'm absolutely shit at it. Come on, look at me, look at my best efforts – they're pathetic. Pretending I've seen a spider, sending in a cake... Is that really the best I can do? They're the tactics of a teenage girl.

I pick up my phone and see that I've got a message from my mum. That's the thing about time differences – I can only speak to people back home at certain times.

> MUM
>
> Hello darling, just checking in. You okay?
> Excited for the wedding?

I stare at the screen for a moment, debating what to say. Am I okay? Not really. Am I excited? Definitely not. But I can't say any of that. Probably best I tell her what she needs to hear.

> LIBERTY
>
> Yeah, I am! Can't wait to see everyone.

It takes her all of ten seconds to reply.

> MUM
>
> Lovely. Everyone's so looking forward to seeing
> you. How's work going?

Another lie will serve me well, I think.

It's going really well actually! Busy, but in a
good way.

I hit send and immediately feel like a fraud. I hate lying to
my mum but I don't want to worry her when I'm so far from
home.

MUM

Good! I'm so pleased for you. Dad says
remember to bring him back a good present.

I can't help but smile.

LIBERTY

Tell him I'll do my best. Love you.

MUM

Love you too!

I'm missing my parents more than usual – probably because
it feels like everything is going tits up, and I know they'll always
love me, even when I'm not exactly thriving.

If I thought my mum had the answers to my problems,
believe me, I would ask, but I've got myself into this mess. Only I
can get myself out.

I stare into space, like the answer might be written on
the wall in front of me, but it only reminds me that the
contract is on the other side of it, safe and sound, and
there's clearly no way I'm going to be able to get my hands
on it.

There's only one thing I can think to do, and I'm not sure
how well it's going to go down, but I'm out of options. I need to
call Paige.

The phone rings for a while – so long I'm about to give up – when finally she answers.

'Liberty, hello,' she says. 'How's it going? Are you enjoying New York?'

'Hello, oh, it's lovely here,' I say. 'Even more spectacular than I imagined it being.'

'Glad to hear it,' she replies. 'And do you have good news for me? Is it done?'

'Erm, well, no, not yet,' I babble.

'Oh?' is all she says.

I swear, I can hear the muscles in her jaw tightening.

'I can't get anywhere near him,' I confess. 'He doesn't really trust me. He's polite, but professional. He keeps to himself. The door between our rooms is always locked – any time it's been unlocked briefly, he's been like lightning to lock it again.'

'Well, that is disappointing,' she says. 'I thought you were more resourceful, given your experience.'

I feel like, even if my role had been more than admin, if I did have investigator experience, it's not about doing sneaky things, it's about figuring sneaky things out. Investigators aren't the ones up to no good, they're the people exposing those who are. She's asking too much, regardless.

'I've tried, Paige, really I have. But he's not giving me anything,' I reply. 'He doesn't even need an assistant, so I'm not even being given work to do. There's just no way to get close.'

'Well, that's classic him,' she replies. 'Not valuing women, for one. And not being reasonable – this is why we're having to sneak around, to get the job done, because he won't be helped.'

'I know that I don't know him as well as you do, but I was wondering if maybe, I don't know... if I just... talked to him? Like, if I explained the situation—'

'No! Absolutely not,' she insists. 'Liberty, I've told you, if he knew what I was doing, he would bury me – and the whole company too.'

Except it's not her doing it, it's me. I'm the one who is having to lie to him.

'And you're part of this company, Liberty – your job and your bonus rely on you getting it done,' she adds. 'Listen to me, okay, I think you need the right motivation. You get this done for me, I'll pay you your bonus the moment you're back in London – five thousand pounds. Just think of the Christmas you could have with that.'

My jaw drops. A five-thousand-pound bonus? Is she serious? I quickly scramble to my feet.

'Really?' I blurt.

'Really,' she replies. 'The heartache you would be saving people – it's worth it.'

Five grand would go a long, long way to helping me get my own place. It's a deposit and a chunk towards rent. A buffer, now that I'm earning again... well, so long as I keep earning, which means keeping this job, which means doing exactly as Paige says.

I flop back onto the bed and stare at the ceiling.

'Okay, so what do I do?' I ask. 'I'm running out of ideas, nothing I'm trying is working. Do you have suggestions, hints, tips...?'

'There's only one sure-fire way,' she says with a sigh. 'You need to woo him.'

I sit bolt upright, like a woman possessed.

'Woo him?' I repeat back to her.

'Yes, woo him, date him – feed his ego, he can't resist that,' she explains. 'Seduce him. Whatever it takes. Get invited back to his room, distract him, swap the contract, and then make your excuses and leave. Don't actually have sex with him, obviously.'

'Obviously,' I repeat sarcastically, but she either doesn't detect my tone or doesn't care.

'I'm not exactly a Bond girl,' I point out. 'Sexpionage isn't really something I'm equipped for.'

And that's putting it mildly. I'm not a naturally sexy person – not that I'm saying anything is wrong with me, or selling myself short, but it's just a fact. I'm the kind of girl who gets trapped in revolving doors, and lifts, who makes scenes at weddings, and trips men on the ice. Any allure I have doesn't manifest as objective sexiness, it comes in the form of a man I just met in Australia asking if I wanted to give a long-distance relationship a go.

'Just pretend,' she says.

Ha! So no reassurances, no pep talks. She agrees with me, but she wants me to fake it. A little white lie might have given my self-esteem a bit of a boost, y'know.

'Fluff his ego,' she says.

'Fluff?' I repeat back to her.

'Yes, you know, like in porn...'

'No?' I blurt with a laugh.

'Bat your eyes, give him lots of attention, compliments, keep eye contact, make sexually suggestive comments – this is easy, Liberty, really it is,' she insists.

Stare at him, but blink at him. Pester him, tell him I want to... what?

'Insider intel,' she offers up. 'Talk about biting him. Men love being bitten.'

Oh my God, do they? I know it's been months since I had sex, but we're not all biting each other now, are we? And, ugh, something about getting advice from a scorned woman about how to seduce her ex-husband is so, so gross. My ick alarm is going berserk.

'You don't have to do it,' she reminds me, reading the silence. 'Just make him think you will, get into his room, make the swap, get out again. Tell him your stomach is bad, you need the toilet, you have to go.'

Get into his room under the pretence of biting him. Leave by excusing myself to have diarrhoea. Forgive me for not feeling great about this.

'I can't believe this is my job,' I blurt.

'Well, it won't be any more, if you don't succeed,' she replies. 'We'll all be out of work – do you know how many people work here?'

'All right, all right, I'll do my best,' I tell her.

It's bad enough worrying about my own job. I don't want other people's livelihoods on my conscience.

We say our goodbyes and hang up. I let my phone drop onto the pillow next to me.

She wants me to woo him. I have to woo him, to keep my job, to save everyone's job. I'm really not up to this, in any sense. I don't feel good about it and I won't be good at it.

How would I even go about it? I suppose I could get all dressed up, make an effort with my hair and makeup, invite him out to dinner, hope he says yes, spend the evening with him, see where it goes...

If I'm being honest with you – and I would never admit this to anyone else – the thought of having dinner with Jordan isn't something I hate the sound of. I'm enjoying his company, I'm fascinated by him, I have a bit of a crush on him in the tradi-tional sense of finding him charming and attractive (so long as I forget everything Paige told me).

I want to get to know him more and, if I could do anything this evening, it probably would be hang out with him, especially since hearing his speech earlier, I'm just so intrigued. I want to hear what he thinks about things – I want to tell him what I think about things and see what he says. I like the idea of a one to one, my own personal TED Talk, getting into that brain of his and see what else is lurking in there.

Yeah, okay, I'll ask him if he wants to have dinner with me. Maybe I'll even flirt a bit, but not because Paige told me to, but because it's on the tip of my tongue anyway.

If it comes up, if I end up in his room, then maybe I'll make the switch. That way it's done and dusted and I can go back to being myself. No harm done.

At least that's what I'm hoping...

23

Dress for the job you want, not the job you have – that's what they say, right? Do you think that applies to men, too? Well, not literally, I'm not saying dress for the boyfriend you wish you had, rather than the one you do, I just mean that if you're inviting someone out for dinner, and you want it to be a date, dress like it's a date.

So, I'm dashing around the shops, weaving in and out of Christmas shoppers, trying to find a dress to disarm Jordan Bill.

I'm after a little black dress, something he's never seen me in before, which will hopefully make him lower his defences, take me out somewhere, and then give me access to his room.

It is absolutely not because I want him to think I'm attractive. And if you believe that, I believe there's a bridge somewhere nearby I could sell you...

It's so lovely to see the city decked out like a department store window display. Twinkly Christmas lights hang between skyscrapers like constellations. Wreaths and garlands grace almost everything that's grace-able (I just saw a dog wearing a wreath around its neck). And there's even a brass band playing

'All I Want for Christmas Is You', infecting everyone with festive cheer.

I start at Bloomingdale's, because: when in New York, right? There's an entire section of designer dresses on the second floor, most of which cost more than my flight here – and I googled it, my flight here was eye-wateringly expensive. A very chic assistant with icy blonde hair and a designer dress of her own follows me, probably because she's ready to assist me, but I've seen *Pretty Woman*. Not that I'm giving escort today, I don't think. I'm saving that for tonight, once I've found the right dress, but believe me, I'll be looking like an incredibly expensive one.

'Just browsing,' I mumble, in case she does think I seem a little sus.

She gives me a reassuring smile and floats away, presumably to help someone who isn't dressed head to toe in the UK high street's finest.

I do pick out and try a few things on. One dress is so tight I nearly crack a rib trying to zip it up at the back. Another has cut-outs that suggest the designer has never met anyone with more than 8 per cent body fat – I try it on, of course, in the privacy of the fitting room, but the holes look more accidental than fabulous. Sort of like I just Hulked out of it.

I have some time to kill, so I try a few places, before ending up in SoHo, where I find a little boutique sandwiched between a bakery and an art gallery, and inside, things are a lot more me. Unique, funky, relatively inexpensive (despite the escort comment I made earlier).

And then I find it, the little black dress of my dreams. It's short and fitted – strapless, but it will look great with my boots and my leather jacket. So long as it fits...

I take it into the changing room and peel off my coat, my

jumper and my jeans before carefully stepping into the dress and, yep, this is the one. It fits like it was made for me.

Hopefully I don't look like a spy, or a Bond girl, just a normal woman, going on a date... even if it's not a real date. I need to keep reminding myself of that.

I stare at my reflection for a little too long and notice that my cheeks are flushed. Great, I'm embarrassing myself in front of myself. I hadn't even realised that was possible.

Wouldn't it be even more tragic, being this deluded, only for him to say no, he doesn't want to go out with me? Well, why would he? And I don't mean that in a self-deprecating way, I mean he's a busy and popular man and I'm an employee that he doesn't entirely trust.

But Paige did say he would date anyone, so with a bar that low, how could I fail?

I suppose we'll see, won't we?

24

If it sounds like a date, looks like a date and plays out like a date, then it's a date, right? That's what I'm telling myself, to keep myself in the right frame of mind, to psych myself up to ask Jordan out.

I'm caked in makeup, I'm wearing an incredibly complicated bra that is doing so much I feel like I should be paying it a salary, and I must have spent forty-five minutes with my straighteners, pulling and twisting my long blonde locks to make curls – curls that will surely drop within the hour, but they'll be there when I ask him out at least. Hopefully that's enough.

Apparently it could snow (but I am trying to look sexy) so I've teamed my black mini dress with my over-the-knee boots. I can throw on my big coat, to head out, but so long as I look fire when I ask then maybe, just maybe, he might say yes. Failing that, if I'm not quite as sizzling as I'm aiming for, then hopefully going out with me will be mildly more entertaining than sitting in a room alone, so he still might say yes.

I strike a pose, leaning on the wall slightly, popping my hip just a little, and then knock the adjoining door.

Unless... oh God. What if he already has plans? What if he's already got a date booked in? He had what I can only describe as groupies fawning all over him after his speech. I wouldn't be surprised if he had a date – I'd be surprised if he had only one date. Shit.

Too late now. I've already knocked. And now I'm staring at the door, wondering whether to panic about the fact he probably already has a date, or that I don't think I know how to flirt any more. The only thing I got from Paige was that I should bite him.

I can hear movement behind the door so there's no time to strategise (I'm probably not going to bite him though) and then it opens, Jordan appears, and his eyes widen.

'Wow,' he blurts. 'Look at you.'

My brain goes blank, my mouth goes dry, I can't move a muscle. I wasn't expecting a reaction from him and it has completely disarmed me. I'm sure no time has passed at all, but it feels like I'm frozen. What do I do? What do I say? How am I fucking this up already?

Suddenly it occurs to me, Jordan's speech from earlier, about knowing your worth. If I tell myself that I'm a £6 bottle of water, then maybe I can convince him of that too. I can do this.

'This old thing?' I joke.

I try to keep my tone light, easy-breezy. I want to seem casual but with an undertone of desire. He needs to know I want to spend the evening with him, if I want him to say yes.

'Are you going somewhere nice?' he asks.

'I thought it might be nice to go out for dinner, see the city,' I tell him. 'I wondered if you had any recommendations for me?'

'I can think of a few places,' he replies, leaning on the doorframe, matching my body language. 'It depends what you fancy...'

What I fancy is him, but I probably shouldn't say that, should I? Unless it will help...

'What I fancy is you coming with me,' I tell him.

And there it is, I've said it. I was bold and flirty and not myself, but the genie is out of the bottle now. Now I need to see what he says.

He raises an eyebrow, like he wasn't expecting me to say that (neither was I) but then he grins, letting me know it's not an unpleasant surprise.

'I'll get ready right now, give me fifteen minutes,' he replies.

There's a spring in his step as he dashes into his room to get ready.

Most surprisingly of all, he leaves the adjoining door open. Shit, it's working, I've got his guard down. It does cross my mind that now could be the perfect time to slink in there, swap the contract (it's in my handbag, it would only take me a second or two to grab it) but the adjoining door is in the main entrance way to our rooms, meaning you can't really see into the main part of the rooms from it, so I can't tell if he's in the bedroom or the bathroom. If he were in the bathroom then maybe, just maybe I could have time to get in there and do it. But if he's in the bedroom, and I casually stroll in while he's changing, what would I say? Or worse, say he walked out of the bathroom and caught me in the act – how would I explain myself?

I know it's going to sound crazy, because I've been trying so hard to get this door open, to get in there and shoot my shot but... well, if I mess this up, if he catches me, then our date won't happen, will it? And I know I'm here for work, not to hang out with Jordan, but I like him, he intrigues me, and if I think with my heart instead of my head, the thing I want the most right now is to go to dinner with him.

Don't look at me like that. The plan was always going to be to try to switch the contracts after we had dinner, so I'm sticking with that, playing it safe. No point messing things up now, by getting ahead of myself.

Soon enough he reappears, dressed up, hair styled and smelling sensational. I don't know what aftershave he's wearing, but diffuse it into my room.

'Ready?' he asks me.

I think so...

'Ready,' I reply. 'So, where are you taking me?'

I grab my bag, following him into his room, leaving together through his door. I glance back at his desk. It's tidy. No sign of any papers.

'I've got an idea,' he says mysteriously. 'A few, actually. We've only got a couple of days left, so let's see how much we can fit into one night. I'm working on something – I'll figure it out as we go.'

'Sounds exciting!' I reply – it really does. I know, I have a job to do, but... you can't blame me for being giddy about this.

Is it weird that I'm excited? And so, so nervous. I know why though; it's because suddenly my objective feels blurry. I know what I should be doing, what my goal is supposed to be. But now I'm not so sure why I'm going on this date – is it business or pleasure?

25

Jordan's dating game is just... unreal. No one can say this man doesn't know how to show a girl a good time. Who knew running a dating app could make you so good at it? It's almost like he's taken tips from the best of the best (and ignored what not to do by the worst of the worst).

We're currently in what he's calling act one of our evening. He's showing me the sights of New York, taking me to see iconic locations like Central Park, the New York Public Library, the Church of the Holy Communion, Columbus Circle – everything feels so familiar, even though I've never been here before. It's strange, isn't it, how movies and TV shows can make you feel like you know a place when you don't.

We're strolling down a residential street when Jordan stops, all of a sudden.

'Okay, where are we now?' I ask.

He looks at his phone for a moment.

'So, this is Perry Street,' he tells me. He puts his hands on my shoulders, to turn my body. 'And that, if I'm not mistaken, is Carrie's apartment, in *Sex and the City*.'

I gasp.

'Oh my God, it is,' I blurt. 'How did you... why... you...'

He laughs at me.

'I wanted to show you the sights,' he tells me. 'And I remember you talking about *Sex and the City* so I found a list of iconic tourist locations that had featured in the show.'

'That's why everywhere seemed so familiar,' I say.

'It's also why we're looking from across the street now,' he replies. 'The article I read said that the people who live in the neighbourhood are driven mad by fans of the show. So, I wanted you to see it, but I didn't want to piss anyone off.'

'I love it,' I blurt. 'I don't need to get closer – I can see it perfectly from here. What a fun angle for a tour.'

'Thanks,' he says. 'I'm taking that as a compliment.'

'It really is,' I insist. 'You can't know how iconic those steps are.'

'Well, I thought you'd get a kick out of it,' he replies.

'I can't believe you researched it,' I say.

'I can't believe that, while I was on the website in the cab, I considered taking a quiz that was apparently going to tell me if I was a Big or an Aiden – does that mean anything to you?'

'It does – and now I really want to know what your answer would have been,' I practically cackle.

'Some things are best left unknown,' he replies. 'Okay, so, now the tour is over, we can move on to act two. The food – it's only a quick cab away, if you've seen all you need to see here?'

'I have,' I tell him. 'This, for me, it's practically a spiritual experience. I want to make so many jokes, but you won't get any of them.'

'Geez, I'm such a Big,' he jokes, clearly having no idea what he's saying. 'Come on, let's eat. I'm starving.'

'Me too,' I reply. 'And I don't even know where we're going.'

Once we're out of the cab, we don't have to walk far before we're at our destination.

'This is Giorgio's,' he tells me.

'The best meatballs in New York,' I say, reading the sign outside.

We're outside a small, unassuming Italian restaurant that looks like it's been here forever.

I suppose I was expecting somewhere glitzy and glamorous, somewhere super *Sex and the City*, where we'd eat sushi off naked waiters and drink overpriced Cosmopolitans. But we're not doing the tourist New York any more, we're doing Jordan's New York, and I can see true love in his eyes as he stares at the place.

We step inside and it's small, but so inviting. It's warm and cosy and filled with delicious smells like garlic, pesto, oregano – God, my hunger really is awakened now.

There's a sports channel on a little TV in the corner, but no one's really watching. There is a table of four older men arguing (in Italian, so I'm guessing based on their tone) over a game of cards, like they're auditioning for a part in a *Goodfellas* spin-off movie.

I love it here already. It's almost as charming as Jordan.

We find a booth and take a seat.

Soon enough a sixty-something Italian man comes over to greet us.

'Giordano! *Ciao!*' the man says, greeting him with a slap on the back.

'*Ciao*, Giorgio,' Jordan replies, standing up to shake his hand.

Giorgio pats Jordan's face affectionately, like they're old friends, then starts speaking rapid Italian. Jordan nods along, before saying a few words back to him, without his usual confidence, like he's not quite sure he's getting it right.

'Ahh, you haven't been practising,' Giorgio says, clapping his hands together.

'I know, I've been busy,' Jordan replies. 'But this, this is Liberty, I've brought her to try your famous meatballs.'

'Lady Liberty,' he quips. '*Ciao, bella.*'

Giorgio gives me a kiss on each cheek.

'I know exactly what to bring you, just you wait,' Giorgio says.

'*Perfetto,*' Jordan replies. 'Hey – how's the family?'

'*Fantastico,*' Giorgio replies. 'Maria, she's getting married, and Antonio is going to be a firefighter. We're so proud.'

'*Congratulazioni,*' Jordan tells him.

'*Grazie,*' Giorgio calls back as he dashes off to the kitchen.

'Okay... What was that?' I ask when we're alone again. 'Do you – somehow – come here often?'

He laughs.

'Yeah, every time I'm in the city,' he replies. 'It's my local meatball place.'

'You live in London, though, right?' I check. 'How have you been here enough to be greeted like a family member back from a war?'

'The first time I wound up here was New Year's Eve 2017,' he tells me.

'Someone brought you here?' I say.

'Something,' he replies. 'The weather. I don't know if you heard about it, or if you remember, but that was when we had the historic bomb cyclone. I've never seen so much snow in my life. The temperature was way below zero, there was snow everywhere, the pavements were almost too icy to walk on. It was my first time here, to set up Matcher US, and I was trying to do all the touristy things but it was all a bust. I went up the Rock, one of the things I had been looking forward to the most, and just stared into a wall of white. It was crazy, I've never known anything like it.'

'I think I remember hearing about it,' I reply.

'Anyway, one night I was out freezing, starving, struggling to get back to my hotel, so I ducked into the nearest place that served food and looked like it would be warm, and it was here,' he continues. 'Giorgio and his wife Lucia sat me down, gave me a plate of meatballs and a glass of red wine, and I've been coming back ever since.'

Right on cue, Giorgio reappears with two plates. Gigantic meatballs covered in a rich-smelling tomato sauce. I can't wait to try them.

Jordan says something to him in Italian.

Giorgio laughs.

'Enjoy,' he tells us.

'What did you just say to him?' I ask.

'I was trying to say I was hungry, but I might have said I was famous,' he replies with a chuckle. 'Anyway, dig in.'

I take a bite and, okay, I feel like I could be in Italy right now.

'Okay, wow, I can see why you come here often,' I reply. 'To a different continent. For a meatball. They're actually worth it.'

'It's nice to have someone to share them with,' he says with a smile and a shrug. 'I don't think people believe me when I tell them they're the best.'

'I can officially vouch for them,' I reassure him. 'So, how many times have you been here? And do they do dessert?'

Jordan laughs.

'I lived here for a while, when we were launching Matcher US,' he tells me. 'So I've eaten here more than a few times.'

'That must've been cool, living here,' I say.

'It was,' he replies... but something seems off.

'Are you sure?' I check playfully.

'Yeah, I mean, the work was great. I love my job,' he replies. 'And the food, obviously. But Paige...'

'Ah,' I say simply.

'She really struggled with the long-distance thing,' he explains. 'Looking back, I understand how she felt, but at the time I just thought she was being irrational, jealous for no reason. She was convinced I was cheating on her.'

I don't say a word, but he must be able to read my mind.

'I wasn't,' he tells me. 'But we were having other problems, we just didn't want to admit it. Hindsight is twenty-twenty, right?'

'Yeah,' I reply, stabbing another piece of meatball – these things are addictive. 'I know that feeling.'

Ben and I had plenty of problems, looking back. The cheating was just the last straw.

'Oh, really?' he replies.

I nod as I finish my mouthful of food, then push my food around my plate a little.

'Are you okay?' he asks. 'Do you want to talk about it?'

'I'm not sure you want to hear it,' I reply.

'Try me,' he insists. 'If you want to, that is.'

He doesn't need to hear about how selfish Ben was. The way he talks about Paige is so mature – I'd probably just rant like a woman scorned. There is one thing I haven't told him though...

'My ex. Ben. When he was... erm... sending photos of himself, to other women, behind my back,' I begin, refreshing his memory – like anyone could forget. 'He... erm... he was using Matcher to do it, it turns out.'

Jordan winces.

'I'm sorry,' he tells me. 'That's not what I want people to use it for. Paige thinks the money is better if we lean into the hook-up angle, but honestly? I want it to help people connect. And, I know it's not very cool or sexy, but I want to make sure our users feel safe.'

'I really admire that,' I reassure him with a smile.

'That I'm more safety than sexy?' he jokes. 'Thanks. I get that some people are going to use it for different reasons, and that's okay, but for the people who are looking for something more serious, I want that to work too. I don't want people on there looking for a partner to be seeing photos of your ex-boyfriend's knob.'

'I felt the same way,' I joke.

After clearing our plates, and talking more with Giorgio and his friends, Jordan says it's time for act three, which is only a short walk away – and a surprise.

'So, are you looking forward to Christmas?' he asks.

'Erm, sort of,' I reply. 'I'll be spending it with my family but, before any of us can get festive, we've got my cousin Hannah's wedding.'

'You don't sound too excited about that,' he points out.

'I don't suppose I am,' I reply. 'I'm not exactly in her good books. In fact, I recently found out she had uninvited me from her wedding – but only when she invited me again.'

I laugh.

'Oh, boy,' Jordan replies. 'What does a person have to do, to get uninvited from a family wedding?'

'So, it was at her engagement party where I found out what Ben, my ex, was up to,' I explain. 'And I didn't find out in the nicest way, so I very publicly imploded.'

'Understandable, given what you went through,' he reassures me.

'Not to the blushing bride,' I reply. 'Except she wasn't blushing, she was boiling red with anger. But I'm back on the guest list, and I'm still allowed to bring a plus one. It just has to be a good one, apparently.'

'Someone said that to you?' he replies.

'Yeah, I'm assuming there will be some kind of quality check on the day,' I half joke, because there might be. 'So, I'm not sure I'll find the calibre of man I need between now and then,' I point out. 'It's a couple of days after we fly back. The last thing I want to do is embarrass myself again.'

'Well, I'm not going to recommend you use Matcher to find a plus one,' he replies. 'I'd feel somehow responsible, if you got a dud.'

'Well, I don't even think I'm going to try,' I tell him. 'I mean, come on, after this date tonight, how is any man ever going to be able to compete again?'

He raises an eyebrow.

'So this is a date?' he teases.

So much for laying off the embarrassment.

'I'm joking,' he replies, nudging me lightly with his elbow. 'I'm definitely counting this as a date.'

'Then it's easily in my top ten,' I point out with a smile. 'It might actually be the only one in the top ten. I feel like I've only been on bad dates, since Ben and I broke up.'

'That bad?' he says. 'All of them?'

'All of them,' I insist. 'Every last one.'

'Go on then, tell me about them, it will make me feel like a regular Prince Charming,' he replies. 'I could do with the ego boost.'

'Well, one time I visited Paris, and I was having an absolute nightmare with a revolving door when this dreamy Frenchman rocked up, saved the day and then took me on a dream date of an evening,' I start.

'You're supposed to be making me feel better about myself,' he points out, still smiling, of course.

'Oh, just wait,' I tell him. 'So we had a lovely time, he showed me the sights, took me for dinner – amazing. But then we got back to the hotel and it turned out he wasn't even French, he was English, there on a business trip, and he thought I might be more likely to sleep with him if I thought he was Henri from Paris, not Henry from Milton Keynes.'

'Ah,' he says.

'Yeah, and the irony there is that I've obviously slept with way more Englishmen than I have Frenchmen, so the odds were in his favour.'

What was supposed to be a funny joke has actually sounded like me bragging about shagging a bunch of English blokes, and not quite as many Frenchmen, when I have in fact slept with zero Frenchmen, so even two Englishmen would make that statement true.

Thankfully he gets the joke.

'It must be so difficult for women to put their trust in men after they've been lied to – multiple times,' he says, shaking his head.

'I mean, what else can you do but hope the next fella isn't a shit like the last one?' I reply. 'The only other option would have been to simply give up.'

I don't mention my other bad dates, mostly because they'll make me look like I've been stalking him (which, I guess I have, I just didn't know it at the time), but while I might not like men who get too serious too quickly, or who bleed on me while they're trying to take off my clothes, it's always going to be the ones with ill intentions who leave me feeling the most deflated.

'Wow, okay, so the bar for tonight is super low,' he confirms.

'It really is,' I tell him.

'Then I think we might be on to a winner,' he replies. 'Here we are.'

Now that we're here, and I'm paying attention, it's obvious where we are. Well, we've been walking and talking, and unpacking the emotional baggage I had intended to leave in my room, but we're here now, at Rockefeller Center, staring at the Christmas tree.

And not just any Christmas tree, is it? It's *the* Christmas tree in New York. The one from the movies, the one you see on the screen, but can't even begin to imagine how it looks in real life.

It's beautiful. It's tall, twinkling, standing proud. I can't resist snapping photos.

'Wow,' I say in a breathy voice.

'Beautiful, right?' Jordan replies. 'I thought you might like it.'

'I love it,' I say. 'I feel like I'm in a movie – and I'm the main character.'

'Happy to take a supporting role then,' he jokes. 'Both off and on the ice.'

'The ice?' I repeat back to him.

'Yeah, here at the rink,' he replies. 'Apparently you have to skate here, it's iconic, but I've never got round to it. I thought we could have a go together?'

I hesitate.

'Ice skating?'

'Well, I don't think they'll let you in with a skateboard,' he jokes. 'What do you say?'

'I should warn you,' I start, getting flashbacks to my time in Nova Scotia, 'I've only tried it once, and it went terribly. The guy I was with, by the end of it, he had a nosebleed, was covered in bruises, and I must have checked the news for weeks, to make sure no one had been found under suspicious circumstances with internal injuries.'

Jordan laughs. Well, I was joking about that last bit.

'Sounds kind of fun,' Jordan says as we head towards the rink. 'I don't know what I'm doing either. I'll bet I'm terrible too. We can be terrible together.'

'You seem like the kind of guy who would be good at everything,' I point out. 'And I don't want you to get hurt.'

'I don't hurt easy,' he tells me, taking me by the hand.

It sends a shockwave through my body.

He might not hurt easily – the problem is, I do, and not just on the ice.

The thing is, I'm having such a great time with him, being in his orbit, so I would probably do anything he suggested. So, once again, I find myself lacing up my skates and hoping I manage to stay upright.

We head out and, to my surprise, I'm steadier than I remember. I'm not saying I'm graceful, or at all impressive to look at, but I'm definitely less likely to cause blunt-force trauma than last time, so maybe I did pick up a thing or two.

Jordan skates alongside me, looking a little wobbly too. It makes me feel less dorky, that he isn't a professional either.

'Okay, this place is unreal,' I say. 'If there was a feedback form for dates, I think you would be getting full marks.'

'Oh, yeah?' he replies.

'Don't you usually?' I joke. 'So, is this your usual date protocol? Tree, meatballs, mild concussion risk?'

'Honestly? I haven't been on a date since my divorce,' he admits. 'So I haven't been on a date with anyone other than my ex-wife since before I was married.'

'Really?' I blurt.

'Yeah. Despite what Paige might be telling everyone, I've been spending a lot of time on my own, trying to get my head around things,' he explains. 'It's not easy. I haven't even been able to eat dinner with business associates, without her assuming the worst – even when she knows where I'm going and who I'm meeting. It's rough for her too, I'm trying to be sympathetic. We're actually splitting the business, in a way, with her taking the UK and me taking the US. I'm hoping things will be easier then.'

'That sounds exhausting,' I say.

'It is,' he admits. 'But here, with you... it's the first time I haven't felt like I need to explain myself. Or feel guilty for moving on. I guess because I know Paige is back in London, I can relax.'

'I get it,' I tell him. 'I thought I was ready to move on way too quickly, too. But then I realised I have this... thing.'

He raises an eyebrow.

'A thing?' he repeats back to me.

'I call it my "ick alarm",' I confess. 'It's not a real alarm, it's in my head, but basically, it goes off every time I go on a date. After my ex, after I realised I was settling for so many of these icks, because I thought I loved him, I decided never to settle again, but it's made me too critical, if I'm being honest. With everyone I date – on the first date – it's only a matter of time before the alarm goes off and that's when I know I'm out. I can't get past it.'

'Interesting,' he replies. 'Has it gone off tonight?'

I stare at him for a second, as the realisation sinks in.

'No,' I admit. 'But sometimes it doesn't sound until someone tries to kiss me...'

'Do you want me to test that theory?' he asks, flashing me that cheeky grin of his.

God, yes.

'Okay,' I say, very calmly for someone who is internally screaming.

He leans in slowly, the way they do in movies, where time

slows down, music plays, and you just know it's going to be perfect...

...until some dude comes flying towards us on the ice and crashes into us.

'Ouch,' I blurt as Jordan and I clatter together, our foreheads bumping. We somehow manage to stay upright, but my dignity is definitely hanging by a thread.

'Yo, I'm so sorry!' the man calls out as he skates off, like his feet have a mind of their own.

We both laugh, partly from relief and partly because, of course, the universe would choose now to intervene, wouldn't it?

'Well, that was subtle,' Jordan says. 'But, hey, if an alarm was going to go off, now would be the time, right?'

'And yet... I can't hear a thing,' I reply.

We skate to the side, well out of harm's way. The lights from the tree glitter down over us, casting pretty reflections on the ice.

'How's your head?' he asks me, tucking my hair behind my ear.

'All over the place,' I say, and then wince. 'You mean from the bump, don't you? My actual head. It's fine.'

He smiles.

'Do you want to give it another go?' he asks.

'I'll chance it,' I tell him.

This time, he doesn't go straight for the lips. He leans in gently, his cold nose brushing my neck. He kisses my skin just once, slow and warm, and I can't help but tilt towards him.

He pulls back slightly, his breath warm against my cheek.

'Still no alarms?' he checks flirtatiously.

I open my mouth to say no – definitely not – but then his phone starts ringing, sounding a lot like an alarm. We both laugh.

'Seriously?' he says, pulling it out from his pocket. He frowns. 'Shit. I've got a bunch of missed calls from work.'

'Call them back,' I tell him. 'Make sure everything is okay.'

'I'll make it quick,' he replies.

I only hear his side of the conversation, but it doesn't sound great.

'No, no, I'm on my way,' he says. 'Tell them to hold tight. I'll be there in twenty.'

He hangs up and turns to me, wincing slightly.

'Liberty, I'm so sorry, there's a crisis, tech problems, they need me,' he replies. 'Can we pick up where we left off later? If it wasn't important...'

'Sure,' I tell him.

I'm gutted, because I really, really wanted him to kiss me, but it's his job, I understand.

'To be continued?' he says.

'To be continued,' I reply.

'Let me get us a taxi. I'll drop you at the hotel, on the way,' he suggests.

We grab our shoes and head to somewhere a taxi can pick us up.

'Any alarms now?' he checks.

I shake my head, smiling.

'Not a peep,' I reply – and it's true.

My ick alarm, my red flag radar, the mental block that usually stops me from moving on – it's keeping quiet. Maybe it's broken, maybe it's confused, or maybe, just maybe, it's met someone it approves of. Someone it likes. Jordan. And I like him too.

26

I'm not even awake properly when I feel a smile stretch across my face.

Last night was, well, I don't know what it was, but I loved it. I loved every minute of it, right up until Jordan got called into work but, to be honest with you, that only left me wanting more. If it was a power move, it worked – although I'm pretty sure it was a genuine emergency.

I mean, come on, we almost kissed, and it felt like the kind of moment that only happens in the movies. Or very, very good dreams. We were so close. Like, centimetres – or seconds, depending on how you measure it.

I know I didn't imagine it, or dream it. I wanted to kiss him and he wanted to kiss me too. That was one hell of a little black dress I picked out.

I roll out of bed, still in a dreamy, hearts-for-eyes haze, and walk over to the door between our rooms. I knock gently. No answer. I try again, louder, but there's still no reply.

He must have gone to the office already, so it really must be an emergency. Well, I don't have anything else to do, so I may as well throw on some clothes and meet him there. Presumably he'll let me in now, no questions asked.

I throw on an outfit and head to Matcher US HQ with a real spring in my step. I know, it's not like I'm going to walk through the door and he's going to pick me up, *An Officer and a Gentleman* style, or pin me to a desk and have his wicked way with me right then and there – I'm not against it, by the way, but I know that it's not very likely.

Jordan is on a call when I get there, so I get to know the other members of the UK team. There's Pete, who is some kind of tech guy, and Bella, who handles PR. It's nice, to hear a few more English accents, to make me feel a bit more at ease. I've never felt more self-conscious of having a different accent, mostly just because it seems to fascinate people here. Well, I'm from York-shire, and that is not the accent they hear in the movies.

Eventually he emerges from a private office, Jordan, in the same shirt he was wearing last night.

He comes over, catches my eye, and smiles like he's genuinely pleased to see me.

'Morning,' he says casually. 'Sleep well?'

'Better than you,' I reply. 'Have you been here all night?'

'Yeah, I got a few hours on the sofa,' he replies. 'But Alison is in now, and she needs her office.'

He nods towards a woman who I recognise as the one he was in the bar with. Hmm, so it really was a work meeting.

'Has the crisis been averted?' I ask.

'Just about,' he replies. 'Tech problem. Some kind of cyberat-tack, but we're out of the woods now, I think. Although I'm sure you'd love to see someone take Matcher down, huh?'

He gives me a cheeky smile.

'If I knew how to...' I joke.

'You know, if you press that big red button in the corner, you can shut the whole of Matcher down,' he replies.

'Oh reeeeally,' I reply, joining in on the bit.

He grins.

'Tempting, isn't it?'

'It might have been, a few months ago, but now I'm happy to let it slide,' I say with a smile. 'I'm over it.'

I know we're only joking around, but I am. People are always going to do whatever they want and no one is ever going to change that by simply flicking the kill switch on one app. There are plenty of others to download.

I lean in closer and lower my voice.

'You've still got my lipstick on your collar,' I tell him, noticing the shade I was wearing last night.

He looks down, startled, then up at me with faux scandal.

'Are you trying to get me sacked?' he jokes.

'It was only a light HR violation,' I point out. 'And I won't tell anyone.'

'They've all been too polite to mention it,' he says. 'But I should probably change, before my meeting later.'

'Do you want me to run out and grab you a shirt?' I ask.

'Would you mind?' he replies. 'Don't trek back to the hotel, buy a new one, and let me know what it costs.'

Going to his hotel room would have been ideal, as far as my mission goes, but I genuinely was just thinking about him needing a shirt.

'No worries,' I tell him. 'Jot down your size and your budget, or whatever, and I'll get right on it.'

'Gosh, is this new girl?' the woman I now know as Alison asks him. 'The one you've been telling me about? She's great – can I steal her?'

'Get your own new girl,' he replies. 'Anyway, you've been with us a while now, I think you might need a new title.'

I laugh, my cheeks warming at the thought of him telling people about me.

'I'll be right back with that shirt,' I say, terrible at taking compliments.

I head down in the lift, my brain buzzing, my smile so wide it hurts, thinking about what Jordan said and... Wait... oh, hang on a minute. Suddenly it all makes sense. They were calling me new girl – NewGirl, my name on WorkM8. It's so, so obvious now. Jordan is MrLoveByte. The guy I've been chatting to all this time. How did I not see it before?

I mentally scroll through every conversation, every little clue I missed.

I grin, giddy, and not only because I figured it out – although honestly, now I'm starting to think maybe I would make a pretty good private investigator – but because it's given me an idea.

I pull out my phone, fire up the WorkM8 app, and write a message.

NEWGIRL

I think you're in New York...

It doesn't take long.

MRLOVEBYTE

I think you are too...

NEWGIRL

I think I know who you are...

MRLOVEBYTE

I think I know who you are too...

God, this is fun.

NEWGIRL

Fancy a drink tonight? Hotel bar?

The reply pings back instantly.

MRLOVEBYTE

I'm going to be working late but I'd love to.
Shall we say 9pm?

NEWGIRL

Sounds good. Guess I'll see you then.

MRLOVEBYTE

Not if I see you first...

I actually squeal. In the street. Like an idiot. I shove my phone in my coat pocket and try to compose myself.

Oh, boy, it's happening. I like him. I can't hide it any more. I really, really like him. And I'm pretty sure he likes me too.

And we have another date tonight. Here's hoping we finally get to seal the deal with that kiss. But how would we not, after I've played such a blinder?

27

By the time I get back to the office, my fingers are purple from the cold, and kind of numb.

Still, I'm clutching the bag with the crisp white shirt I bought for Jordan, to replace his lipstick-stained one. It must have happened just before our almost kiss, when I had my face pressed into his neck. Is it weird that I find it sort of sexy? Like, I don't know, I've marked my territory or something. Somehow it feels different to when Ben would leave his beard hairs all over and I'd end up with them stuck to my foundation.

The office is still alive with activity – the UK team still set up in a pop-up office in the conference room.

Bella is on the phone – I don't think I've seen her off it yet, not even when she introduced herself to me – and then there's Pete and another guy called Karl who appear to be elbow deep in code right now.

And then there's Jordan, whose face lights up when he sees me. He's on the phone too, but not for long.

'I'll call you back,' he says as he hangs up the phone. 'Hello.'

He really does seem genuinely pleased to see me, and it makes all of my internal organs feel sort of fizzy.

'Hi,' I reply. 'Your shirt, boss.'

'Why thank you,' he replies. 'Do you have a minute?'

'I work for you,' I say, stressing each word.

He laughs.

'In here,' he suggests.

Alison's office must be free again, so I step inside with him. I've no sooner closed the door behind me when I turn around and see him standing there, shirtless, grinning at me.

'So, what did you decide on?' he asks.

'What?' I reply, mildly lost for words. I just... his body... wow. His tattoos almost look as though they tell a story. I've only got to look at them fleetingly, but I want to get a closer look. Problem is, if I get that close to him, I think my priorities might change.

'The shirt,' he prompts me. 'Something with stripes? Something floral?'

'Oh, no.' I laugh as I get my thoughts back on track. 'A plain white one. I'm trying to get a rise, not the sack.'

'You'll get a rise,' he replies, almost like he has his tongue in his cheek. 'Which reminds me. Tonight... I was thinking about picking up where we left off, at the ice rink, but I'm thinking we might have to do the whole date again...'

'Like *Groundhog Day*?' I reply.

'...but I'm thinking we might have to do the whole date again...' he says again, which is the most adorable joke.

'I don't know, as perfect as last night was, doing it again feels like cheating,' I point out.

'Not the same date,' he replies. 'I'm working on a plan for another one – an even better one.'

'Last night won't be easy to top,' I remind him as he buttons up his new shirt. 'How are you going to do that?'

'I don't know, I think what I had planned for the finale might have swept you off your feet,' he tells me. 'So, what are you going to do until then? You know the hotel has a spa…'

I love how he drops a bomb like that and then swiftly moves on.

'You don't need me here?' I reply.

'You may as well go and enjoy yourself,' he says. 'Save you sitting around here watching us talk tech.'

'Well, if I'm definitely no use here, I'll see you in the hotel bar at nine?' I say – I swear, I can practically smell the spa's essential oils in anticipation of my arrival.

'Sounds good to me,' he replies. 'I'll get things wrapped up here, get changed, and then knock your socks off.'

'Sounds like it's going to be big,' I say.

'Well, now you're just trying to make me say something dirty,' he replies with a laugh. 'See you at nine. I'm looking forward to it.'

'Me too,' I tell him.

As I leave the office, I can feel my heart beating, knocking against my ribs, almost like it's trying to say to me: Did you hear that, Liberty? He called it a date. We have a date!

He did, didn't he? My brain heard it as well as my heart, so I know I'm not imagining things.

Don't get me wrong, I'm excited to pick up where we left off, but the thought of having a whole date first, before we get to give that kiss another go, sounds like it's going to be one big, long tease. A delicious kind of torture. I'm going to need a day in the spa to try to keep calm.

Even if he doesn't plan as much stuff for tonight as he did

last night, honestly, finally getting to kiss him will make it worth it, and I'm not going to let anything get in the way this time.

Hopefully...

28

Tonight feels so different to last night. Last night I was nervous – tonight I'm petrified.

I guess it's because last night I didn't know what was happening, whether I was doing it for business or pleasure, but tonight it's clear. It's a date – a date where we are going to kiss. I just wonder how long it will take for one of us to cave, or if we'll both wait for whatever perfect moment Jordan will have no doubt carved out for us.

Standing in front of my hotel room mirror, I double check my eye makeup, smooth down my dress, and spritz on more perfume, because I'm convinced it's worn off since I applied it fifteen minutes ago. Then I stare at myself, giving myself a long, hard look, and I don't want to be all soppy and daft but, honestly, I would probably cry if I didn't think it might ruin my makeup, because the reflection smiling back at me isn't the usual one; it's a girl with hope and optimism, not the sad sack who honestly feared every man would hurt her, or disappoint her, or ultimately cheat on her. I really do feel good about this one and it's been so, so long since I felt that way. It's kind of nice.

I'm scared, but in a good way. I'm not worried I'm going to mess it up, or that he's going to be nipping to the lav to AirDrop snaps of his dick to everyone in the hotel. It's that nervous excitement as you start to fantasise about what the rest of your life might look like with someone, usually when you first get together, and the butterflies in your stomach can't stay still.

I grab my bag and head down to the hotel bar. I love that we haven't just been getting on in person, but that we had that first digital spark too – not that it was flirty, but it's like we were drawn to each other. Plus, we got stuck in a lift together, and whenever that happens to a couple in the movies that shit is as good as locked in for life. Nothing says happy ever after like a meet-cute in a broken-down lift.

The bar is dimly lit, as always, which really does reassure me that Jordan didn't see me that night, when I was lovingly observing (that sounds so much nicer than stalking) him and Alison. I do a casual scan of the room, looking to see if I'm the first one here – I am ten minutes early – but there's no sign of him.

'Liberty.' A voice snaps me from my thoughts.

'Pete,' I reply. 'Hello – did you get the app sorted?'

I'm surprised to see him but it makes sense that we would all be staying in the same hotel.

'Just about,' he replies. 'Honestly, I leave London for a couple of days and it's chaos. At least it's a working trip, so we could use Matcher US HQ to sort it.'

'That's good,' I reply. 'Jordan will be pleased then?'

'Yeah, he's got a real spring in his step today for some reason,' Pete says with a shrug.

I think I know why...

'That's great,' I say.

'So, what can I get you to drink?' he asks me.

'Erm...'

'And do you want me to call you Liberty or NewGirl?' he adds.

Wait – what? Surely not... This is just me, trying to find something to worry about, looking for problems where there aren't any because I'm too scared to move on – as bloody always.

'Oh, haha, yeah – Liberty is fine,' I tell him.

That's what it is. Just me, panicking, imagining the worst-case scenario.

'Good, because it might be weird, if you called me MrLove-Byte all night,' he says with a chuckle. 'One of the lads in the office chose the name for me – cringe, I know.'

Fuuuuuuck.

'You look beautiful, by the way,' he tells me.

'I... er... thanks.'

I don't know what else to say. I mean, clearly, I'm a shit private investigator and whatever I do for work moving forwards it should absolutely not be that. Why oh why did I think it was Jordan? Of course it's not going to be Jordan, the boss, pissing around on an app meant for the workforce. I leapt to a genuine cliff of a conclusion, just because he called me new girl which – news flash – is what I am, and now I'm slowly falling back to earth as reality sets in. I have a horrible feeling the impact is going to be catastrophic.

'Sit down,' he says, nodding towards the bar stool. Then he turns to the barman. 'What do you recommend?'

'I make a mean Manhattan,' he replies.

'Two of those then, please,' Pete says.

'Erm, hi,' Jordan says as he appears between the two of us, and all at once the air changes.

'Actually, make it three,' Pete tells he barman. 'I definitely owe this man a drink, after the bonus he gave me today.'

Jordan glances between us.

'Oh, thanks,' he says to Pete as he takes a seat next to me, leaving me sandwiched between the two of them. 'So, you're celebrating, eh? What are you getting up to tonight?'

'Well, I'm taking this one for a night out,' Pete tells him, nodding towards me.

I notice Jordan's eyes widen for a split second.

And this is it. The impact. And boy does it hurt.

'You two?' Jordan replies.

'Yeah, I know Paige doesn't like us getting close, but you know it won't affect my work,' Pete reasons.

'I didn't think you two knew each other,' Jordan says.

'Turns out we've been chatting on WorkM8,' Pete says. 'Funny, isn't it?'

Jordan doesn't laugh.

'I should, uh, leave you to it then,' Jordan says.

Shit, shit, shit – what do I do?

'Have your drink first,' Pete tells him. 'We don't mind, do we, Liberty?'

I open my mouth to speak but I can't get any words out.

'Three Manhattans,' the barman announces.

Pete hands them out.

'To a great day and hopefully an even better night,' Pete announces, raising his glass.

Oh, this can't be happening. What have I ever done that was so bad that karma thought she could do me so dirty?

'So, what are you two up to tonight then?' Jordan asks, knocking back at least half of his drink in one gulp.

He makes it sound like an innocent question but I know it isn't.

'I'm open to ideas,' Pete says. 'I want to show Liberty the

sights so, you were the local, if you've got any recommendations, I'm all ears.'

Jordan rests an elbow on the bar.

'Well, if it were me...' he starts. 'Maybe something fun, like a *Sex and the City* walking tour. For dinner maybe somewhere small and full of heart, not somewhere touristy – there's a place called Giorgio's that does great meatballs. Then, I don't know, maybe a trip to Rockefeller Center, for ice skating.'

I glance at him but he's not even looking at me.

Pete lets out a scoff.

'That sounds... I mean, no offence, but a bit naff, doesn't it?' Pete replies. 'I'll let you off, because you were married, but *Sex and the City*? Meatballs? Ice skating? That's not how you treat a girl like Liberty. She wants something classy, don't you?'

'I—'

'She doesn't want to go to some family restaurant, not in New York,' Pete continues.

'Fair enough,' Jordan replies. He knocks back the last of his drink. 'Well, I'll leave you kids to it.'

'Have a good one,' Pete calls after him. He waits until Jordan is gone before he says anything else. 'He's lucky the ladies love him for his looks and his money because that sounds like a crap date.'

'I don't know, he seems to do okay,' I point out in his defence.

'Yeah, lots of women want him but, between us, he's lost his bottle, since his divorce,' Pete tells me. 'But Paige is a bit of a mad woman – I don't know if you've noticed. She'd put me off women for life too.'

I know that this isn't a date – not on purpose, anyway – but my ick alarm is sounding, proving that it still works, and the only person who doesn't trigger it is Jordan. Oh, and he thinks I've ditched him for Pete, which is just wonderful, isn't it?

So Jordan isn't the playboy Paige made him out to be, Pete was right about that, but he was wrong about him being a crap date because, honestly, hands down the best date of my life – I mean, bloody hell, the number two spot probably goes to the con man formerly known as Henri, so clearly the competition isn't even close.

Jordan is the one for me, my dream date, as cringe as it sounds. I have to find him.

'I think I might have to go,' I say, grabbing my bag like it's a parachute and I'm about to launch myself out of a crashing plane.

'What? Why?' Pete replies.

'I feel sick,' I tell him. 'Really sick.'

'Can I get you some water?' he suggests. 'It might pass.'

'I don't think it will,' I reply. What is it going to take to put him off? 'I'm having a monster period right now. Just... the worst of it all of it. I really do think I'm going to throw up.'

You can tell a lot about a man based on how he reacts when you drop the P word. I swear Pete actually leans back in his chair, like I have some kind of contagious disease.

'Right, well, that can't be helped,' he says, sounding like he sort of thinks I could help it, if I tried really hard.

It's an old excuse but a good one. The kind where you don't want to be put off by something so simple, but you're relieved you can say it at any point and hopefully get out of whatever situation you're in.

With his blessing, I leave, hurrying out of the bar and into the lift as fast as my legs will take me. God, I hope Jordan went straight to his room, because I need to talk to him right away. I just need to explain and then I can put everything right. This doesn't need to be a misunderstanding, this is just one of those things where I tell him what happened, and we have a laugh about it, right? Right?

I knock on Jordan's door. He doesn't answer – I don't give him enough time to, to be honest – so I knock again. Screw it, this is an emergency, so I keep knocking until he opens it.

'Erm, hello,' he says, surprised it's me – or maybe surprised I was smacking the crap out of his door until he opened it.

'Can I come in?' I ask. 'We need to talk.'

'Yeah, okay,' he says, heading back in. I follow him, letting the door close behind me.

He's wearing his shirt but he's rolled up his sleeves, undone a few buttons and kicked off his shoes, like this is him for the night.

'I wasn't expecting to see you,' he says. 'I thought you were on a date.'

'Well, you thought wrong,' I reply.

'Pete seemed to think it was a date,' he counters.

He's trying not to let it show, but he definitely seems bothered. I mean, yeah, anyone would feel bothered if they made a plan with someone, then turned up to see them doing it with someone else, date or not, but Jordan seems really bothered. Upset maybe, or disappointed – maybe a bit of both.

For a few seconds we just stand in silence as I think about how to explain myself. The truth is a good start, obviously, but I need to make sure it comes out right.

'I didn't ask Pete out on a date,' I say eventually.

'He said you were talking on WorkM8,' he replies.

'Yeah, and we were,' I continue. 'Just about work and stuff, until earlier today, when you called me new girl – that's my username on there – so I stupidly assumed I had been talking to you, and that was your way of letting me know.'

He doesn't respond at first. He just looks at me, his expression totally unreadable.

'I swear, I wouldn't have...' I break off, shaking my head as I try to find the right words. 'I wouldn't have made a plan with Pete knowing that it was him. I really thought it was you. I thought we were... picking up where we left off last night. That's why, when you mentioned it to me in person, I gave you the same time and location. I felt even more sure it was you.'

'So, for no reason other than me calling you the new girl, you assumed you had been chatting to me on an app?' he checks. 'You didn't know the name of who you were talking to?'

'Well, only the username – MrLoveByte,' I reply.

He tilts his head slightly, still not really giving much away.

'You really thought that I would have the username MrLove-Byte?' he says in disbelief.

'Okay, when you say it like that...' I rub my face with both hands. 'I didn't really think that bit through.'

Finally, a flicker – the slight curl at the corners of his mouth. I narrow my eyes at him, trying to read him. Eventually he starts laughing.

'I am on WorkM8, but under my actual name,' he tells me. 'MrLoveByte wouldn't make a great name for the boss, would it?'

'Probably not,' I reply. 'So... you're not mad at me?'

'Mad?' he says. 'Why would I be mad? You've explained, it makes sense, all good.'

'All good?' I say in disbelief.

'Do you want me to shout at you or something?' he asks. 'Get really jealous and punch a hole in the drywall?'

'I mean, to the second one, kind of, yeah, because that sounds hot as hell,' I reply. 'I'm surprised, that's all. You're taking this really well. In my experience, things don't usually go smoothly. Or end well. It's just my luck, to have things go tits up, and really unlikely that they'll simply go right again, by magic.'

'Well, perhaps this isn't your luck,' he replies. 'Perhaps it's mine.'

I smile at him.

'Maybe,' he continues, walking slowly towards me, 'it's not going right by magic. Maybe everything is fine – better than fine. Great, even.'

The air between us shifts. It doesn't just warm – it heats up rapidly. He's close now – not too close, but close enough that my breath feels heavy.

'It's only a misunderstanding,' he replies. 'One that is easily explained. It doesn't need to be a thing, just, you know – MrLoveByte? Really?'

I laugh.

'I really thought it was you,' I insist.

He stops in front of me.

'And here I was thinking I was special,' he continues.

'You are,' I say immediately, too honest to stop myself.

He watches me, his eyes darting back and forth between mine and my lips. 'I thought you'd be able to tell. That if you were talking to me, you'd know...'

'Looking back, there really was no reason to think it was you,' I practically whisper. 'But maybe that was just... wishful thinking. I mean, everything so far has felt like a fairytale. And wouldn't it have been the most magical thing, if it was you?'

He laughs softly, shaking his head.

'Not everything's a fairytale, Lib,' he says.

Oh, I like it when he calls me Lib. He's so close now I can feel the warmth coming off him. He brushes my cheek with the backs of his fingers, his voice much lower now.

'If we'd kissed on that rink,' he says, pausing for dramatic effect as his hands find my waist and he pulls me closer, 'with the music and the fairy lights then, yeah, maybe it would've been a fairytale.'

His eyes lock on mine. I feel like he's looking into my soul.

'But if I kiss you now, here... with that bed just feet away' – he leans in, his lips so close to mine I swear I can feel them – 'then I can promise you, it wouldn't be a fairytale, it would be a different sort of movie altogether.'

There's nothing coy or sweet in the way he's looking at me. Nothing Cinderella about it – unless you're spelling it with an S.

It feels like we're at a point of no return. That all of the cat and mouse games, the flirting, the dates – like it's all led to this moment.

I swallow hard, my heart pumping at a million miles an hour, and say the only thing I can think to say – the only thing that feels right – is...

'Prove it.'

And then he does.

He kisses me like he's been waiting all week – all month – for permission. Like everything we've been through has been nothing but foreplay and, if it was, wow, it worked.

His hands are on the small of my back, in my hair, on my face, like he can't decide where to hold me so he tries everywhere. And then he starts kissing my neck and I know I'm done for.

I don't know whether he pushes me back onto the bed or if I throw myself, but I'm on my back now, him kneeling between my legs as he carefully lowers himself on top of me so that we can keep kissing.

He's right, it would have been a lovely first kiss, if we had done it at the ice rink like he planned, but this is something else. Something so much hotter. Something that tells me the last piece of the puzzle is in place, that we have that sexual chemistry that is such a vital ingredient.

I fumble with the buttons on his shirt as we kiss – something I don't think I could have got away with at the ice rink – and then I feel him lifting my dress so that it's up around my waist. Yep, okay, that one I'm certain you can't do in public.

Everything we're doing just feels right though. Just so easy, and sexy, and somehow in the moment, but full of possibilities, like the better it gets, the more excited I am for the next step, here in this bed and in the future. I'm imagining having his hands on me every day, and it sounds like heaven.

And most importantly of all, what there is absolutely zero sign of is my pesky ick alarm. It's definitely never let me get this far before. I don't even feel like it approves of Jordan, or like it's a thing at all, it's just gone. I feel fixed. Like I'm not pretending any more, or trying too hard to make something feel right – it is right. What more could I want?

29

Waking up, it doesn't take me a second or two to come to my senses, or remember where I am, because last night is still swirling around in my head; in fact, I think I even dreamt about it. Even after Jordan and I fell asleep, he was still on my mind.

Which is why it's so strange that I've just woken up here, in his bed, all alone.

I blink as my eyes adjust to the morning light streaming through the gap in the hotel curtains. I sit up, pushing my messy hair from my face, my heart immediately pounding with that weird, irrational panic that hits you when someone disappears after you spend the night together – I imagine. This has never happened to me before.

'Jordan?' I call out, voice still croaky with sleep.

No answer.

'Jordan?' I try again – still nothing.

I shuffle out of bed, wrapping one of the plush hotel robes around myself, and head towards the bathroom.

'Jordan?' I say as I poke my head around the door, but it's

empty. He's not in here. He's nowhere to be seen. I'm in here alone.

And for a split second – and I really do mean a split second – I wonder if I dreamt it all. That maybe I had a few too many cocktails to drown my sorrows and then made it all up in my head. But then I spot my bra hanging delicately off the corner of the TV and remember how we both laughed when Jordan threw it and it landed there.

I puff air from my cheeks and rub my eyes. With no sign of Jordan, I glance around for a note – something that explains why he's not here, but there's no sign of that either. The only thing I can see, laid out on the desk, with a pen next to it, is the contract.

I look and it's still unsigned. So I'm not too late – plus, I have the correct version in my bag still, I'm sure...

I reach in and grab for it and, yep, sure enough, it's here.

I'm here, alone, the contracts are both here; I could swap them in a split second and it would all be done and dusted.

All I'd have to do is swap them. Just a little switcheroo. No one gets hurt. My job is secured. Paige is happy. Jordan gets to move on with his life – which is what I really want.

Except... I don't know, it just still doesn't feel right. It doesn't feel honest.

I stare at the new contract in my hand. All I have to do is swap them, just slip one into the other's place, cram the dodgy one in my bag and walk away.

It sounds so simple and yet I just can't do it. I can't bring myself to switch them behind his back. Jordan trusted me enough to leave it here with me, in the open. And he opened up his heart – and his bed – to me over the last couple of days. It might be a victimless task, but it still feels manipulative.

I can't help but think of Ben. Of all the ways he lied to me, misled me, kept me in the dark. I remember that suffocating feeling of realising I didn't know what was going on in my own life, of being lied to, betrayed in the worst ways. I hated it. I wouldn't wish it on anyone – least of all Jordan.

So if this costs me the job, then so be it. Let Paige sack me. I would rather be unemployed with my pride and my honour intact, and still be able to look Jordan in the eye, than risk it all for a job. I'd move back in with my parents – I'd sleep in their bed with them – before I'd do anything behind Jordan's back, even if he would never know it had happened.

I like him. I really like him. I care about him more than some crappy – frankly weird – job. I know what I need to do, and it's not swapping these contracts. Paige will just have to sort out her own mess.

Suddenly I hear the door opening so I shove the contract back into my bag and hurriedly kick it to one side before diving back on the bed.

'Morning,' Jordan calls out. 'Oh, great, you're awake. I come bearing coffee and bagels.'

'Oh, just what I need right now,' I reply. 'You're a mind reader.'

'I thought I'd surprise you,' he says. 'And let you catch up on your sleep – I didn't let you get much last night.'

'Where did you go?' I ask, smiling. 'I was worried for a second, when I woke up, and you weren't here.'

'It is my room,' he reminds me. 'I was always going to come back – you know that. I went to the best bagel place in Manhattan. We're going home soon so I couldn't let you leave New York without trying one. The coffee is great too.'

He hands me a cup. It's still so warm, and it smells amazing.

'Are you okay?' he asks, watching me. 'You don't regret—'

'No, no, no,' I insist, interrupting him, because that's the last thing I want him to think. 'I think I was just freaked out, that you weren't here.'

'Well, I'm here now,' he says with a smile. 'And with bagels – cream cheese and lox. You'll love it.'

We dig in and honestly, I could cry at how good it tastes. He's not wrong, they really are the best bagels.

'So... I've got a meeting in Leeds,' he tells me between bits.

'Leeds... in Yorkshire?' I say in disbelief.

'Yes – I've got a meeting with the founders of RedFlags – that app where people warn each other about bad dates. We're talking about collaborating on something.'

'That's cool,' I reply. 'The world definitely needs that.'

He nods in agreement.

'So, I'm leaving earlier than planned, tonight actually. I'm taking a private flight, so I can be there to make a meeting,' he says like it's the most casual thing in the world. 'So, I was wondering... do you want to come with me? I know you've got the wedding in a couple of days. It's in Leeds, right?'

I nearly drop my bagel.

'You want me to join you on your private jet?' I blurt back to him. 'You're asking me like that might be a question people say no to...'

'It's always good to check,' he replies. 'I figured I could drop you at the wedding – well, close enough.'

'I'd love that,' I tell him. 'Talk about arriving in style – not that you can drop me at the venue, without a parachute, which my cousin would hate. But, yes, ignore my nervous babbling, I would love that.'

'Great,' he says with a laugh. 'And... if you're still looking for a plus one...'

I raise an eyebrow.

'You would come with me?' I squeak.

'I scrub up all right,' he jokes. 'And I've got a black tux with me – because you never know, in New York.'

'You had me at scrub,' I reply. 'I would love you to come with me.'

He genuinely looks as happy as I feel right now.

'Perfect,' he replies. 'Well, I've got a couple of meetings to wrap today, some unfinished business to put to bed, but how about I have a car take you shopping? Spend your last few hours in New York in style?'

'Why are you so perfect?' I ask him.

He just laughs.

'My recent reviews haven't been quite so glowing – so thank you,' he jokes. 'But, really, you're worth it. You deserve all of it.'

I pretty much launch myself at him, knocking the bagel wrapper from his lap, wrapping my arms and legs around him and squeezing him tightly.

'Well, that's adorable,' he says.

'I'm just in a really good mood,' I tell him.

'Good,' he replies.

I'm not just in a good mood, and it's not just that I'm excited either; I think the main thing I'm feeling is relief. I am so, so glad that I didn't swap the contracts. I could have done, so easily, and he probably would have never known, but I would have known, and I could never have lived with the guilt.

The longer you tell a lie, or keep a secret, the harder it gets to undo, and the more damage it does when it finally comes out.

I'm so happy I didn't go through with it. I was only doing it for my job, for my future, but things just look and feel so much brighter now. I've definitely made the right decision.

Finally, it feels like my luck might have changed.

30

I always think it's one of those silly, jokey things people say, when they declare that they're living their best life, but today I get it, I totally get it, because that's what I'm doing. It's a real thing.

I've spent today dashing around the shops of New York, killing time while I waited for Jordan to wrap things up at work. I bought a dress I definitely couldn't really afford, tried on shoes I'll never be able to afford, and walked the streets like I was Carrie Bradshaw – just without the weekly sex column or her inexplicably generous credit limit.

Now I'm in the back of a black limo, acting like I belong, being whisked off to the airport where I will be – just let me clear my throat, before I say this – catching a private jet back home. And with Jordan, no less, and I honestly can't believe he's real. That he wants to fly with me to Leeds. To go to Hannah's wedding with me. Surely that would freak most men out, so early on? But not Jordan.

Oh, and not only is this great news for me, because I actually really like him, but it's good news for the wedding too. Because

Jordan is the kind of man you want on your arm. He's got that easy charm that everyone laps up, he can talk about anything and sound like the smartest man in the conversation – I can see him now, working the room, chatting to my relatives, making my mum swoon, and laughing – even if it's just politely – at my dad's dad jokes. Who knows? He might even find them funny. Stranger things have happened lately.

I don't think my family are going to believe he's real – I don't even think they believe I'm going to show up. They know I've been working in New York, but I've barely spoken to them.

Actually, now feels like the perfect time to call them and drop the bombshell. To let them know that not only am I coming, but I'm bringing a plus one.

I call my mum.

'Hello, love,' she says. 'Everything okay?'

'Hi, Mum! Yes. How are you? Is Dad there?' I check.

'He's right here,' she says.

I can hear him in the background, yelling.

'Tell her if her flight's mysteriously delayed again, we're sending in a search party,' he calls out.

'Hilarious,' I reply. 'No. No delay. I'm actually on my way to the airport now.'

'Thank God,' Mum says. 'You've had us wondering.'

'Well, not only am I coming,' I start, barely able to contain my excitement, 'but I'm bringing a plus one.'

There's a pause.

'Oh,' she says cautiously. 'Who?'

'You know the dating app I've been working for?' I reply.

'Oh, God,' Mum blurts.

'Please tell us you're not resorting to some freak you found on the internet,' Dad calls out.

'Wow,' I say dryly. 'Charming. No. I'm bringing Jordan – my boss.'

There's another second or two of silence.

'Your boss?' Mum confirms.

'The one who owns the company?' Dad chimes in, suddenly sounding a lot more interested.

'Yeah,' I reply.

'Well, look who's landed on her feet,' Mum teases.

'Is he good enough for you?' Dad checks.

'He's amazing,' I say. 'Honestly. I think you'll both love him.'

'Do you love him?' Mum teases. 'And can I tell your Auntie Eleanor? She keeps asking, to confirm numbers. She's finalising the seating plan and she's convinced you're coming solo.'

'Tell her. Tell everyone,' I say, grinning. 'We're flying to Leeds. He's got business there first, but we'll be in by the day before the wedding.'

'Oh, love, that's great,' Mum says. 'So happy for you. Can't wait to see you. And Jordan, of course. Fly safe.'

'I will,' I reply. 'Love you.'

'Love you too,' they shout back at the same time.

I hang up. We're finally at the airport and, even while the driver unloads my bags, I can't stop grinning like a psycho.

I'm heading into the airport when my phone starts ringing – it's Paige.

Shit. She's probably calling to check up on me, to see if I've done what she asked and switched the contracts out. Obviously I didn't, and I have no intention of doing so. I know, I'll lose my job, one way or another, but I care far more about protecting what I have with Jordan. That means more to me than any job.

Of course, I won't tell her about the two of us. It's not my place. Plus, she would probably explode.

I answer brightly.

'Hello, Paige,' I say.

'You didn't do it,' she replies. She doesn't even say hello, so I already know it's going to be bad.

'I'm sorry, it's just—'

'I asked you to do something, Liberty. And okay, sure, you could have not done it. Not ideal. But it would have been better than what you've done,' she rants.

My heart sinks.

'What do you mean?' I reply.

'You left both contracts in Jordan's room,' she says – she sounds so angry she might explode regardless. 'The one he was supposed to sign, and the one we were trying to swap out. He's seen them both. He called me – he's furious. He knows exactly what we were trying to pull.'

Oh, fuck. It must have fallen out of my bag, or maybe I didn't stuff it back in properly, but it doesn't matter, does it? The point is he's seen it. Shit. I wasn't going to do it – I couldn't do it. God knows what he thinks of me now.

'I didn't... I...'

My mouth is almost too dry to form words.

'Liberty,' she snaps. 'You didn't think. You fumbled it. You messed everything up.'

'Did you try to explain?' I ask desperately. 'Does he not understand that we were only fixing a mistake?'

Paige laughs. It's not a nice laugh. It's spiky and cold and cuts right through me.

'My God, you're naïve,' she says. 'This was a business play, and you've just tanked your career. Well done.' She sighs. 'You're fired, by the way.'

'I'm...'

'The rest of the team are staying in the US,' she talks over me. 'I heard you were flying back with Jordan. You're not. I've booked you a hotel room at the airport for tonight. You're flying in the morning. Alone. And I don't ever want to hear from you again – don't expect a reference.'

She hangs up.

For a moment I stand on the spot, staring straight ahead at nothing in particular.

My phone buzzes again.

It's MrLoveByte – or Pete, as I know him now.

> **MRLOVEBYTE**
>
> Is it true you tried to scam Jordan out of the company?

I think I'm going to be sick.

> **NEWGIRL**
>
> No! What are you talking about?

> **MRLOVEBYTE**
>
> He's here now, trying to sort out the mess.
> We've seen the contract you were trying to
> switch in. It would've ousted Jordan completely.
> Gave Paige the US too.

I reply quickly, my hands shaking as I type.

> **NEWGIRL**
>
> She told me it was fixing a typo. I didn't know
> she was planning that.

I stare at the screen, willing a reply. Nothing.

Then I type:

> **NEWGIRL**
>
> Did Jordan sign it before he realised?

I hit send but nothing happens. Then I get an error. Is it my signal? Something wrong with the app? Then I realise, I'm logged out. I've been booted out. Wow, Paige acts fast. Unless it was Jordan who kicked me out. He must be so mad at me. I'll bet he never wants to speak to me again.

And I don't have anyone's number, so I can't message Jordan, or even Pete.

Oh, I'm such an idiot.

I make it to the hotel Paige booked – a modern, minimalist, super cool room with views over the runway that, ordinarily, would make my day, but I can't think straight.

I've lost my job, I've humiliated myself, by being completely oblivious – because now it's so easy to see that Paige was using me, trying to get me to scam Jordan out of the company, and I just blindly went along with it, because I thought we were part of the same sisterhood, done wrong by no-good men. I wonder if she even believed the things she was telling me about Jordan, or if she was lying, to turn me against him, to get me to do her bidding.

Jordan must think I betrayed him. Played him. Lied to him. God, I hope he doesn't think that everything I said, when I opened up, was a lie. I really hope he doesn't think I only slept with him to make the contract switch.

I just have to face it. He knows. And worst of all, he's right to think I was involved, because I was. Even if I didn't mean to be, even if I didn't know the facts, even if I changed my mind. I've been so stupid. I don't know how much Jordan hates me – I'd imagine quite a lot – but I hate myself even more.

And with thoughts like these, who needs enemies?

31

First class isn't quite as exciting on the way back.

The seat still reclines into a bed. The champagne still flows and sparkles in equal measure. Warm flannels are still being handed to me with tongs – and I have another pair of pyjamas. But it all feels... hollow. Like I've been downgraded, somehow.

The vibe is ruined. It's not that the holiday is over – although that's always a shame – it feels like everything is over, and it's all my fault. My one stupid, honest mistake has ruined it all.

I stare out the window as the plane levels out above the clouds.

I wonder what Jordan must be thinking right now. I feel haunted by the look on his face, the one I'm imagining he made when he found out, when he realised it was me who was sent to betray him.

I'll say it until I'm blue in the face – I didn't know that the plan was for me to betray him, but he doesn't know that. God, I wish I could tell him. The best I can do is tell the empty seat next to me, the one he would have been in if we were both taking our original flights home.

I wish I could have explained myself, told him what I thought my job was, and that this was all Paige manipulating me, but I feel like I've missed my chance, and I'll bet the longer he sits with it, the more mad he probably gets at me. He's never going to forgive me, is he?

And the bloody annoying thing is that I didn't make the swap, I chose him. I was never going to do it.

I sigh and lie back in my seat, trying to appreciate the quiet luxury. The calm. The pillow that smells faintly of lavender. The food and drink that is seemingly never-ending.

Up here, life feels like it's on pause. All time is free time. I could nap, I could watch movies, I could eat, read books, listen to music – do all the things I don't feel like I have time to do in my day-to-day life.

Instead I'm just beating myself up, and even a first-class beating sucks.

I should be on top of the world right now. I should be heading back to the UK giddy with my new man, looking forward to introducing him to my family, taking him to my cousin's wedding...

Instead of touching down with a man, I'm bringing bright red eyes, picked-at skin on the sides of my thumbs, and a pretty fucking bleak outlook on all things love and marriage. Not ideal for a wedding. My puffy eyes are really going to clash with the dress code colours.

Which only reminds me – what the hell am I going to tell everyone? Because stupidly I already told them that I'm bringing Jordan, an absolute dream date, and now I'm going it alone again. That needs explaining, whether I want to or not, and the truth simply is not an option.

I pull out my phone and open the notes app. If people ask – and they will ask – why Jordan isn't with me, I need to give them something quick. Light. Believable. Anything but the truth.

Tech problems could work – a massive cyberattack, perhaps? Saying he's working isn't enough; it sounds like he cares more about work than me or the wedding, which isn't good. It would need to be something big and scary – but wouldn't something like that make the news?

I could say he was ill, I guess, but where would I say he was? Hospital? People might want to visit him. And why would I leave him, if he was ill? That makes me look bad.

I could borrow any one of the icks, for any of my failed dates – I could say he fell, he was a liar, he was too intense. I suppose I could always tell everyone that he broke up with me. I don't think anyone would find that hard to believe, but then I would feel like I was making things all about me, garnering sympathy, when really I want the day to be all about Hannah. She deserves to have a wonderful wedding day free of drama – especially from me.

I suppose I'll just stall at first, say he's working, he's in meetings but he's coming after, and then on the day I'll just drop a last-minute bombshell, something small but impossible to counter, like a flat tyre. These things happen, no one can help them, there's no drama, it's just disappointing, that's all.

The reality isn't disappointing though, is it? It's devastating.

I'm going to put on a brave face. I have to. I'm going to show up to the wedding, smile until my cheeks ache, drink just enough to feel warm, but not weepy. And I'll lie through my teeth when people say, 'Where's that new man of yours?'

But what I won't tell them is the truth, that he's gone, and that it hurts more than I thought it would.

More food arrives – something beautiful but overly garnished. I push it around, trying to feel grateful.

I can't though. It's all wasted on me today. Not even the free food and unlimited movies can cheer me up.

I might be in first class but my heart – not to be overly dramatic – is hanging off the outside of the wing by a thread.

And sooner rather than later, life will be off pause, I'll touch down in reality, and I'll have to deal with it.

Shit.

32

I sigh so heavily as the taxi pulls up outside my parents' house that I actually think I up the price on the cabbie's meter.

'Here we are, love,' he tells me.

I really have missed the Yorkshire accent. There's something so welcome about it, so friendly. I've never met this man before in my life and yet I feel like I know him. I'll bet he drinks Yorkshire Tea, watches rugby league, drinks pints, says hello to his mates by giving them a hard slap on the back and saying, 'Nah then, lad.'

It's nice to see a familiar place too, my parents' house, the street I grew up on. You know when going home feels like coming home? Back to where it all began, somewhere you can decompress, reset, figure out where you're supposed to go from here. The mothership – but not in the cringe way people refer to their mum, I mean like I'm an actual alien, and I'm returning to base to, like, I don't know, decontaminate? I'm sleep deprived and jetlagged. Is it showing?

I can see Mum at the window, practically tearing the curtain off the rail in her attempt to watch out for me. Seeing the taxi outside, she dashes for the front door – but not before straightening her curtains. She is expecting guests, after all.

Oh, how the mighty have fallen, eh? I'm dragging my suitcase up their driveway, on my own, struggling because I collected it from baggage claim with a broken wheel. To think, I've spent a week enjoying first-class travel, five-star hotels, drivers taking me wherever I needed to go. And now I'm here, alone, struggling.

I thought this was going to be so different. I thought I would have Jordan with me, handsome as ever, excited to charm my parents in that way only he can do, getting to know them a little before we all went to the wedding as one big happy family. Serves me right, for getting ahead of myself, for letting my imagination run away with me. I felt so hopeless and demoralised after Ben, I never thought I'd dream again, so it's been nice, to not only act like everything was going to be okay, but to believe it too. I guess I was kidding myself.

Oh, and I'm so knackered. I didn't sleep at the airport. Obviously. I sat awake in my impossibly quiet hotel room overlooking the runway, watching the planes take off and land, trying to decide if that glow in the distance was the Manhattan skyline. If it was, it felt like looking into a snow globe. A bubble. Its own little world – and Jordan's still in there somewhere. Probably hating me. Probably trying to work out how I could be so stone cold, to sleep with him, all while being part of the coup.

Paige really played me. She spun her tragic story – months of being cheated on, a brutal divorce, trying to save her business and mend her heart at the same time – and I, in my soft, sad, squishy, too-trusting state, just... believed her. She told me she'd accidentally deleted a few clauses in the contract – and I believed her. She told me all that horrible stuff about Jordan, and, all together now... I believed her!

I joked about corporate espionage, like I was being cute. But really? I helped her try to swap out a legit, legally sound contract with one that would give her the whole company, leaving Jordan with nothing, totally screwing him over. Can you get in trouble for something like that? Legal trouble, I mean. Morally I feel well and truly bankrupt.

The worst thing is that Jordan actually cares about Matcher. He talks about connection, love, helping people. And Paige? She just wants to keep capitalising on the chaos. The hook-ups, the ghosting, the never-ending parade of dick pics.

Ugh, and I helped her, because I needed a job, and I felt bad for her. Thinking about it, it's probably why she hired me in the first place. She didn't need an expert in espionage, she needed someone sad and skint. Someone who would do whatever they were told without asking questions. She didn't need a super sleuth, a criminal mastermind. She needed someone naïve, desperate for a job, who would do her bidding for her. The fact I was heartbroken didn't hurt either.

And now I've not only put Jordan's company at risk, but I've betrayed his trust. It could have been so easy. He liked me. I liked him. We were both finally ready to move on, to trust again, and I've blown it. He'll probably never trust anyone again, and I'll never trust myself.

Mum opens the front door before I get to it, almost taking it off its hinges. You can tell she's excited. She's all dressed up – Dad too.

'Here she is,' she says, arms open. 'Oh, love, it's so good to see you.'

I force a smile.

'Hi, guys,' I reply.

'Welcome home, kid,' Dad says.

They both come out to hug me, full of warmth and welcome, but then they realise I'm alone.

Mum peers behind me, scanning the taxi as it pulls away.

'Wait, where is he?' she asks, her smile dropping. 'Where's Jordan?'

I give her a tired smile.

'Hello, Mum. Dad. Lovely to see you too,' I say sarcastically.

She catches herself.

'Sorry! Hello, of course. Give me a cuddle,' she says. 'It's just, well, where is he? I've got the guest room all ready, I've made lasagne...'

Oh, God, I can't do it. I can't tell them. Not now. Not yet. It's only been twenty-four hours since I was bragging about bringing him. How the hell am I supposed to tell them that I've fucked it up already?

'He's stuck in Leeds,' I lie quickly. 'He's got meetings, loads of them, he's working on something new. He's still hoping to get here in time for the wedding though.'

Now, why would I go and say a thing like that? Giving them hope. Maybe I'm trying to give myself hope, which is a special kind of stupid.

'Oh,' Mum says, clearly disappointed.

'Did you tell people he was coming?' I check, casually as I can.

'Yes,' she replies. 'Auntie Eleanor, Hannah – and I know your gran is excited to vet him.'

I smile, even though it feels like a punch to the stomach.

'Great,' I reply.

'Well, the lasagne's almost ready,' she says, still peering at me like I might produce Jordan from inside my suitcase, like this is some sort of fake-out. 'And the guest room is all ready for you.'

'Thanks, Mum,' I say sincerely. 'I'll nip up, dump my things, freshen up quickly.'

'Don't be too long,' she says with a smile. 'We've missed you.'

'I've missed having someone to sort the Sky box,' Dad calls after me jokily. 'Your mum's recorded 108 episodes of *Emmerdale*. We're running out of space.'

'I told you, I'm going to catch up at some point,' I overhear her reminding him as I head upstairs.

I head into the guest room, which used to be my bedroom, and while it's changed a lot as far as the décor goes, you can still see the ghosts of my childhood, if you know where to look.

The hot-pink walls are long gone, replaced with something neutral and grown-up, but you can still tell I was here. Like, that little dent in the plaster, over there, from where one of my friends threw my Aqua CD like a frisbee, hitting the wall, making a ding.

It could be fixed though – filled, sanded, painted over properly, like it never even happened. But they didn't. They left it there. Even with a fresh coat of paint, the damage shows, like an old war wound, a brave face painted over it.

Is that me now? Damaged. Brushed over, but trying to look okay. Putting a brave face on, but being undeniably damaged. I'm being dramatic, I know, but I'm having a pity party, so if you could leave me to it...

Time for dinner, I guess. I don't want my mum or dad realising that anything is up, and I'm worried they'll see straight through me. At least I have a good excuse. I'm tired, I'm jetlagged, I'll be fine tomorrow – well, that's what I'll tell them.

Downstairs, Mum is serving up giant portions of lasagne with a side of focaccia. I don't know if I'm starving or feeling sick or what. I'm all over the place. It does smell good though.

'Perfect timing,' she tells me. 'Take a seat.'

I do as I'm told. I should try to eat something.

'Come on then,' Dad says, handing me a glass of red wine. 'Tell us about New York, make us jealous.'

I force a smile.

'I've had such a great time,' I tell them. 'It's a fascinating city, so alive, so full of energy. The office was so much bigger than the one in London, with views of the skyline, surrounded by other tall buildings, I can't even describe it. It's almost like there are layers and layers of the city, from the floor to the sky. Life doesn't simply exist on the ground.'

Dad laughs.

'I'm surprised you came back,' Mum teases.

'And miss the wedding of the year?' Dad jokes.

'I've met some really interesting people – some cool locals,' I continue. 'I had the best meatballs from this little Italian place called Giorgio's, where Giorgio himself served us.'

'We'll have to plan a trip,' Dad says.

'I've always wanted to go,' Mum adds. 'Is it like it is on TV?'

I smile to myself. As much as it hurts, it's nice to think about what Jordan did, taking me on a silly *Sex and the City* tour.

'It really is,' I reply.

Mum reaches out and puts a hand over mine.

'I'm so glad you had a nice time, darling,' she tells me. 'You deserve something good after... after what happened. After everything.'

As she smiles, I notice her eyes welling up.

'I'm just so pleased you've had a nice time, you've got a job you enjoy, and you've met a nice man,' she says. 'That's all – ignore me.'

And now I'm filling up but they're not happy tears. It's like I'm in mourning.

'Give over, you two,' Dad teases. 'You're putting me off my lasagne.'

I eat a mouthful of lasagne to avoid having to say anything.

Eventually we carry on chatting and eating, them asking me questions about the city, me trying to answer without blubbing. They both seem so happy for me, so proud of me. It's making this feel so much worse because I really did almost have it all, didn't I? A cool job, a good man, a heart that wasn't broken.

And I lost it. Just like that. In a New York minute.

I thought I'd be safe, hiding in my parents' guest room, keeping my head down before the wedding.

Turns out I was wrong, because I can hear a knocking on the door and Hannah calling out my name.

She's not going to go away; she knows I'm in here, and if she thought I was sleeping, well, she wouldn't still be knocking.

I pull myself to my feet and answer.

'Heeeey!' I say brightly. A little too brightly, maybe.

'You made it,' she replies.

'Of course,' I say, refusing to read anything into her choice of words, because I have enough problems.

'I have something for you,' she says.

She opens up a small box to reveal a yellow flower on a pin.

'Everyone is wearing them,' she tells me. 'This is yours. It's symbolic.'

'Lovely,' I reply. 'What does it symbolise?'

'Well, just, like, flowers, growth, new beginnings – I don't know, the florist really convinced me though.' She pauses to laugh at herself. 'Also, I just really like yellow, so the more yellow the better, right?'

'Right,' I reply, although I can't say I've ever had that thought.

I pick up the flower, twirling it between my fingers. I guess it is symbolic, in a way. It's cheerful. Hopeful. Everything I'm not currently feeling.

'Soooo,' Hannah says, far too casually, plonking herself down on my bed. 'What time's your man getting here tomorrow?'

I pause. She's watching me. I can tell. That slow, creeping curiosity, laced with a hint of suspicion.

'Jordan?' I say, aiming for breezy, as though she could be talking about one of my other men. 'Oh. He's... he's not sure yet. He's so busy with work stuff, in Leeds, he's doing something new and it's taking up a lot of his time.'

'Hmm,' she says, playing with the tassels on one of Mum's decorative pillows. 'You wouldn't think he would be too busy for you though...'

'He says he's coming,' I insist. 'It's just... if he gets held up... in his meeting.'

'Right,' she says, dragging out the word in a way that makes my back itch.

There's a silence. Not long, but pointed. Then:

'You know, we've all heard a lot about Jordan,' she says. 'Your mum has told my mum, who has told me...'

'Oh, yeah?' I say, carefully popping my flower back in its box, so that it's safe.

'Yeah,' she says, smiling in a way that suggests she thinks he might be too good to be true.

It's not that he's too good to be true, I'm just too shit to hang on to him.

'I can't wait to meet him,' she continues.

'I can't wait for you all to meet him,' I reply. 'He is real, you know.'

'I never said he wasn't real,' she says, all innocent. 'Just... you know, if you had made him up, that's not unusual, I've seen it in romcoms.'

'I didn't make him up,' I say quickly, too quickly, trying to awkwardly laugh it off. 'He's real. He's... very busy. But he'll try to come. If he can.'

'All right, Lib, relax, I'm only messing,' she says. 'So... we still might see him tomorrow?'

I nod again, trying to smile.

I leave out the part where I know, with absolutely soul-crushing certainty, that we will not see him. Not a chance.

But it doesn't matter. What matters is that they believe he's busy. That Hannah believes it, and doesn't think this is me acting up because it's her wedding, trying to steal sympathy, or attention or whatever. I want to show her that's it's all okay, so she can enjoy her day in peace, and I can go back to keeping my head down.

'Well. If he shows, I look forward to meeting him,' she says. 'If not, I look forward to mocking you mercilessly until one of us dies.'

'Thanks for the support,' I reply, fairly sure she's joking now.

She gives me a hug and heads for the door, stopping just before she opens it.

'I can't believe I'm getting married,' she says.

'It's going to be great,' I reassure her.

'Yeah,' she says, sighing, her shoulders relaxing.

I don't know whether she came just to bring the flower, or to reassure herself I wasn't going to be a problem, but clearly her work here is done.

Tomorrow's going to be perfect and I'm going to be a contender for cousin of the year, because I'm going to smile, drink prosecco, make excuses for my fella who is so sad he couldn't make it, and then I'll go home, back to my parents' place and then...

And then I don't know. Shit. But I'll worry about that once the wedding is over.

34

The morning of the wedding is bright and crisp – cold, but not in a way that is unpleasant or wet or icy. The sky outside the hotel room window is actually blue, which is nice. There's always a worry, with winter weddings, that they will be dull. Well, not in this family, but you know what I mean.

We're at a country hotel just outside Leeds, the sort of place with grounds and deer wandering about like they own the place, and really tiny, fancy little foods, rather than the cosy staples you want at this time of year. I can't remember what food I chose, but I know that it wasn't fish and chips, or steak and ale pie.

I'm here, I'm in my silky mustard dress – as per the dress code for women. Men are to wear black suits, which is easy; most men have a black suit. I did not, however, have a mustard dress, so I had to buy one. Not sure I'll ever wear it again, but at least I'm not a bridesmaid, so I got to choose a fit that suits me. April, Hannah's bestie, is wearing her mustard bridesmaid dress, and it's far too frilly for my liking. I'm so glad she never asked me.

Today is going to suck, frills or not, let's face it. It should have been my big redemption arc. Me swanning in, fresh back from New York, fancy new job, handsome man on my arm. That was supposed to be the story, after what happened at the engagement party. It was going to show everyone that I was okay now. That what happened in the summer was just a blip, not who I was. I guess I was hoping that, if people were going to be talking about me, it would be for good reasons, rather than gossiping about what happened before. I don't want to be known for that – as the dick pic girl, who exploded with rage by the toilets.

I can already feel the glances. Is that Liberty? Didn't she have a bit of a breakdown last time? And maybe I'm imagining it, maybe this is me projecting, but I'm already tired of defending myself in my head. I know things are bad when I'm rehearsing my arguments.

I'm currently in Hannah's hotel suite, sitting in a velvet armchair in the corner, sipping prosecco – the breakfast of champs.

Hannah's sitting centre stage, in front of the mirror, checking her curls are still secure. She seems calm but excited. Not nervous at all.

The room is full of women – everyone giddy and full of prosecco, so you can imagine the volume level. My mum, her usual breezy, chatty self, is passing around pastries, which will hopefully sober up some of the older ones, but leave me with my buzz, the one that's going to get me though the day. Auntie Eleanor is perched on the edge of the chaise, sitting awkwardly, trying not to crease her outfit. Gran looks gorgeous in her twin set, with her big hat (not as big as Auntie Eleanor's though – hers is so big it's got its own seat by the door). And then there's April. Hannah's best friend. Who had a wedding in the south of

France last summer that, if you believe her, was attended by a minor royal, a footballer, and two runners-up from *Love Island* (different seasons – not sure why that matters).

'I mean, yes, technically we had fireworks,' April continues, examining her nails, 'but classy ones, not tacky ones. We flew in an opera singer from Rome – you really struggle, to find quality in the UK these days... although I'm sure your wedding will be great, Han.'

'Thanks,' Hannah says with a smile.

I think I'd be taking offence from that, but why get upset on your wedding day?

'No one had fireworks back in my day,' Gran says. 'Well, not unless people had too much to drink and started spilling family secrets.'

'Remind me to buy you a few cocktails,' I joke.

She gives me a wink.

'I really can't wait,' Hannah blurts. 'I don't even care about the fireworks. I just want to be married. Honestly. I know it won't always be perfect, but we're going to buy a bigger house, have babies, start our family right away, not leave too long between each kid.'

'How many do you want?' Mum asks.

'At least four,' Hannah replies.

'Wow, and I thought one was a handful,' my mum jokes.

'I was an angel,' I protest playfully – although I'm sure I was. I'm more chaotic as an adult, to be honest with you.

It's nice to hear that Hannah has a plan. She knows what she wants and she's starting strong, going all out to get it. Sure, it might not pan out that way, but she's looking to the future and she's excited.

My heart feels heavy. I have no relationship, no job, no dreams – no hope.

And of course I'm sitting in a room full of married (or very soon to be) women. The one sad single girl listening to everyone being excited for the future, or reminiscing about the past.

Whatever way I look, it makes me feel sad. I feel like a tornado, leaving chaos in my wake, knowing I'll destroy wherever I head next – but not the wedding, I'm going to be on my best behaviour today. I want things to be perfect for Hannah. That's why I've told people Jordan is still held up, but he sends his apologies.

My brave face is firmly on, now I just need to work out the prosecco dosage to keep it there.

It's going to be a long day.

35

I'm taking a detour, on my way from the hotel to the events building, to grab my mum's lipstick from the car.

My dad rolled his eyes and told her to wear one of the other six in her handbag – which could be an exaggeration or it could be true – but she's bought a special one, to match her mustard dress, so I volunteered to go grab it, just to have a breather, to get away from the wedding chaos, even if it's only for a minute.

It's a bit of a trek to the car park, where the event parking is. It's out of the way, in a sort of woodland clearing, under the canopy of the trees. Even bare, they're so tall, it's like being in a cage.

I don't have a coat on, because we were only supposed to be walking to the events area, and I didn't want to be carrying a coat around with me all day. My God, it might be a bright day, but it's freezing, and the deeper I walk into the woods, the darker it seems.

There's no one else around, just rows of cars catching pops of light filtering through the trees, and it's so silent, the kind of quiet where your ears start looking for things to hear, imagining all sorts.

You know that old question: If a tree falls in a forest and no one's around to hear it, does it make a sound? Does that apply to all noises? Because I've got all this stress and frustration inside of me, and this feels like a good spot to just... let it all out.

What about if a woman screams into the void, mid-breakdown, on the morning of her cousin's wedding? Will anyone hear it?

Only one way to find out.

'Ahhhhhhhhh!'

It bursts out of me, loud, primal even, and totally ridiculous. I half-expect a bird to drop out of a tree in shock. Animals to wake up from hibernation – a bear to pop out and maul me. Go ahead, buddy, make my day.

My breath clouds in front of me. My heart slows. Weirdly... that did help. Who knew?

Maybe if it all gets too much later, I'll come back out here and scream again. And again and again. Between that and prosecco, maybe I can get through today.

'I know family weddings are rough,' a voice calls out, amused, from behind me. 'But that seemed a bit overdramatic.'

It sounds like Jordan but... it can't be, can it? I turn around, half expecting to have completely imagined the voice altogether, but there he is, standing there, looking like a dream in a black suit.

'Hi,' he says, smiling like he's just popped his head through the adjoining door.

I blink at him.

'Is it... really you?' I blurt.

He laughs.

'Why wouldn't it be?'

I take a few shaky steps towards him. 'Because I've had a lot of prosecco already, to the point where screaming in a car park felt like a good idea,' I point out. 'But also because I assumed that you hated me. That you'd never want to see me again...'

He shrugs, but I can tell he's trying to suppress a smile.

'I can see why you might've thought that,' he replies.

I don't think – I just run. I throw my arms around him, and I'm so relieved when he catches me and holds me close. Even if he did hate me, I don't care. I never thought I'd see him again. It's so good to see him.

'Sorry I'm late,' he murmurs into my hair.

'Better late than never,' I whisper. Then I pull back slightly, so I can look at him. 'I didn't think you were coming. Or that you even knew where to find me. How did you...?'

He grins cheekily.

'I don't want to add to the narrative that all men are creeps, but with just a little mild stalking... I found your former employer, from your file – Paige must've deleted your number – and so I called your old workplace. Spoke to a guy called Ben – is that *the* Ben?'

'The one and only,' I tell him.

'Well, I told him I was your date for the wedding, but that I didn't know where it was... or your number... and he sent me here. Thinking about it, I'm lucky he gave me the right place.'

I laugh, but my face falls as reality sets in. My stomach tightens.

'Tell me you didn't sign the contract. The bad one,' I blurt.

He nods.

'Actually... I did.'

Shit.

'Jordan, I'm so sorry, I didn't—'

'Don't worry,' he cuts in gently. 'I saw both versions. I read them both. Silly of Paige to think I wouldn't read the contract before I signed. It was obvious, even without two in the mix, that she was trying to sneak in a clause giving her complete control of Matcher US. Like I wouldn't notice. Anyway, I called her. Called her out. She admitted everything. Said she deserved it. Then she ranted about you messing it up, how she should've told you her plan, offered you more money...'

'She told me I was fixing a typo,' I say, for what it's worth.

'I know,' he says. 'I'm sorry she dragged you into it. But I also know you, Lib. You wouldn't hurt me. Or anyone. Not on purpose. That's not who you are.'

I'm trying not to cry but I can feel my eyes filling up. Oh, I have far too much eye makeup on for this, unless I want to turn up to the ceremony looking like an emo.

'She's always been like this,' he continues. 'Jealous, ruthless, manipulative – impossible. I realised I couldn't work with her any more. Not even with the Atlantic between us. So I sold Matcher to her. Cashed out, to start again, but on the condition that I could poach the team I wanted, because I'm starting something new. Collaborating with RedFlags in Leeds. We're building a new dating app – one with a rating system, so that bad users get strikes against their name. Red flags – or maybe even "icks" for lesser offences. Fewer creeps. More accountability. It will be bigger and better than Matcher.'

'Like TripAdvisor, but for people who date?' I joke.

'Exactly,' he replies. 'And it means I'll be in Leeds for a while.'

'Oh, really?' I reply. 'And am I one of the people you poached?'

'No, of course not,' he replies firmly. 'Paige already sacked you – you're a new hire. If you want a job? I already know your references. I'll ignore Paige's, obviously.'

My smile grows.

'I'd love that.'

He takes my hand and shakes it playfully.

'Good. Look, I know we should probably talk more, about everything, but later, yeah? After the wedding?'

'Shit, yes, the wedding, we'd better go,' I say – my mum will just have to do without her lipstick. I'm sure she would rather wear a slightly different shade than have her daughter walk into the ceremony late.

We turn together and head back towards the hotel, our footsteps in sync. Just as we reach the doors to the function suite, the music inside starts to play. Oof, crisis averted. Imagine if I'd walked in late, with Jordan. Hannah would've thought I was doing it to show off.

Inside, we slip into our seats, with seconds to spare. My mum spots us, eyes wide, smile beaming. My dad gives Jordan a nod and a handshake as he sits down next to him, eyebrows raised in amused approval. He's passed the initial vibe check; that's a big relief.

And then the ceremony starts, kicking off the day, and just like that, my nightmare is a dream again.

Today might not be so bad after all.

36

I don't think I've ever been to a winter wedding before. Well, people usually opt for the summer months, preferring the warm glow of the sun – and probably the security of knowing a freak snowstorm isn't going to derail the big day by stranding the guests and/or having them slip on the ice.

Thankfully although it's cold, the weather has been kind, so everything just feels so cosy and festive and positively Hallmark movie-esque. If I ever get married, I think I'd probably opt for a winter wedding too – so long as enough time had passed by for Hannah not to accuse me of copying her.

The function room is decked out for the wedding and for Christmas, which only makes it all the more beautiful and sparkly. At a summer wedding it might seem like too much but, here, with Christmas only a matter of days away, it feels exciting.

Twinkling fairy lights hang from the beams like stars, evergreen wreaths and holly wrap around the pillars, and there's a twelve-foot Christmas tree standing proudly in the middle of the room that really is a showstopper. It's not the Rockefeller

Center tree, but it looks like it's trying to give the bride a run for her money by stealing the show.

The most perfect thing of all though – and admittedly this is nothing to do with the wedding – is that Jordan is here. We're sitting at our table, eating, chatting, having a lovely time. It means a lot, that he came, but things are still fresh enough between us to give us that cute nervous energy and magnet-like attraction to each other. Whenever our elbows so much as knock, it's like lightning striking us. When our eyes meet, we can't help but smile. Everything just feels so right.

'Can I have your attention, please?' the best man calls out as he takes the mic. 'I'm Fred, the best man, and I guess it's my turn to give a speech...'

Fred, who I don't really know, already has his bowtie loosened and the top button of his shirt open – he's giving off a Michael Bublé kind of vibe, except he doesn't quite have the voice to pull it off. Not unless Bublé usually speaks with a south Leeds accent.

He taps the microphone in a way that I'm not sure is necessary in the year 2025.

'Can you hear me at the back?' he calls out.

A few people cheer. The less kind ones lightly heckle him.

'Right, I'll keep this short and sweet – like the groom's attention span,' he announces. 'And his—'

He doesn't get to finish his sentence before Hannah elbows him, not all that subtly, which gets more of a laugh than his joke was going to.

'Your cousin doesn't take any prisoners, does she?' Jordan whispers to me.

I stifle a laugh, nudging his leg with mine beneath the table.

'Anyway,' Fred continues, 'me and this lad here have been

mates for over twenty years and I never thought I'd see the day he managed to convince a girl to marry him.'

Oof, it's so awkward.

'And now he's got Hannah,' Fred continues. 'So he's probably going to spend his weekends at IKEA, and we all know what that means, right?'

I really don't think we do. I don't think anyone does. And hilariously he carries on his speech without telling us.

Jordan and I giggle together like a couple of school kids at the back of the coach on a school trip. I smile to myself, despite the car crash happening at the top table, because I feel like I have a partner in crime. Someone who sees things the way I do. Who finds the same things funny. Who I know will always make everything fun. I wouldn't be having such a good time with anyone else today. Definitely not with Ben, who was originally supposed to be my plus one. Ben never really got me – I never really got him either though. He never laughed at jokes – or even pretended to. He'd sit through a speech like this and probably check the score of something on his phone, holding it just below the table so no one saw, oblivious to the fact everyone could tell what he was doing and probably thought he was a tosser.

Jordan is different. He's here nudging me, whispering jokes in my ear, and making what is frankly the worst best man speech in history feel like something I'll remember forever – for good reasons though. I couldn't ask for a better partner in crime, could I?

When it's finally over, we're all allowed to mingle. People disperse, buying drinks, dancing – now the party can finally start.

My parents drift over to where we're standing at the bar, both grinning at us, unable to hide how happy they are.

Dad smacks Jordan on the back in that way dads do when they approve of the man their daughter is seeing.

'And to think, we weren't sure you were going to show up,' Dad says with a glint in his eye.

Jordan smiles.

'I worried I might not make it,' he replies. 'I had to get an emergency filling yesterday, after breaking my tooth.'

'Ah, I know the drill,' Dad says, grinning at his own dad joke.

To be fair, that was a good one.

Jordan laughs, which earns him points.

I appreciate him making excuses for me, about why he was late. He's really got my back.

'So, Jordan, what are you doing for Christmas?' Mum asks him as she sips her wine. 'Spending it with family?'

'No, my parents are total Grinches,' he replies. 'They go on a cruise every year to avoid Christmas. I thought about joining them, but... I don't know. It doesn't feel right to me. I love Christmas.'

Mum's eyes flick to me and then back to him, and I already know what's coming.

'Well, if you don't have plans... you're more than welcome to spend Christmas with us,' she says casually – although you can tell she's really hoping he'll say yes.

I squeeze Jordan's hand to let him know I'd like that too. He glances at me and smiles.

'I'd love that,' he says. 'Thank you.'

Dad chuckles, lifting his beer.

'Wait until the end of the night,' he warns him. 'See if you still feel the same after you've met the entire circus.'

'Oh, I'm sure I'll love everyone,' Jordan says confidently.

Christmas at home is always a bit of a circus, but in the best and most chaotic way. My mum starts planning in November and pretends she isn't, which means we spend three weeks eating 'just a few picky bits' that she's absolutely been hoarding since Halloween. And it's tradition that my dad, who eats everything put in front of him, complains about how much food my mum has bought. Between us, and the extended family, it's not like there's ever food left over; nothing goes to waste. Isn't it funny how dads are usually two sides of a coin – a grumpy old man and a comedian who constantly cracks dad jokes? You wouldn't think two personalities could exist in one man, but my dad wears it well.

Every year it's the same: Gran and Grandad come to stay – always bringing boxes of local biscuits from the island they live on. Auntie Eleanor comes by with a bottle of sherry 'just in case anyone fancies one later' and proceeds to use it as her main form of hydration from the second she arrives until my uncle drives her home. Hannah brings Samuel now – and Samuel brings Monopoly, which I hate. I think that man loves Monopoly more than he loves my cousin.

When I was younger, I used to wish we were one of those polished happy families where everyone quietly got along but, to be honest, the friction keeps things spicy. It makes it easier to hold the ones you love the most the closest. Plus, I might hate Monopoly, but I do love to see Samuel's face when someone beats him.

There's something comforting about knowing exactly how the day will unfold. The noise, the warmth, the arguing over who left the Quality Street tin empty except for the toffees – only for some weirdo to pipe up that the only one involving zero chocolate is their favourite. As if.

Having Jordan around for all of that mess – and him not leaving – sounds great to me.

'Here she is,' my dad announces as Hannah joins us. She's

been doing the rounds, trying to get to everyone, so I guess it's finally our turn.

'Liberty,' she squeals, giving me a slightly-too-tight hug – she's definitely making the most of the prosecco. 'Sorry, I feel like I've barely seen you! And you must be Jordan. I've heard so much about you. Thank you for coming.'

'Thanks for inviting me,' he replies. 'You look beautiful, by the way. Absolutely stunning.'

Jordan smiles and I could swear Hannah swoons a little. So his charm works on everyone then. She blushes – she's literally a blushing bride.

'Well. You can stay,' she jokes.

Dad drags Jordan into a conversation about something sport-related – and it sounds like he's holding his own, so that's a relief. Not that I care about sports but getting used to my dad's constant chat is easier if you're invested.

'He's great,' Hannah whispers to me. 'I'm so happy for you. Especially after everything that happened.'

'Thanks,' I reply. 'I'm really glad I got to be here – for you. And Jordan is right, you look unreal, Han. You deserve every part of this amazing day.'

She squeezes my arm.

'Whoever I go talk to next isn't going to be able to top that,' she tells me before she moves on to the next group.

Just as I'm finishing my drink and trying to decide what to have next, I notice Auntie Eleanor making a determined beeline for us. Oh, joy. This will be the real test for Jordan. I'm practically bracing.

'Liberty,' she says. 'I feel like we've barely spoken since this morning...'

We haven't spoken at all since this morning.

'Hi, Auntie Eleanor.' I smile, trying to show her that I come in peace. 'Have you met Jordan?'

'Not yet.' She turns to him like she's about to give him a performance review. 'So. What do you do, Jordan?'

'I work in tech,' he tells her. 'Dating apps – I'm just about to launch a new one actually.'

'Another one?' she says, eyebrows raised. 'Isn't the market saturated?'

'Name five,' I suggest.

'Possibly,' Jordan tells her, not giving her a chance to react to my remark. 'But we're trying to do things differently. Safer. Smarter. More honest.'

Auntie Eleanor makes a vaguely approving noise – or maybe her huge hat is just cutting off the blood flow to her brain.

'And what are your intentions with our Liberty?' she asks him.

Our Liberty? It's not like her to take ownership of me.

'I'm really enjoying her company,' Jordan tells her, happy to answer the question. 'She makes me laugh, she keeps me on my toes, and every day I spend with her, I want to know more.'

Auntie Eleanor stares at him – I don't know if she's doubting his word or maybe she's simply struggling to believe that anyone could feel that way about me.

'Well, good luck to you both,' she says.

And with that vague threat of a blessing, she leaves as quickly as she appears.

As soon as she's out of earshot, Jordan leans in to my ear.

'Good job I didn't tell her my actual intentions,' he replies. 'Not for tonight, anyway.'

'I'm looking forward to finding out what those are,' I reply as I plant a kiss on his cheek.

His smile widens, and I rest my head briefly on his shoulder, thinking – for maybe the millionth time today – that I'm so happy he turned up.

Eventually the lights dim just enough and the band starts playing the kind of jazzy Christmas covers that make you feel like you're in a festive romcom.

Jordan takes my hand.

'Shall we dance?' he suggests.

'Why not?' I reply.

He leads me out onto the dance floor and we sway slowly under the fairy lights, my cheek against his chest, his warm hands on my waist. It's one of those moments that you wish could last forever.

'So,' he says quietly. 'Have you thought any more about my job proposal? Still happy to take it?'

'What can I say? I love working for you,' I reply. 'What about... everything else?'

'As far as I'm concerned, everything else is great,' he tells me. 'We'll figure it all out together. As long as I'm with you, I've got what I want.'

'Me too,' I say.

'I've never felt like this about anyone, not this quickly,' he says. 'I know it's early days, but I'm excited to see where it takes us.'

'So am I,' I say, snuggling closer to him.

I feel fixed – as cringe as that sounds. Complete again. But while this might be the end of the story about how we got together, really it's the beginning of the story of us. We're only on the first page. Neither of us knows what the future holds, but we're walking into it together.

37

ONE YEAR LATER

I swipe. And swipe. And swipe.

App dating never seems any less bleak, does it?

Men holding fish. Men posing with cars. Men in the gym. Bios that say things like 'no drama queens' and 'I hate kids'.

I sigh dramatically. This is why getting back on the apps feels so demoralising. There's just so much to swipe through in the hope of finding someone decent enough to go for a drink with.

I swipe again. Then again. Then – oh, we've got something.

I notice a profile that has been flagged for aggressive messages by no less than three users. I'm delighted to hit the ban button – in fact, I stare into his beady eyes and grin back at the photo of his smug smile as I watch his profile disappear.

'Ugh. Another one,' I say, shaking my head.

'Really?'

'Yep, third one today,' I reply.

'At least we're weeding them out,' Jordan says, spinning in his chair to look at me.

I lean back and stretch my arms over my head with a sigh.

'It is weirdly satisfying,' I reply. 'I feel like a superhero, doing my bit to protect people.'

'Oh, yeah, you're basically Batman,' he jokes.

'Batwoman,' I reply.

'Why not?' he says, laughing to himself.

Flagd, our new app, is doing well. Better than well, actually. It turns out that safety is something that a lot of people value so we've had loads of sign-ups. Yes, we've got bad eggs, but it's early days, and we're weeding them out really quickly. It's my favourite part of my job, checking who has red flags, banning users for bad behaviour.

'Speaking of dates...' Jordan says, wheeling over to me on his desk chair, 'I'm taking you out tonight, buying you dinner. And when we get home, I'm going to give you the massage of your dreams – it's stressful work, being Batwoman. I'm going to relax you.'

'Oh, yeah?' I raise an eyebrow, standing slowly and circling around the back of his chair. 'That's very generous of you.'

'I'm a very generous man,' he replies, leaning back against me.

'Thing is,' I whisper, wrapping my arms around him from behind, pressing a kiss to his neck, 'I don't want to relax.'

'That,' he says, standing and turning to face me, 'can definitely be arranged.'

I smile as he pulls me in and kisses me.

Living with Jordan is just so easy in all the ways that matter but still so exciting – I'm somehow relaxed but at the same time it's like I never know what's going to happen next. Only that it's always all going to be okay.

We work really well together too. Who knew building a dating app with someone you're actually dating would be the recipe for success? Well, that and teaming up with RedFlags, to make sure no one is getting dick pics they don't want.

I know that I should probably still hate Matcher (I think it was more that I hated how people used it, to be honest with you) but it's hard to hate the app that, technically, brought me and Jordan together.

And people say app dating never leads to true love.

I guess sometimes, if you're lucky, and you're keeping your eyes (and I guess your heart) open, then true love will be easy to spot when it does happen to cross your path.

It's like I always say, finding someone isn't the end of the story. It's the beginning.

And I can't wait to see what happens next.

* * *

MORE FROM PORTIA MACINTOSH

Another book from Portia MacIntosh is available to order now here:

https://mybook.to/PortiaMBackAd

ACKNOWLEDGEMENTS

Thanks to Megan, my editor, and the rest of the team at Boldwood HQ for all of their wonderful work on *A Lot to Unpack*.

I had so much fun writing it – thanks so much to everyone who takes the time to read and review not just this book, but all my books. It means so much to me.

I couldn't do any of this without the support of my wonderful family. Thanks so much to the amazing Kim, Pino and my incredible gran, Aud. Shout-out to my brilliant brothers – James and Joey. Thanks as always to Darcy for being by my side. Finally, huge thanks to Joe, my husband, for all of his love, support and hard work. I love you all so much.

ABOUT THE AUTHOR

Portia MacIntosh is the million copy bestselling author of over 20 romantic comedy novels. Whether it's southern Italy or the French alps, Portia's stories are the holiday you're craving, conveniently packed in between the pages. Formerly a journalist, Portia lives with her husband and her dog in Yorkshire.

Sign up to Portia MacIntosh's mailing list for news, competitions and updates on future books.

Visit Portia's website: 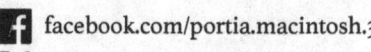www.portiamacintosh.com

Follow Portia MacIntosh on social media here:

- facebook.com/portia.macintosh.3
- x.com/PortiaMacIntosh
- instagram.com/portiamacintoshauthor
- bookbub.com/authors/portia-macintosh

ALSO BY PORTIA MACINTOSH

Off The Record

Love On Tour

Always The Bridesmaid

Drive Me Crazy

Truth or Date

It's Not You, It's Them

The Accidental Honeymoon

Never The Bride

Summer Secrets at the Apple Blossom Deli

Snow Love Lost

Here Comes the Ex

Honeymoon For One

My Great Ex-Scape

Make or Break at the Lighthouse B&B

The Plus One Pact

Stuck On You

Faking It

Life's a Beach

Will They, Won't They?

No Ex Before Marriage

The Date Escape

Snow Place Like Home

Just Date and See

Your Place or Mine?

Better Off Wed

Long Time No Sea

The Break Up Plot

Trouble in Paradise

Ex in the City

The Suite Life

It's All Sun and Games

You Had Me at Château

Wish You Weren't Here

Too Hot to Handle

Going Overboard

A Lot to Unpack

Boldwood
EVER AFTER

x♡x♡

JOIN BOLDWOOD'S
**ROMANCE
COMMUNITY**
FOR SWEET AND
SPICY BOOK RECS
WITH ALL YOUR
FAVOURITE
TROPES!

SIGN UP TO OUR
NEWSLETTER

HTTPS://BIT.LY/BOLDWOODEVERAFTER

Boldwood

Boldwood Books is an award-winning fiction publishing company seeking out the best stories from around the world.

Find out more at www.boldwoodbooks.com

Join our reader community for brilliant books, competitions and offers!

Follow us
@BoldwoodBooks
@TheBoldBookClub

Sign up to our weekly deals newsletter

https://bit.ly/BoldwoodBNewsletter